NIGHTMARE SYNDROME

WILLIAM MARSHALL

NIGHTMARE SYNDROME

THE MYSTERIOUS PRESS

Published by Warner Books

A Time Warner Company

Mysterious Press books are published by Warner Books, Inc.,
1271 Avenue of the Americas, New York, NY 10020.

 A Time Warner Company

The Mysterious Press name and logo are registered trademarks of Warner Books, Inc.
Printed in the United States of America
First printing: June 1997

10   9   8   7   6   5   4   3   2   1

Library of Congress Cataloging-in-Publication Data

Marshall, William Leonard
    Nightmare syndrome / William Marshall.
        p.   cm.
    ISBN 0-89296-574-6
    1. Feiffer, Harry (Fictitious character)—Fiction. 2. Police—
Hong Kong—Fiction.   I. Title.
PR9619.3.M275N54   1997
823—dc20   96-42015
                                                                    CIP

This is for Alexandria Knights
13 August 1995

The Hong Bay district of Hong Kong
is fictitious, as are the people who,
for one reason or another, inhabit it.

NIGHTMARE SYNDROME

LIFE, AND LIM

Looking across Hong Kong island from the New Hop Pei Cove Typhoon shelter in Hong Bay, the night was a white and blue and yellow and orange kaleidoscope of light from all the buildings along the shoreline and, in the cupola of the sky, ablaze with constellations of stars.

Standing by the railing of the aft deck of the moored floating restaurant *The Pearl Princess*, itself lit by a thousand colored bulbs hung from stem to stern, Mr. Lim had a half-smoked panatela cigar in his hand, but, gazing at it, he could not remember if he had been smoking it or not or merely holding it for someone, and let it fall into the water between the boat's hull and the pier and watched as it fizzed out, became dead, and floated away into the darkness to the stern.

Behind him in the main banquet room, he could hear the sounds of people talking, the clashing of trays of plates and cups and bowls from an army of waiters serving a thick, wonderful-smelling spicy Mongolian hot pot, and the high, sibilant sound of a three man Chinese *wyang* string orchestra playing a well-known song from the classical opera—the name of which he could no longer remember.

The night was full of lights from all the great buildings along the shoreline, but he did not know what any of the buildings were or when they had been built or even the names of any of the streets they were in and he looked away from them back to the water to see where the cigar was.

Like memory, it had faded and gone.

Standing silhouetted in the lights, he was a thin, almost emaciated old man wearing an expensive English Savile Row silk suit and handmade matching Thai silk tie, but as he put his hand into the side pocket of his coat to see what was in there, he did not know whether it was his or someone else's and he had merely borrowed it for the occasion.

All there was in the pocket was a single white piece of printed cardboard the size of a business card, printed in embossed black characters and letters, first in Chinese and then in English.

Attention POLICE:

If this old gentleman is found wandering,
please contact daughter—day or night—
at phone number on back of card.

On the back, there was a single phone number printed in large characters and numbers. It was a low number, probably somewhere up on The Peak, the highest part of the entire island of Hong Kong, but he could not visualize a room where the phone might be or the table it might be on and, like all the thoughts in his mind, it was a thought that came from nowhere and went nowhere, and he let the little card fall into the water and watched it float away into the darkness like the cigar.

He was eighty-five years old: he knew that. He had been born one year before the fall of the last emperor of China in 1911, but he could not remember anything that had happened in the last almost forty years since after he had woken one morning on his cot in his one-room electrical repair shop on Great Shanghai Street in 1949 and heard on the radio that Mao Tse-Tung and his Communists had taken control of Peking and the old Nationalist government of General Chiang Kai-Shek had been defeated and, with their army, fled to the offshore island of Taiwan.

He could not remember what the occasion on *The Pearl Princess* he had worn the expensive suit to was.

Standing there amid all the lights of the night, he could not even remember his own name.

The farther away things were, the clearer, and his body still remembered what his mind could not. The memories were etched there, like a map of his life. He put his hand to his face and winced as his fingers touched a deep semicircular scar under his right eye from his first job at the age of eight in the fields along the border with Old China in the New Territories at Fanling.

Kicking back eighty percent of his daily wage to the uncle who had gotten him the job, he had worked twelve hours a day at one of the duck farms that in those days exported over a thousand dried and salted duck carcasses a day by train to the restaurants and great private houses and mansions in Canton.

He knew there were a thousand a day because, as the youngest worker there, he had the least complicated job—killing the thousand ducks a day by wringing their necks one bird at a time—and because, with the kickback to his uncle, eight hundred was the minimum he had to kill before he was paid anything at all for his labors.

The day one of the birds had smashed itself free from its rattan cage and a razor-sharp spearpoint of the exploding wood had sliced his face to the bone, he had reached number nine hundred and twelve and, still bleeding, had had to go on killing another eighty-eight times before he could feel that the day had any meaning to him financially and he could stop and wipe away the blood.

He knew the ducks he killed were dressed and dried and salted when they were put into wagons on the train because after he had finished at the farm at dusk he had another job, carrying and loading blocks of salt into the salting works next to the railroad freight yards until midnight.

There, working at two cents a block, he learned to count a second time, and, this time, paying back not a simple number like eight cents in every ten to the person who had gotten him the job, but thirty-three and a third percent of the first two hundred and fifty blocks, twenty-five percent of the next fifty, and a mere twelve and a half thereafter, he learned to *calculate*, to understand profit and profit margins, and, as he worked, to think and plan.

Standing looking at the lights with his mind only half-lit, touching at his hands, he remembered things of childhood and youth.

And nothing else.

He supposed from the card he had found in his pocket that he had a daughter, and therefore, somewhere in his life, he must have had a wife, but he had no recollection of her at all, and if she still lived he did not know where she was or what she looked like, or if she was dead whether he missed her or not.

He remembered that his first real business venture when he

came in from the New Territories after the Japanese had invaded China in the 1930s and all the great houses and mansions and restaurants in Canton had been closed, was the renting out on Empress of India Street of the headphones of a crystal-set radio he had had built so passersby could keep up with the hourly news of the war on their way to and from work.

His place of business was a square of the pavement three-foot by four-foot: his stomach and upper arms still carried the scars from where on at least six occasions he had had to defend it from claim-jumpers with razors and crystal sets of their own.

He remembered the war and the Japanese Occupation and how he had moved inside to his first roofed premises with a full-time contract from the Imperial Army Signals Corps to block out the international and long-range wave bands on all the private radios seized and brought to him by the Occupiers so they could not receive broadcasts from Radio Free China in India; the Japanese paying ten virtually worthless New Hong Kong cents a time, and the people who wanted their returned, blocked-off radios unblocked again, paying, each time, the two dollars in gold.

That little enterprise had almost cost him his life, but all he could remember about that was the frozen terror of the moment the Japanese had put him in a line of people to be shot and the blood and brains from the next man in line drenching his face and neck like a river as he was killed, and he could not remember how he survived or why the officer with the pistol either did not shoot him next, or missed, or, thinking he was already dead when he fell down with the shock and the gore, had simply moved on to the next in line.

But he could not remember. He could not remember what had happened at all.

He wished he knew the names of the buildings in front of

him or the names of the streets they were in, or who he was and why the buildings and the streets were important to him, and he put his hand in the other pocket of his coat to see if he carried a wallet or an identity card or anything that might have his name on it.

Attention POLICE:

If this old gentleman is found wandering, please contact . . .

It was another card, the same as the first.

He put his hand into his inside coat pocket and there was another, and in the pocket of his shirt another, and in his pants pockets two more, and he supposed, with his eyes blinking at the thought of it, that whoever his daughter was she must love him, and instead of throwing the cards away, out of respect for her he put them all back carefully in his pockets where he had found them.

He wondered if she was inside at the banquet and he tried to think how, if there were a lot of tables, he could go back in there without sitting at the wrong table and embarrassing himself.

He wondered, gazing up at the stars, why, if she worried about him so much, she had even let him come out onto the deck in the night in the first place.

His body, as it had done all his life, told him what he wanted to know, and with the increasing pain in his bladder crying out for relief, he turned and went back into the passageway of the boat to go where he had originally meant to go unaccompanied: the toilets in the men's room.

Night and stars and lights and forgotten lives: in his tiny triumph, feeling for a moment young again and in control of his own life, he went down the passageway and opened the door of the men's room and went in.

And saw what was in there.

Hong Kong is an island of some thirty square miles under British administration in the South China Sea facing Kowloon and the New Territories areas of continental China. Kowloon and the New Territories are also British administered, surrounded by the Communist Chinese province of Kwantung. The climate is generally subtropical, with hot, humid summers and heavy rainfall. The population of Hong Kong and the surrounding areas at any one time, including tourists and visitors, is in excess of six and a half million people.

And saw what was in there.

The New Territories are leased from the Chinese. The lease is due to expire in 1997, at which time Hong Kong is slated to become a special, semiindependent region of the People's Republic with the promise of a peaceful blending of British parliamentary rule of law and the Chinese Communist People's Army to enforce it—and if you believe that is going to happen peacefully, you will believe almost anything.

And saw what was in there.

Hong Bay is on the southern side of the island, and the tourist brochures advise you not to go there after dark.

And when at last someone came to find him, Mr. Lim, who owned almost all the buildings he had been looking at in all the streets along the shoreline, as well as properties all over Hong Kong and in Kowloon, a chain of electrical discount supermarkets that spread all over Asia and down to Australia, four television stations in Taiwan and two in Singapore and one in Malaysia, and was guest of honor at the monthly banquet of the Hong Kong Millionaires' Club, had sunk to the tiled white floor of the men's room and begun to cry and, at the awful horror of it, drawn himself violently up on the floor into the fetal position, and as even his body lost the last of its memories, and everything that he had once been disappeared into the nothingness of age and senile decay, in final humiliation, wet himself like a baby.

I.

IMPORTANT!

To: All Senior Station Officers, Royal Hong Kong Police Force

From: Office of the Government of Hong Kong, London

Re: Peaceful Transition of Authority in British Crown Colony of Hong Kong into Other Hands

At his desk in the Detectives' Room of the Yellowthread Street Police Station, Hong Bay, Detective Senior Inspector Christopher Kwan O'Yee thought that the one thing he had always admired about the British was their seemingly effortless ability to make everybody else on earth feel like pure scum.

Soon it will come to pass that, after ninety-nine years of uneventful and

serene administration of the Colony of Hong Kong by the British gov-ernment . . .

(Leaving aside opium wars, Tong Wars, two world wars, riots, murders, mayhem, assassinations, kidnappings, revolts, shoot-ings, knifings, bashings, bludgeonings, and other assorted un-serene events too trivial to mention . . .)

. . . will end, and Another Hand will turn the wheel to windward and direct the fortunes of the then ex-Colony and its people . . .

O'Yee, scratching his head, said softly, "Gee, who could that be, I wonder? The Swiss? The Boola-Boolans? *Tonga?*"

. . . namely . . .

It was the third time he had read the communication that morning. For the third time he waited in a lather of expectation for the answer.

. . . the Chinese.

In his wonderment, O'Yee, slapping at his forehead and al-most knocking his glasses off, said, "Good God! Who would have thought *that?*"

As is well known, the British peoples, in one way or another, have had a long and happy association with the Chinese . . .

Seizing Shanghai, sacking Peking, introducing opium . . .

... and it is important that we continue this association up to the very end by continuing to be cognizant of the particular characteristics and national traits of the so-called Celestial Race that distinguish them from other peoples and taking the appropriate actions early to accommodate these characteristics and traits.

For instance, as is well known, all Chinese are—as our American cousins would say—height-challenged, often deficient in eyesight, and, in many ways, totally unfamiliar with Western technology, particularly at the massive lower stratum of society ...

That was to say, they were short, blind, stupid, and there were a lot of them.

O'Yee, not even pure scum but, as half Chinese and half Irish-American, even less than scum, said with his glasses fogging up in gratitude to whoever had written The Great Epistle From the Gods lying on his desk, "Thank you. Thank you very, very much."

... in short, even the simplest object or structure, so familiar to all of us, may constitute a grave danger to them ...

What that meant was that they were so fucking stupid they didn't even know what a door was.

Therefore, to this end (the continuance of this long and happy association of the past), and as a sign of friendship and good intentions in the future, the following immediate steps will be taken in all Police Stations and Departments in the Colony:

1. All criminal records, papers, files, dossiers, photographs, notes, etc., liable to Misinterpretation by people unfamiliar with the Western

European style of writing and communication, and therefore liable to confuse them, will be viewed by the Senior Administrative Officer in each Station and, where appropriate, sent by armed courier to Head-quarters to be held prior to the peaceful Handover at which time they will be destroyed . . .

The good old British: they were going to be thoughtful.

2. All weapons and dangerous objects, including guns, knives, swords, hatchets, axes, clubs, whips, chains, bludgeons, blackjacks, grenades, gas cannisters, poisons, germ cultures, parangs, machetes, and other manner and types of weapon and instruments of bodily injury seized from the indigenous population over the last ninety-nine years and still held in Evidence Rooms or in Station Armories, shall be gathered up, crated in wooden crates, and sent to Headquarters by common carrier to—for reasons of security—the fictitious personage of (Address) "Mr. George Gunn" . . .

Well, that would fool any spies the old Yellow Peril had around the place. That extra *n*, especially when squinted at via deficient eyesight, would definitely make any short, stupid, John Chinaman looking at it think the box contained nothing more than used Yeti parts.

Crate to be marked in order to facilitate rapid sorting: ATTEN-TION ARMORY.

The good old British: they were going to be orderly.

. . . after all, no one would wish any of our Chinese friends to come to harm through the accidental discharge or slash of a weapon during

the period when—in their simple joy—drinking and revelry might be involved and caution thrown to the winds . . .

And the yellow ape-men celebrated in the streets by tearing up the trees and throwing bananas at each other.

. . . we should always remind ourselves that as the original guardians of the affairs of the Colony, it is our duty to leave it in a state that will reflect well on our many years of stewardship and serve as a model and inspiration to the coming Other Hands . . .

They were going to be good.

. . . and as a general guideline, in all we do in the time in advance of the Handover to Other Hands, it would perhaps not be inappropriate to keep uppermost in our minds those immortal words of the poet Andrew Marvell written upon the death by beheading of His Majesty King Charles in 1649:

> *. . . [they] nothing common did, or mean,*
> *Upon that mem-or-able scene—*

They were going to be good and orderly and civilized and kind and selfless and poetic.

There was more, pages and pages of it, but at his desk, staring wide-eyed down at it, O'Yee could not get his squinty, deficient Chinese eyes to move past the last two lines to read any more.

The British . . . The folks who brought you The Charge of the Light Brigade, The Massacre on the Somme, The Defeat at Dunkirk, and the loss of the entire continent of North America as only a few of the high points in their thousand-year history of complete and utter bungling and incompetence . . . they were going to be *noble*.

At his desk, O'Yee said in horror, *"Oh, no!"*

—He knew something awful was about to happen.

Something awful had already happened.

> *3. A minimum of two detective officers will—prior to a Quali-fied Person coming from London at a later date to view items held in Evidence Rooms, etc.—carefully examine and where necessary dis-mantle all pieces of plumbing in the various stations where, over the last many decades, objects of value (diamonds, sapphires, gold, plat-inum, silver, etc., for example) may have fallen, been lost, or in the case of the Criminal Elements, been discarded or "ditched" to avoid detection . . .*

Something awful was still happening.

It was happening two floors below in the sub-basement.

It was happening at the base of the battery of open church-organlike ends of the oldest toilet pipes on the face of the earth that, through a maze of links and connections and joints, came out one floor up in the basement in the holding-cell area at the oldest row of filthy, stained, cracked, blocked, backed-up, re-volting, and generally retch-making prisoners' toilets in the his-tory of the world.

There was a noise in the pipes like a giant burp, and the awful thing came sliming and slithering down the center pipe and with a squelch landed on the sub-basement floor an inch from De-tective Phil Auden's rubber-booted foot.

Auden said in the sudden stench of the thing that would have killed any ordinary man, "Oh, my God!" Auden shrieked a foot away from the pipe, "What the hell was that?" He looked down and it was still moving—twitching. It was a green-and-black lump. It was alive. Auden screamed up the pipe, "It's still moving!"

The voice of He Who Was Safe a floor above in the cells came booming down through the pipe like the voice of God. God had an upper-class English accent—which would have hardly surprised the man who had written Item 3 of the IMPORTANT! order that had gotten them down here in the first place. Up there, ramming hard with a long flexible steel rod at what was probably another of God's little creations stuck halfway down the pipe next to the center pipe, Detective Inspector Bill Spencer yelled down the cast-iron speaker tube, "I don't know what *anything* is!" He sounded a little disappointed. "All I can do is push the rod down the pipe until I feel something caught in there, and try to free it! You're the one who gets to see it when it goes through, not me!"

Well, lucky old him. Auden glanced down at the lump. It had gone. Auden yelled, "It's gone!"

"You've lost it?"

"I didn't lose it! It *went!*"

"What was it?"

"I don't know what it was! That's why I asked you what it was in the first place!" The sub-basement was a nasty dark place running with slime and full of drains and grates and dark, dark corners. All he had to protect himself were coveralls and rubber boots. Auden shrieked, "It's like the spaceship from *Alien* down here! It could be anywhere!" Two floors up, in his desk drawer in the Detectives' Room he had his .357 Magnum Colt Python loaded with hollow-point bullets. Even if he could get there fast enough, it wouldn't be enough. Somewhere behind him, there was a ker-plunk! Auden shrieked, "It's moving!"

"Try and see what it is!"

"I don't want to see what it is!"

There was something wrong with Spencer. He was an enthusiast. Spencer yelled down enthusiastically, "Phil, the whole history of Hong Kong is written in the stuff stuck in these pipes! You never know what you might find!"

Oh, yes, he did. Oh, yes, he did. Oh, yes, he did. From the center pipe there was a scraping sound and Auden shrieked up to him before he sent down the Thing That Lived's older brother, "For God's sake, don't push anything else down until I—" There was a squelch, then a sound like a rush of water, and Auden shrieked in panic, "Bill! Don't—"

And then a thud.

And then a scraping sound again and another squelch.

Spencer yelled down in answer to the unfinished sentence, "What?"

He didn't know what the sentence was. Probably, the sentence was Death. Suddenly, everywhere in the sub-basement, there was another sound: a sound like very—very—heavy breathing.

Spencer yelled, "I didn't do anything!"

There was a clang.

Spencer yelled down, "What was that?"

It was the Ooze Creature from Hell putting on its armor.

Auden thought he shrieked back, "I don't know what it was!" but he didn't. He opened his mouth, but nothing came out.

Then there was a clang, then a scraping, then a squelch, then, all at once, a clang-scrape-squelch and what sounded like the entire brick wall of a ten story building falling down. Auden, knowing for sure this time he said it, said, *"Oh, my God!"*

Spencer shrieked down, "What was that?"

He didn't know. His brain didn't work anymore.

Spencer shrieked, "It didn't come from the pipe! It must have come from somewhere down there in the slime where you are!"

He knew that. Auden said, not loudly enough to carry up the pipe, "Yes."

He knew that. He knew it hadn't come out of the pipes in front of him. He knew it had come from the walls. Behind him.

Spencer shrieked down, "Phil? Are you still down there?"

He knew who Phil was—he just couldn't place him for a moment. Auden said, "Yes."

"Phil—?"

There was a squish, squelch, rush, clang, scrape, and then a hissing sound.

Auden said sadly, about to be eaten, "Oh, gee . . ."

"If it's not coming from the pipes, it must be coming from one of the floor grates where the drains are!"

Auden said, "Oh." Some tiny part of his cerebellum was still working. Unfortunately, it was the part capable of comparing what might have come out of a five-inch-diameter effluvia pipe in front of him with what might come out of a half-visible five-foot-diameter sewer-drain grate in the complete gloom behind him. Auden said in answer to some question or other—probably whether he knew "Phil"—"Oh, yes. Okay . . ."

Scrape!

Clang!

Auden said, "Oh, shit!"

"Phil—!?"

Squish!

Auden said, paralyzed, "Oh, God—!"

Crash!

"Hang on! I'm coming down!"

Squelch!

Scrape!

Clang!

Squish!

Rumble!

Auden said, at the end of his life, "Oh, Lord!"

Then, squish! Crash! Squelch! Scrape! Clang! Squish! Rumble! *THUD!*

And then, under his feet, the entire earth moved.

In the sub-basement, Auden, Meal of the Month, *plat de jour,* said like a lobster about to be popped into the pot and scalded alive, "Oh . . . *no!!"*

Starting to rock back and forth in his chair at his desk—no Dunkirk or Charge at Balaclava or Surrender at Yorktown for him—O'Yee shouted to the wall of the Detectives' Room and whoever had written the Missive from the Master Race, "Oh, no, no, no, no, no! I saw that movie! It was called *Assault on Precinct Thirteen!* It was where the poor dumb L.A. police lieutenant following orders from above obediently goes to a police station they're closing down, crates up all the weapons he might need to use in an emergency in the place, and what happens? Some crazed civilian who's too shocked to say what happened to him turns up at the door followed by half the gangs in the entire city of L.A. armed with everything from single-shot .22 pistols to .50 caliber belt-fed Vulcan mini-guns to kill him and anybody else who's stupid enough to still be in the place!"

At his desk, O'Yee said to the chinless little twerp who thought he knew better than a man with five thousand years of Chinese civilization and culture running through his veins and a thousand years of Irish cunning coming in at the capilliaries, "Oh, no, no, no, no . . ."

Shouting at the wall, like the dumb cop in *Assault on Precinct*

Thirteen, O'Yee, shaking his head, losing his grip, said definitely, "Oh, no, no, no, no, no!"

Peering into the open drain in the glow of Spencer's flashlight, Auden said, not wanting to know, "Well, what is it?"

He got a grip on himself.

In *Assault on Precinct Thirteen*, all the poor dumb cop had in the decommissioned station was one female clerk working the telephones that didn't work anymore and one female detective hanging around talking to the clerk and wondering why the telephones didn't work anymore.

And then, because that was all he had, by halfway through the movie, he had a crazed, mute civilian, two temporarily free death-row murderers, a slew of dead bodies, and half a million crazed gang members climbing in the windows and shooting everything that moved to shit.

No comparison.

Passing through the corridor by Uniformed Section, he had at least twenty armed and determined Hong Kong cops, telephones that always worked because—someone who knew what they were talking about had told him—they were linked to satellites around the earth or in space or somewhere—and faxes and computers and radios and every other modern modernity known to Science, all manned by people who knew exactly what they were doing.

And the station was not in East L.A. where the gangs were, it was in southern Hong Kong.

. . . where the gangs were.

But they were nicer gangs.

They were Chinese gangs.

Cultured gangs.

He was being dumb.

Almost at the door of the Evidence Room, where all the guns, knives, clubs, and assorted weapons of war that had been seized from the nice Chinese gangs in almost ninety-seven years of nonstop slaughter were kept, O'Yee stopped to get an even firmer grip on himself.

He was Chinese. He was Irish.

They were not people who got excited over nothing.

Crate the weapons—who cared? Why not?

O'Yee said, "Right. Crate the weapons. Why not? What could happen?"

Turning, he went back down the corridor towards all the good people in the Uniformed Section of the Station to ask about crates.

It was a ten-ton aerial bomb at least twenty feet long and two and a half feet in diameter wedged sideways in the smashed-down brick wall of the ancient sewers of the Station with one of its fins sticking straight up in the air and the other two bent and buckled in among the bricks. It was huge, painted blue-black, with no markings on it at all.

In the sub-basement, gazing at it with a strange light in his eyes, Detective Inspector Bill Spencer said in an awed whisper, "It's a *bomb* . . ."

He looked down at it and something happened to his voice and it became the voice of a nine year old unwrapping his Christmas gift and finding in it the one thing he had always hoped to get, thought he never would get, and now, had got. Spencer said, so happy his voice quivered, "It's a *bomb!* . . ."

Spencer said with his little hands forming fists around the flashlight, "Oh! . . ."

It was not even a word. It was a sort of sigh.

Spencer said again, "Oh—!"

All his life, all he had ever wanted to be was Brave Bomb Disposals Bill. All his life, all he had wanted to do was wear a microphone around his neck and, as he slowly unscrewed the detonator and all the world wondered, say carefully and slowly so that if he—and it was just jolly bad luck if it happened—was blown to bits, the next Johnny in line would know how to proceed: *I-am-now-unscrewing-the-detonator* . . .

Spencer said, "Oh . . . Oh . . ."

It was A Bomb.

Spencer, so happy he could not even speak, said breathlessly, "Oh . . . oh . . . *Oh!* . . ."

In his joy, wanting to share his gift with his friend, with a trembling hand, Spencer passed over the flashlight to Auden so he could look at it too.

Uniformed didn't have any crates. They didn't have any crates because they didn't think they were moving out of anywhere for a while and when they did move out when the Chinese Communists came, they expected it only to be a day or two for the sake of appearance and then they'd all move back in again and things would go on the way they had always gone on.

Good old Uniformed. Good old backbone of reality. Good old mollifiers of the mass-hysterical. Good old—

On his way back to the Detectives' Room, O'Yee, smiling and nodding to himself, said to the anonymous IMPORTANT! Penner of the Approaching Apocalypse, "See? This is Hong Kong. This is China. Things happen differently here. There's a difference between colonization and infestation, and all you ever did here was colonize us."

Us?

And why not?

In this world, you had to know who you were.

He was O'Yee.

O'Yee said in Cantonese, "Damn right!"

He said happily, feeling better about everything by the moment, "Begorrah!"

He went back to the Detectives' Room to read more of the communication and—with a larklike laugh at his lips at its utter lack of lore—ignore it all completely.

In the glow of the flashlight, looking down into the sewer, Auden said in a gasp, "Oh, my God!"

It was a Bomb.

A big one.

It was the same sort of thing as the Colt Python in his drawer in the Detectives' Room two floors above—only bigger—and in this case, aimed at him.

Auden said in a gasp, "Oh, my God! It's at least a ten-tonner— a Second World War German Satan bomb, or a British Grand Slam, or an American—" He couldn't contain himself. He had seen pictures of them in his copy of *Jane's Every Lethal Weapon Known to Man Since the Beginning of Time*. Auden said, staring down at it with eyelids stuck open in horror, "It's a fucking, great, huge, live, enormous, massive, fucking—*bomb!*"

From somewhere behind him in the gloom out of the flashlight's circle of light, a voice that sounded a little like Spencer doing George C. Scott doing General George Patton said in an odd, dreamy voice, "All my life I have wanted to lead a large body of men in a last desperate battle. All my life I have wanted to be the man who defused a great, huge, live, enormous, massive . . . *bomb!*"

He took a step into the circle of light and his face lit up in light and dark shadows like a papier-mâché geographer's globe of the moon, with two gleaming eyes at the thirty-eighth parallel. Spencer said in his quiet Churchillian way, "Phil, all my life has been but a preparation for this one moment—"

He took it in. Still staring down at the Bomb—it was a *Bomb!*—Auden said as if he had not taken it in, "What?"

"Yes." He was so happy. He patted Auden on the shoulder to share his happiness. Spencer said, "I know about these things."

He tried to think. He couldn't think. Auden said, "What?"

"I know how to defuse this bomb."

"Oh." Somewhere deep in Auden's mind, a brain cell said to Auden to remind him, "You read a book too, once." It was a good book, a book with a blue cover he had found in his uncle's attic in London. It was called *What You Should Know in the Event of an Air-Raid, HMSO, 1941.* It was full of words.

The words were Bomb. Death. Death on a Wide Scale. Shrapnel. Massive Explosion. Death on a Very Wide Scale, Blast. Concussion. Destruction. Injury, Concussion, Mass Slaughter. Death, Injury and Destruction on an Extremely on a Very Wide Scale. Auden said, "What?"

"Yes!" He wanted him to be part of it. Spencer said happily, making the good fellow gaze at him in astonishment at his pure, unbridled munificence, "Yes! And you can help! You can hold the bomb while I do it!"

It was a Bomb. Auden said, aghast, "Oh! Oh, my *God!*"

Spencer said, "Oh . . . *Yippee!*"

Almost falling over each other in the slime and muck on the sub-basement floor in their rush, they both ran together towards the stairs to be the one to get to O'Yee first to give him the good news.

2.

If anyone was watching from any of the rear windows in the massive monolith of the St. Paul deChartres Hospital on Empress of India Street, all they looked like were two people sitting on a stone bench contemplating the spiritual things of life in the Zen Buddhist stone-and-sand garden provided by the hospital for the purpose—one a female surgeon wearing green operating-room scrubs, and the other a tall, fair-haired man wearing a white suit and striped tie.

Perhaps they were talking about life and death, and grieving: the doctor, a slight figure in her late thirties or early forties with etched lines under her eyes from a lifetime of living in hot, unprotected places, kept looking over to the Mortuary building off the Pathology wing and the unmarked undertaker's pick-up hearse parked outside its side entrance.

The garden was a place of peace and tranquility and serenity. In her case, it seemed to have failed to achieve its purpose, and as she glanced back and forth, then back and forth again, she drummed her fingers on the arm of the bench.

She was an emergency-room surgeon: It was stencilled on her scrubs below the neck and again on the shoulders of the sleeves.

The garden was raked daily in different symmetrical patterns and whorls of sand around the rocks; representations of some aspect of the never-beginning, never-ending, interconnected nature of the universe. This morning, it had been raked in long, perfectly parallel, shallow wavelets, representing the nearness of all living things in the spiritual life and, at the same time, their distance from each other and solitude in the physical one.

Still drumming on the arm of the stone bench, not looking at him at all, in a voice so soft it seemed she was afraid of offending someone, Doctor Rebecca Pickering asked with her attention still focused on the Morgue, "Are you thinking of staying on after the takeover, Harry? Or going?"

He knew her personally hardly at all. His wife was the chief pharmacologist in the hospital and he only knew her through her.

All he knew about her was that, like his wife, she had grown up in East Africa when it had been a British Colony, been thrown out when it ceased to be a British Colony and become Uganda, gone with her family to Rhodesia, and, unlike his wife and her family, been thrown out of there when it became Zimbabwe, and then, he thought he remembered his wife telling him, moved on to work and study in the United States for a year or two, and then, when her visa and work contract expired, been thrown out of there as well.

Maybe that was why the voice was so soft: She had learned that to be unnoticed was best.

Answering her question, Detective Chief Inspector Harry Feiffer said equally softly, as if it were a matter of conspiracy, "I'm not sure. It depends how things play themselves."

He waited, but she kept watching the side entrance of the Morgue and did not reply.

Feiffer asked, "How about you?" By nationality, she was English. He thought she could always go back there.

"My husband's Chinese. He wants to stay on." And so she had, therefore, nowhere to go. Doctor Pickering, still gazing at the Morgue, still drumming her fingers, said softly, "The only place that has to take me in by dint of passport is England." There was a movement at the back of the hearse and she leaned forward a little to watch it. "I've never been there. Have you?"

"Once."

"What was it like?"

It was dreary and dark and, compared to the life and sound and smell and vibrancy of the East, it was a country painted not in all the colors of the rainbow, but in unrelenting, soul-numbing black and white. Feiffer said, "It was cold and it seemed to rain all the time."

The movement at the Morgue was the undertaker and the mortuary attendant bringing out a body on a stretcher. Working together, they slid the stretcher into the back of the hearse and then both went in after it and closed the doors behind them.

Because the undertaker worked in a highly competitive business, and because the Morgue attendants had a nice little racket going informing this particular undertaker ahead of anyone else when someone died in the hospital, it was where a little money was going to change hands.

She had been thinking, not only about the Morgue, but about the garden. Doctor Pickering, turning suddenly to Feiffer as the undertaker and the attendant both got out of the rear of the vehicle and the undertaker went around to the driver's door to go, said in a voice that sounded firm and loud and decisive, "You know, Harry, the thing about living on the brink, at least according to the Zen Buddhists, is that the balance is perilous . . . but the view is so spectacular!"—and somewhere deep and se-

cret inside her, there was an entire dimension different to anyone else's brought on by years of soft voices and alienation neither he nor anyone else—perhaps not even her husband—would
ever know anything about. Glancing back to the Morgue as the
attendant went back inside to his little office off the corridor
that led into the cold rooms and the autopsy theater, Doctor
Pickering said, "I'm sorry to have called you at home, Harry, but
I think there's something you ought to see before it's gone."

Across the square from the garden, as the hearse pulled out
and turned in the direction of the street, and the door to the
Morgue closed, she stood up and, as if it was all she needed to
go anywhere in the place, touched unconsciously at the stencilled
words Emergency Room Surgeon on her scrubs and, pinned
below it, the hospital nameplate reading *Rebecca Pickering, M.D.*

Already on her feet and starting to move, Rebecca Pickering
said urgently, "Come on. Quickly. Before that venal little bastard
in the Morgue gets on the phone again and half the undertakers
in Hong Kong swarm over here and start fighting like the goddamned vultures they are for the right to get in there and take
what's inside away—!"

*4. Pursuant to (3), when a Device or Object that may endanger
life or limb on a large scale is located, while reasonable efforts should
be made to ensure the safety of the local indigenous/aboriginal popu-
lations from harm, the question of unreasoning and counterproductive panic should be properly weighed before communicating its
discovery to the masses.*

That meant don't tell old Charlie the Chink anything because,
if you do, he's liable to go berserk and come at you with a meat
cleaver.

Standing on the top step of the Station with a loud-hailer in his hand, O'Yee said with a look of Superior Knowledge on his face, "The little you know . . ."

Below him, in the street, there were people everywhere—*his* people—Chinese people: people working and dealing and selling and living and crowding and . . . and being Chinese, hundreds of them, thousands of them—in the clatter and crash and color and life and smell and heat of Yellowthread Street, buyers, sellers, loaders, unloaders, walkers, saunterers, amblers, perambulators, packers, pickers, pedestrians. There were shops, stalls, storehouses, smells—the smells of spices and sweat, smoke. There was movement, sound, a roar of a thousand voices all talking and negotiating and treating and trading at once: in their intercourse and presence there were ten thousand years of history and culture and learning and lore and loudness.

They were the people of his ancestors.

Wallowing in his own Chineseness, O'Yee, doing his duty as per *4. Pursuant to (3),* said into the loud-hailer as loudly as he could, "—BOMB!"

The local indigenous/aboriginal population, instantly panic-stricken to a man, took not one blind bit of notice.

He did his duty again. O'Yee yelled again, "—*BOMB!*"

Nothing.

O'Yee said to IMPORTANT! He who knew nothing, "See? This isn't East L.A., this is Hong Kong. This isn't *Assault on Precinct Thirteen*—this is Yellowthread Street Station, Hong Bay. This isn't where the phones all suddenly go dead . . ."

Down in the slime by the bomb—just cleaning up a little—Spencer said with a strange, glassy look on his face, "I-am-now-cutting-the-unmarked-unidentified-wire-that-seems-to-lead-from-the-bomb-into-the-sewer-wall . . ." and with a single click all the phones and faxes and computers in the Station instantly went dead.

"—this is where Celestial Civilization and the Sanity and Reason of the oldest race on the face of the earth reign! This is where—"

Lowering the loud-hailer, O'Yee said softly, "Tax Department raid . . ."

God, how he loved those kind hearts and gentle people.

Turning back from the suddenly emptied, ghost town of a street, O'Yee went in to share his admiration with the seventeen heavily armed uniformed cops in the station before using one of the phones in the Detectives' Room to call the army bomb-disposals people to come and disarm the bomb.

There were no heavily armed uniformed cops in the Station—they were all gone.

There were no phones—they were all dead.

Hong Bay, East L.A./Yellowthread Street Station, Precinct Thirteen: unreasoning and counterproductive panic. O'Yee, alone in the place in the silence of a tomb, said as an order to himself, "Don't panic!"

All he needed now was a mute, half-crazed and terrified civilian to rush in with half the gangs in the uncivilized world hot on his heels with guns and meat cleavers to kill him.

But, although he waited stock-still for a full half minute, no one even vaguely resembling that description rushed in or even strolled in.

They didn't have to.

Standing behind the open door of the Detectives' Room and therefore invisible, he was already there, mute, terrified, half crazed, and, with his hands up against his chest like a dog trying to balance on its hind legs to please its master, completely, utterly, deeply, soundly, asleep.

*　　*　　*

In the autopsy room of the Morgue, Doctor Pickering pulled back the sheet on the gurney parked against the wall by the sliding main doors, and Feiffer looked down into the face of something from another world.

Feiffer said in a gasp, "God Almighty!"

It was not a man. It was some sort of grotesque caricature of a man, twisted naked on the bed of the shining steel gurney with all the muscles in its face locked in a cavernous open-mouthed shriek with long lines of blood and tissue and skin dried on it like melted makeup. In the left eye socket there was no eye. In the right, the orb of an exploded eyeball hung down onto the cheekbone, connected only by a ragged network of ragged and blood- and fluid-soaked viscera. At the neck, where the head was twisted away to one side, all the blood vessels were swollen and black and bulging. The face was unrecognizable: from the top of the forehead to the sides of the mouth, it had been clawed open in eight long, deep claw marks.

As Doctor Pickering handed him the edge of the sheet and stepped back, Feiffer lifted the sheet to expose the full body and saw the claw marks again, this time running laterally across the body below the breastbone. From the color of the skin, the body was Chinese; from the parchmentlike wrinkling of it around the breasts and armpits, an old, old man. He looked at the hands, and the nails were long and carefully manicured—a man of substance who did no physical work—and then he looked again and saw all the blood and tissue caught under them like little flecks of paper and confetti.

Standing back a little, watching him, Doctor Pickering shivered once. Maybe it was just the cold. Then, for some reason, Doctor Pickering said evenly, "He was brought in via Emergency last night at about nine." There was undoubtedly paper on the patient, but she either didn't need it or didn't have access to it. "His name is Tam Kwan Yu, aka Kenneth Tam, age eighty-three, company director, with a home address on The Peak."

He was a tiny, birdlike creature, maybe five foot four or five in height with, around the awful sewn-back cut on his head where the surgeon had taken the top of the skull and scalp off to get at the brain, wisps of white hair.

"—according to information the Emergency Response crews got on the scene, he was discovered on the floor in the first-class men's rest room of the floating restaurant *The Pearl Princess* about 8:45 P.M." She shivered again, but it was not from the cold, or fear—it was from something else. "The man who found him could offer the paramedics no information at all as to what happened. He was well into his eighties himself, and senile, and the crew had to sedate him until his own doctor could come and make arrangements to take him away for treatment."

In over twenty years as a homicide and major-crime detective, he had seen a lot of dead bodies. He had never seen anything like this one. It was like looking at something in a museum from another era, another culture, another epoch, something dead and silent for centuries. It was the body, not of a modern rich man who wore tailored silk suits and handmade bright polished leather shoes, but of an Ice Man, something caught and crushed and twisted and distorted under a glacier millennia ago. Doctor Pickering said, "The cause of death, apparently, in the absence of the family allowing an autopsy to be performed, was a massive stroke accompanied by a catastrophic heart attack and widespread and violent hemorrhaging in at least eighty percent of all the veins and arteries in the brain, as well as what appears, again without autopsy examination, to be a sudden and instantaneous asthmalike shutting down of almost the entire bronchial tree and both lungs."

Feiffer saw her touch at her side again. Doctor Pickering said with no tone in her voice, "He was attending a monthly dinner of the Millionaires' Club. Evidently, the rest room for people like that is covered from wall to wall in mirrors and when the old man found him, he looked a lot worse than he does now."

"Is it a homicide?"

Doctor Pickering said, "No, according to the Death Certificate and Pathology and this hospital, no other person was involved."

In which case, it occurred to him to wonder why he was there and what she wanted from him, but she was gazing into the distance or deep inside herself, thinking about something not in the room but somewhere else, and he did not ask.

"Was it a fit? Or a seizure? Or a—"

"No. There's no typical evidence of any sort of known—"

"What about poison, or—"

"No." Doctor Pickering said for the second time, "No, there's no evidence of any outside agency being involved. Or any sort of foreign substance or solution or invasive procedure or external trauma. According to the Death Certificate that will be issued later today so the family can come and claim the body, he died of natural causes."

"What about his eyes?"

She was silent for a moment, perhaps wondering whether or not he knew what she wanted from him, perhaps wondering whether she even knew herself.

For the first time, she looked down directly into the dead man's face.

As if, at the sight, something in her side hurt, she winced with pain, and, talking not to Feiffer, but to the dead face as if it could hear her, Doctor Pickering said in a strange, sad, lost, confused voice, "Well, that's the thing, isn't it?" Turning to Feiffer with a look on her face he could not read at all Rebecca Pickering said softly, "Judging by the skin and other matter still caught under his fingernails, Harry, either before or after or during whatever it was that made his entire body *explode*, he clawed his entire chest apart and both of his eyes out himself!"

Down in the slime by the bomb, with O'Yee's shrieks still ringing in his ears, Spencer said with a strange, hurt look on his face, "I-am-now-reconnecting-the-clearly-marked-and-easily-identifiable-Hong-Bay-Telephone-Company-wire-that-does-not-lead-from-the-sewer-wall-into-the-bomb-at-all, but-leads-from-the-sewer-wall-into-the-main-telephone-and-computer-and-fax-terminal-of-the-Station. And waiting for the army Bomb-Disposals team to arrive."

He reconnected it and, with a click, all the phones and faxes and computers came back on again.

Spencer said in the tone of a small, disappointed boy, not looking over his shoulder to where Auden was, but up to the roof of the sewer where, three floors above, O'Yee was, "Mistakes can happen to anybody! Nobody's *perfect!*"

Certainly, the man behind the door of the Detectives' Room wasn't. No more than five foot two, with a face like a gargoyle, he looked, as he waited there with his eyes closed, gently dozing, like a demon gathering his strength to strike.

As if she was still thinking, not of the man in front of her, but something else, Doctor Pickering said into the air, "When I saw him in the ALSV he looked even worse than he does now—"

The ALSV was the Advanced Life Support Vehicle. Feiffer asked quickly, "Do you mean he was still alive when he got here?"

"No. I pronounced him DOA in the back of the truck." It was

all part of the nightmare. Doctor Pickering said, "Normally, the ALSV has a crew of four and two of them carry the patient in while the other two stay in the vehicle in case there's a rapid-response call, but in this case, one of the crew—the one who's detailed to stay in the back with a DOA—was so terrified he wouldn't even get back in and he came back to the hospital, I gather, about two hours later, dead drunk."

It was enough. In the awful place, with his skin starting to crawl at the sight of it, Feiffer said as an order for her to tell him what she knew, "Rebecca, what really killed him? Do you know—*or don't you?*"

The Demon Behind the Door was dressed in jeans and a plain gray T-shirt and no shoes.

The Demon was an odd nut-brown color with big, powerful hands. And, tucked away in back out of sight in the belt of the jeans under the overhanging shirt, it carried an axe.

She could not stop her lower lip and chin from trembling, and in the silent, cold room, Feiffer could hear her breathing getting faster.

Rebecca Pickering said, "*Fright!* He died of *fright!* He was *frightened* to death! He died of sudden, awful, unreasoning terror!" She touched at her side and looked, not at Feiffer or the dead thing on the gurney, but into the distance, away to something else, to somewhere else, to another time. Doctor Pickering said into that place, "Years ago, thirty years, a hundred years, a thousand years ago, a million years ago when I was a child in Africa, when I was five, my family and I went to stay with friends on their farm for a week in Kenya and I talked them into letting me sleep for the first night in a tent out in the native village." She would not look back and her mouth was trembling. "And just before dawn something woke me and I looked up half asleep and saw something black and I thought it was one of the village Kikuyu girls who'd come around to see who I was—which was the general idea—and make friends with me— But it wasn't. It was a panther."

In the awful, cold room of the dead, there was only silence.

Rebecca Pickering, no longer five, said in the soft voice of a five year old, "I had on my pajamas with the little white-and-red flowers on them, but the top had come up and all of my stomach was bare, and the panther had its nose against my tummy sniffing it."

Taking a step forward to her, Feiffer said to comfort her, "Rebecca, I'm sorry if I—"

"No!" She still did not look at him. She put her open hand out like a traffic policeman to keep him away. "And I looked at it out of the corner of my eye and it saw me and it looked at me and all I wanted to do was wet the bed, but I was afraid to make any noise and because of the pressure on my bladder, my stomach started shaking and I—and it came so close to my face that all I could see was its huge yellow eyes and feel its breath on my face and smell the smell in its throat of something rotten and dead it must have eaten during the night, and then it pulled its face back a little and, very slowly, looked at me from one side of my face to the other, and then, when its face moved past mine, it stopped and looked at me out of the corner of its eye the way I was looking at it. And then—"

She closed her eyes for a moment, "And then—" And then she turned back to Feiffer, "And then, very quietly, not making a sound, it drew back and padded out of the tent and it was gone, and I thought—I thought, maybe it was a dream, and I thought—and I couldn't hold myself any longer and I wet the bed, and in the morning when one of the maids came from the big house to get me for breakfast she saw it and she told my parents and they told me I was too little to sleep away by myself and I—" Rebecca said, "And I never told them, and I never— And I—"

"Was it a dream?"

"I don't know!" The creature on the gurney looked like something from another world. "*Is that?* I don't know! I don't know!" Rebecca said suddenly, "Harry, I still dream about it! I dream about it every night! And I don't know if it was real or not!" She stabbed her finger in the direction of the dead man's face—"I know that face! It's the face of someone looking out of the corner of her eye at a panther! It's *my* face! But I was five! I survived it! But he didn't!"

Doctor Pickering said suddenly very quietly and professionally, "Harry, he's the third one in the past eight weeks: all male, all with every organ and cell and blood vessel in their bodies exploded, all rich, powerful people, all certified by the hospital as dead from natural causes, all taken away quickly by the family, and all—"

She looked at the face—"And all, all of them, looking exactly—exactly!—like *that!*"

It was why he was there, why she called him in.

Rebecca Pickering said desperately, "Harry, he saw something out there, something awful . . . and whatever it was that he saw *killed him!*"

At last, after all those years, she finally asked someone, "Find out. Find out! Find out what it was. Find the panther! Find out—will you? *Please?*"

3.

High Noon at Ground Zero.

Well, actually, ten past ten, four slimy, muck-filled, evil-smelling, brick-lined feet below ground zero.

Balancing carefully on the rim of the sewer hole to keep his shoes from getting dirty, the Bomb-Disposals man, a vision of resplendence in carefully pressed, positively gleaming British Army uniform, gazed down into the muck and the trogs inhabiting therein. Under his peaked cap, he had a face like a pained prune.

The Bomb-Disposals man said in an upper-class accent so clipped it could cut watercress sandwiches at a single slice, *"Who are you?"*

One of the trogs moved. It was the Auden trog. Trog Auden had an English accent too. It was the sort of English accent that could call cows in from the filthy fields. Auden said, "Auden."

He winced and looked even more pained. The BD man said with something on his face that was supposed to be a smile, "Captain Hetherington-Smith, Army BD." He looked at the other trog.

He had a nice accent. Spencer, looking up, said with a smile, "Bill Spencer, Royal Hong Kong Police."

The look on his face became a smile. It became a nod. The BD man said with a sigh of relief, "Ah, good morning, Bill— Captain the Honorable Roger Hetherington-Smith, bomb-tinkerer and all that." He kept smiling at Spencer. He ignored Auden completely. "Fella up in the office says you've got your-selves a little whiz-bang or something stuck down here in the jolly old mud."

The voice that called in cows—the stinking peasant standing hunch-backed and grovelling at the side of the medieval lane as the procession of great knights went off to the Holy Land— said with a snarl, "We haven't got a little whiz-bang, we've got a fucking great twenty-five-foot-long fucking *bomb!*"

Half submerged in the mire, there was a long dark shadow that looked like a long dark bomb. Leaning over the rim another fraction, the BD man pursed his lips and looked at it. On top of the bomb, laid out and gleaming, was every tool Spencer had been able to find in the entire station. The BD man, gazing at them too, said with a pleasant smile, "Hmm, eclectic set of tools, hey, Bill?" He looked at the cannon fodder his ancestors had sent into battle at all the great defeats in the history of the British nation for almost a thousand years and said helpfully in case the poor lower-class object thought it was a brand name, "*Eclectic*: it means a number of apparently unrelated objects or ideas picked out from various sources." Maybe it wasn't enough. Hard for the steaming masses to think in abstract terms. "You know, the two gas-pipe wrenches and the gunsmithing screw-drivers and the ball-peen hammer and the office staple gun and the jolly old plastic box of paper clips and all that—*Eclectic*: it's from the Latin *eclo*—"

Spencer said gently, "Actually, Rog, from the Greek *eklektikos*, meaning—"

"Meaning *picked out*." The BD man, right the first time about Spencer, but checking just to make sure, said happily, "Oh! Yes! Quite right! Full marks! Well done, young William! Must have been dozing away in class at the old school when they covered that one, hey?" There was some sort of growl from the gnarled peasantry standing next to Spencer, but he ignored it. "That the old bomb there, is it?"

The mucky peasantry said, dripping muck, "No, it's a fucking cream bun we ordered in from the local fucking baker's shop for morning fucking tea at the fucking Savoy!"

Spencer said, "Yes, it's the bomb." He patted the black monster. "No markings on it at all. At first, I thought maybe it was a World War Two German Satan bomb, but I think the fins are the wrong shape." He liked patting it. He patted it again. "Possibly a British Grand Slam, but I think they were longer and thinner." He stopped patting and began caressing. "American bomb maybe, or Japanese? What sort of bomb is it?"

"Hmm." He cast his expert eye along its lines and identified it in an instant. Captain Hetherington-Smith said, "Jolly *big* one!"

It was all the confirmation he needed. Spencer said happily, "Yes." There was a quiver in his voice. It became a tremor. It became a fervent prayer. Spencer said modestly, "Um, Rog—um, one has actually done a little studying-up on bomb disposal . . ."

One had? Jolly *good!* Hetherington-Smith said, still smiling, "Bit of good fortune on my part then. Jolly busy this morning up at barracks pulling apart a whole lot of old tank ammo some idiot left stacked up against a tin wall in the fuel depot so a little pressed for time." He flicked a casual finger at Auden to order him to charge the guns at Crimea and do or die. "Be a good chap, would you . . . um? . . ." whatever his name was, "—and just cut along through the slime there and stand at the end of the thing so I can get an idea of the shape of the nose, would you?" The peasant said something, but he didn't hear what it was. "Jolly good! Now put your arms around the circumference of the thing so I can—" Hetherington-Smith said, "Yes, standard old bomb, Bill. Just pull the fuse out of the nose, and then steam out the TNT or whatever it is inside and it's all done." It smelled down there. "If one has done a studying-up, one shouldn't have any trouble at all. I'll try to send someone along a bit later to check up, but one should find it a piece of cake, shouldn't one?"

He was going to be Brave Bomb Disposals Bill. Spencer, not trembling, not quivering, but positively vibrating, said in his joy, "Okay, Rog. Whatever you say!"

"Jolly *good!*" He glanced at his watch. "Well, tempus fugit, and all that. Well, one might as well make a start then, Bill, hey? Do or die, hey? Into the valley of death rode the six hundred and all that . . . and, of course—jolly good luck to you both!"

And then, still smiling, having dealt with that little matter of empire in his usual decisive manner, turned smartly on his heel, stepped back from the rim of the sewer opening into the darkness, and was gone.

Ah, the grand old days of the Divine Right of Kings and the positively sublime Silence of the Gnarled Peasantry.

Unfortunately, gone forever.

In the sewer, the gnarled peasantry roared, *"Spencer! Lay-one-little-finger-on-the-goddamned-bomb . . . AND I'LL KILL YOU!"*

Auden, starting to slosh back through the slime, shoving the nose of the bomb to one side as he came, said in a voice that could lop trees, *"If you so much as even—"*

The bomb, like he himself, didn't like being shoved to one side. Bouncing back off a loose section of the sewer brickwork and bringing it down in an avalanche of bricks, it came back and mowed Auden down and crashed into the other side of the brickwork and then came back and mowed him down again.

Auden said, "Oh!"

And then, it came back and moved in the other direction and mowed him down again.

Auden, on his back, reaching up to grab the nose as it went by, said, "Oh! Oh—!"

Auden, hanging on for dear life as the entire thing hit the brickwork again, came loose from the brickwork, and then suddenly straightened itself and careened down the sewer into pitch darkness, said like a man being taken for a quick ride into the Twilight Zone on the bottom of a runaway roller-coaster, "Oh! Oh—! Oh! . . . OH!"

Going, sliding, being taken on a fun ride to oblivion by a live twenty-five-foot-long, ten-ton bomb four feet below the surface of the earth, and getting deeper by the second, Auden said in utter terror, as the bomb turned a corner in a surf wave of slime and, hitting a solid brick wall, sent up a tsunami of brown, green, black, and all the shades in between of muck, mire, morass, and a millennia-old mountain of malodorous matter, *"OH, MY GOD!"*

It was the sound of a human body hitting a solid wall at the same time as the nose of a bomb and sending up a tsunami of brown, green, black, and all the shades in between of muck, mire, morass, and a millennia-old mountain of malodorous matter.

Then there was a silence.

Then there was not.

In the darkness, from somewhere deep inside its long slime-covered, unmarked blue-black-painted body, the bomb said loudly, clearly, unmistakably—like Frankenstein's evil monster just happy to be reanimated and alive again—". . . tick-tick-tick . . . *whirr!* . . . "

Maybe it was just the Morgue and the dead man in there, or Rebecca Pickering's talk of things that had happened a long time ago, but sitting in his car in *The Pearl Princess's* car park on Beach Road and gazing out at the junks and sampans moving like ghosts out to the South China Sea against a slate-gray sky, Feiffer could not escape a feeling of transitoriness and loss that had come across him when he had left the awful room and walked back to his car past the sand-and-rock garden in the hospital.

All along the shoreline of the car park where *The Pearl Princess* lay permanently moored, there was the stone wall of the typhoon shelter, built for protection and fortification out of the granite the entire island of Hong Kong itself was built on—like the island itself, with only two years to go before the takeover, no longer properly maintained, and, here and there as he looked at it, starting to crumble.

He glanced at the restaurant, and the bunting lines of lights that cobwebbed the entire vessel from end to end, now all dark and lifeless, looked, not as they did at night, like a celebration of life and power and money, but merely sad, colorless lines of lightbulbs.

Once, *The Pearl Princess* had been the premier passenger ferry of the old Kwang-Lee Pearl River Shipping Company's fleet that ran the six-hour Hong Kong–to–Macao route and back again four times a day and, in the days when China was still closed, as the boats passed perilously close to the mouth of the Pearl River and the gunboats and armed junks moored there along the shore, gave their passengers and tourists a brief, tantalizing glimpse of what was then a secret nation of almost a billion human beings, before turning away and heading for the safe Portuguese-leased waters of Macao.

No more. Now, the trip to Macao, which to all intents and purposes was no longer a Portuguese settlement founded in the days of the great explorers and privateers, but merely, like Hong Kong, a convenient and politically correct export outlet for the Communist Chinese state factories to the capitalist markets of the West, could be made by hydrofoil in less than an hour and a half and, with the high-speed wash blasting back against the hermetically sealed windows of the craft, with no distraction to the eyes or mind of anything except the soothing Muzak piped through the loudspeaker and the carefully muted and insulated humming of the aircraft engines that powered the craft.

He looked across at *The Pearl Princess*, and, like all times past and remembered, it was a fossil.

As he was himself. Born in Shanghai, when that too had been run by foreigners, to an English family who had not lived in or ever been to England for longer than two weeks in three generations, all he knew and had known all his life was the greatest fossil of them all: *Sinocolonialis*—Colonial China—the mad, unspeakably arrogant notion that the people of the largest, most populous and ancient civilization on the face of the earth were but a nation of small children incapable of disciplining or governing or organizing themselves without the firm but benign hand of a Mother Country and monarch ten thousand miles away regulating their every move.

On what had once been *The Pearl Princess* there was a small army of coolies in shorts and ragged T-shirts scrubbing the decks, bent down over mops and buckets or on their hands and knees with brushes—unceasing, uncomplaining: the Eternal Chinese, Old Hundred Names, all patiently dreaming the same dream of the prosperity of a big-bellied old age through a lifetime of hard work and commerce.

His mind kept wandering back to Shanghai where he had been a boy after the war and to his father who had seen out the last few years of the place in the International Settlement as a policeman, but whatever it was that had set him to thinking about it had nothing to do with Shanghai, and all the pictures of the place and his father in his uniform would not stay in his mind and kept fading.

All he kept seeing in his mind was the look on Rebecca Pickering's face as her lip trembled and the tears welled up in her eyes.

All he kept hearing was her voice, "Harry, he saw something out there, something awful . . . and whatever it was that he saw *killed him!*"

And he had heard the words once before, somewhere else, but they had nothing to do with here and now, and they were, in his mind, not even words at all, but whispers, and he could not think where or when or why he had ever heard them.

The sand-and-stone garden in the hospital had something to do with reflection and loss and grieving, and maybe it was just that.

Harry, he saw something, something awful . . . and whatever it was that he saw killed him!

It meant something.

It meant something, not only to Pickering and the dead creature on the Morgue gurney, but also to him, but, as he got out of his car to go to the boat to talk to the security officer about the death of Tam Kwan Yu, aka Kenneth Tam, age eighty-three, millionaire of The Peak and, if he knew anything about it, the similar death of a man named Yuan Fook Chee, aka Frederick Yuan, age eighty-one, also of The Peak, also a millionaire, a week before, and, six weeks before that a man named Ronnie Wong, age thirty-five, he could not think what it was.

In the long, dark, dank sewer, all he could hear was silence.

Taking a single step forward into the darkness, Spencer said in a small voice, "Hello? . . ."

Taking yet another careful, wary step down the dark, secret, silent passageway, Spencer said softly with a mixture of fear, apology, deep humiliation, and utter terror in his voice, "Hello, Phil? . . . Are you in here anywhere? . . ."

He was in there behind the door of the Detectives' Room: the mute, mad civilian from *Assault on Precinct Thirteen.*

Turning and seeing him as he walked forward, stiff-legged and with his arms outstretched a single step at a time, O'Yee said in horror, "Jesus, Joseph, and Mary!"

The mad civilian from *Assault on Precinct Thirteen* wore a T-shirt and jeans and no shoes and he had a nut-brown face like a wizened demon.

Stuck in the belt of his jeans at his back, sticking out over the hem of the T-shirt, he had an axe and in one of his wizened, clawlike hands a folded-up piece of paper.

And as he came forward, to judge from his breathing and his closed eyes, he was sound asleep.

In the center of the room by his desk, watching him as he came forward a single step at a time, O'Yee, ready for every emergency, paralysed with horror, said over and over, "Oh, Jesus! Oh, Jesus! Oh, Jesus!"

The folded-up paper, clearly, was meant for him.

As the creature from another world came forward like a sleeping goblin, still with its eyes closed tight, it pushed the paper out a little so O'Yee could come towards him and take it.

It was just the garden in the hospital and the dead man and the grayness of the day, that was all it was, and as he crossed the car park towards the gangplank of *The Pearl Princess* to find someone to talk to about the circumstances of the death of Kenneth Tam the night before, Feiffer put the sounds of whispers and secrets and hidden half-remembered things and his place in it all out of his mind to concentrate on what was real and known and remembered and, like *The Pearl Princess* itself in the hard, unforgiving light of day, not strange or wonderful or significant at all, but merely drab and ordinary and easily, clearly, understandable and explicable.

All he had left from all his lovely tools was his flashlight, and, aiming it down into the cave, Spencer lit up the fallen brickwork on both sides of the sewer where Auden and the bomb had gone.

It was a very long sewer, and even at the very end of the light's range, he could see no sign of the bomb or Auden at all.

The vaulted ceiling of the sewer was a little under head-high and as he went forward something awful brushed against his hair and then fell off behind him into the slime with a splash.

Then whatever it was swam away.

Spencer said hesitantly, not too loudly in case Auden had found a little safe nook somewhere in the passage and was close, "Phil? Are you here? . . ." and then whatever it was that had swum away, swam back and scuttled up the side of the sewer wall behind him with a series of what sounded like wet, teeth-gnashing noises.

Spencer said, a little louder, "Hello, Phil. It's me: Bill Spencer—"

There was an utter silence.

There was a noise a little like something wet and finned and scaled coming up for air, then a gurgling noise as it went down again.

All he could see ahead of him in the sewer was darkness.

It was all his fault!

Spencer said, wanting to jump up and down and make his little hands into fists with the humiliation of it all, "I'm sorry! I'm sorry! I'm sorry!"

Nothing.

Not even a gurgle.

Spencer said, "I'm sorry! I promise, I won't touch the bomb again! I'll get Hetherington-Smith in here—to hell with his tank rounds against a tin wall!—and I'll make sure he— I promise! I'll go away upstairs and I won't even look at the bomb or even think about it and I'll—and I'll—" He took another step forward and saw the dark shadows of the bomb's fins bent and twisted against the smashed-down wall of the sewer. Spencer said, louder, *"Phil!* Are you there?"

In the shadows at the nose of the bomb where it had been halted by a wall across the passage, there was some sort of evil oozing blob. In the gloom, Spencer could not tell if it was Auden or just an enormous lump of dripping slime stuck against the wall.

It was Auden stuck against the wall in an enormous lump of dripping slime.

The lump of slime that was Auden blinked, and then a hole appeared in the slime, a twisted, lopsided, half hole.

It was half of Auden's mouth. (The other half wouldn't open because there was the nose of a bomb stuck in it.)

The mouth, making exactly the same gurgling noise as all the other creatures too vile to think about that lived in the slime, said, "Deshoez hair bome . . ."

He sounded ticked off. He sounded so ticked off, Spencer could even hear the ticking.

Spencer, ready to throw himself into the two feet of effluvia flowing around his rubber boots and drown himself if Auden thought it might help, said in an orgy of apology, "Oh, God, oh, God—oh, God! . . . I'm really, really . . ." Spencer said, "Oh, God, *I'm sorry!*"

There was a silence, then the half mouth spoke its immortal words. The half mouth, forming the words one by one, said slowly and clearly and succinctly, "Dryfrooz sir bloon . . ."

"What?" Clearly, the bomb was jammed up against his chest and the poor old chap couldn't breathe. Spencer, going forward to help, then hearing a sound that sounded like someone jammed up against a bomb who couldn't breathe who nevertheless would kill him if he came forward to help, said desperately, "I won't come forward! I won't come anywhere near you! I won't do anything! I'll get Christopher O'Yee to get Hetherington-Smith and then I'll go away for the whole day and then I'll—"

Maybe it was working. The sound of the ticking stopped.

Spencer said, "Okay? All right?" He turned to go. Spencer said, "See? I'm going! I'm going now . . ."

"Negruze ferr zom—!" The mouth stayed open. "Sedoos ne—"

Spencer said, "What?" He took a step forward. "I'm sorry, I just can't—"

And then the ticking started again.

Auden said with a supreme effort, "Grenoose err mom! Mefrooz yerr glom—! Te-fuse zhe pomm—!"

Spencer said, "—What?"

"Denooz therr bomb . . ."

"What?"

"Defoon the blom . . ."

"What?"

"*Defuse the bomb!* DEFUSE THE BOMB!"

He could hardly believe his ears. What a big, noble man he was! Overcome with emotion, Spencer said, shamed in the presence of the Noble Soul, "Okay!" He had to say something. Spencer said, "Oh, thanks! Thanks! Oh, *thanks very much!*"

Oh, frabjus day! Calloo, callay!

"*DEFUSE . . . THE BOMB! DEFUSE THE—*"

Spencer said in a whisper, "Oh, boy, oh, boy, oh, boy!"

"DEFUSE THE BOMB!"

Turning on his heel, Spencer said in his glee, "Oh, thanks, Oh thanks, *Oh thanks!*"

Full of joy and the new confidence of a forgiven man, as he ran back through the sewer to get all his lovely tools out of the slime, he was so busy chortling he did not even hear the ticking suddenly stop, and then with a whirr and a new, urgent loudness, start ticking again.

In the Detectives' Room, staring at the still-sleeping ghastly little creature coming towards him, O'Yee, like the sage Chinese that he was, took in the situation analytically and considered his options.

It didn't take very long.

O'Yee, opting for option number one and recoiling in horror as the paper was thrust into his hand by The Thing's claw, said sagely and analytically, "*. . . Aarrgghh!*"

4.

He was like his boat, past his prime and double-decked with chins, but, again like his boat, camouflaged to all but the closest scrutiny by a beautifully cut, gray English three-piece suit and expensive, slightly slimmer than currently fashionable handmade blue Thai-silk tie.

At eleven in the morning, he wore a white boutonniere in the lapel of his jacket. At eleven in the morning, he had the faint but expensive smell of jasmine about him.

In the panelled upper-deck entrance lobby to the first-class dining room of the floating restaurant *The Pearl Princess*, Wilfred Wing, age fifty-five, the owner and host/manager of the place, said in perfect, almost unaccented English, "Wilfred Wing, at your entire disposal." He smiled again.

He was a Tanka—Feiffer heard it in the slight rising tone of his voice—one of the boat people who for generations had lived aboard their fishing junks and lighters and sampans and from one generation to the next (at least, until the last two generations when the fishing in the South China Sea had dried up from competition from the Japanese) had never come ashore.

He did not look at but touched at the band of his gold Rolex and, having made sure it had been noticed, discreetly tugged on the cuff of his snow-white silk shirt to hide it and avoid an unseemly and immodest show.

Feiffer said, "Detective Chief Inspector Feiffer, Yellowthread Street Station. I'm conducting a routine investigation of the death on board your vessel yesterday evening of one Tam Kwan Yu, aka Kenneth Tam, age eighty-three." He saw the man mentally file his name and rank away in his mind for possible future use. Feiffer said pleasantly, "I'd appreciate it if you'd answer a few questions and let me see where he died."

"Certainly." His tone did not change. If he thought Feiffer a man worth remembering he did not show it. "Please, come this way." He took a single step backward, still smiling, and pushed open the heavy narra-wood door at the end of the entrance lobby and stood to one side to let Feiffer go in.

Feiffer said in a gasp, "Good God!"

"Yes." He was proud of how far he had come as the grandson of an illiterate and constantly vile-smelling and fish-stinking fourth deckhand on a fishing junk he did not own and would never own.

Wilfred Wing, surrounded by the opulence and magnificence of the enormous room modelled in exact detail on the great dining and entertainment hall of the emperor's Imperial Palace in the Forbidden City in Peking, said with a polite smile, "Yes, and of course, this is only the *public* first-class dining room. The late Mr. Tam and his friends from the Millionaires' Club, as they do every month, met elsewhere, in private"—he flowed his hand across the panelled and carved wood of the walls of the place past the great hanging crystal-like lanterns and the long dark-wood tables and carved chairs of wonderful craftsmanship mounted with silver and pearl to a single closed door by a gold-and-silver-framed glass display case holding on display what could only have been a collection of genuine blue Ming dynasty bowls and vases—"there, behind that door, over there."

He had come a very long way. He had come from dirt and filth and hopelessness to opulence and magnificence.

Moving just a little ahead of Feiffer on the most wonderful hand-sewn dragon-motif carpet Feiffer had ever seen in his life—so large it covered the floor of the entire enormous room almost wall to wall—Wilfred Wing, unlocking the door with a little gold-plated key from his waistcoat pocket, said, still smiling, "They met in here, in the private banquet room."

The public room was all splendor and show.

He opened the door and switched on the lights in another enormous room that was all sumptuousness and *money*.

Well, at least—unlike most people—he knew where he was in his life. He was in a deserted police station in a deserted street with a live ten-ton bomb ticking away two floors below his feet while two complete numbskulls sloshed away in the slime working on it with a box of paper clips.

And standing facing him with hands like claws, he had a sleeping demon with what looked like an axe stuck in his hip pocket.

It was only too clear to him where he was in his life. He was in the Hades lunatic asylum where they locked up people too dangerous to be let loose in Hell. In the Detectives' Room, O'Yee said in a whispered prayer, "Oh . . ." and read the message on the folded-up piece of paper the sleeping demon had thrust into his hand.

The message on the folded-up piece of paper the demon had

thrust into his hand, making everything even clearer and simpler, said in a single line of nice, big, bold, easy-to-read print:

Irec Algr Amasc Afmm Icba Atta Emma Zip.

He read it again and waited for it to sink in.
It sank in.
O'Yee said in utter, complete, uncomprehending-where-he-was-in-life horror, *"Aaarrghhh——!"*

Down in the sewer the situation was also clear, if somewhat slimy, muddy, effluent, and as dark as a mouthful of fused bomb nose cone.

It got worse. Bending down over the cap of the bomb where he had given it a whack to loosen it, Spencer said in a mildly surprised tone, "Hmm. Didn't seem to move much." Spencer said, again, "Hmmm . . ."

Taking up his screwdriver and ball-peen hammer and getting a good solid hold on the screwdriver across the bridge of Auden's nose, he gave it another whack and lit up the entire sewer in a shower of sparks.

Spencer said, "One more time! . . ." He glanced quickly to the slime that was Auden's face in case he had accidentally hurt the man with the blow, but he hadn't. Auden was silent and uncomplaining and he knew that at the very least, if he had hurt him and Auden was just being brave, at least he would have seen his eyes blink with the pain.

He hadn't hurt him. He didn't see the eyes blink.

As Spencer, happy as a clam, drew back the hammer for yet another mighty whack, the eyes in the slime above the mouth in the slime with the fused nose cone of a ten-ton bomb jammed in it, merely stared.

And stared.

And as the hammer fell and bounced the tip of the screwdriver off the metal of the fuse in yet another nova of sparks—this time blue and white and yellow—went on staring.

It wasn't a replica of the great eight-hundred-table dining and entertainment room in the emperor's palace: it was the emperor's private personal dining room for himself and fifty friends—maybe not even a replica, so rich and brocaded and gold-leafed it could have been the real thing moved lock, stock and breathtaking jade-panelled and barrel ceilinged directly from Peking.

Wilfred Wing said, "A party of fifty. Seventeen members of the club, twenty of their guests—their lawyers, their accountants—and thirteen inside security staff. The banquet consisted of eighteen courses beginning with spiced ducks' tongues, deep-fried puffer fish, Szechuan sesame beef, and Mongolian hot pot and continuing through a range of various dishes until the serving of Hunan lychees and deep-fried Shanghainese grasshopper marinated in mao-tai." He said before Feiffer could ask, "The staff consisted of eight cooks and twelve kitchen hands who did not enter the room, and thirty waiters, all employed by me."

Maybe it was the meal that had killed him. But then, because of what it was and how old they were, it had all probably come in bite-sized pieces, more for the saying that one had had it served and could afford to have it served than the actual serving or eating of it.

Wilfred Wing said, "The banquet began at seven o'clock sharp and terminated at ten."

"Without, presumably, Mr. Tam, who at that stage was lying dead in the toilet—"

"Yes." It fazed him not at all. "And without Mr. A. K. Lim, the CEO of the Enterprise Mass Media group of companies, another member of the club, who discovered the body. Both gentlemen were dealt with by their security staff without upsetting the progress of the banquet."

It would have taken the ambulance people at least fifteen minutes to get there. "Are you saying Tam's security people moved the body?"

"No." He was unflappable. It was how he had gotten to be the friend of the rich. "No, they merely contacted me about the late Mr. Tam, explained the situation, and I had that particular rest room closed for repairs and opened another in the first-class dining room. Mr. Lim I invited into my private quarters and offered him the hospitality of my best English leather sofa on which to rest."

"Did you see Mr. Tam's body yourself?"

"No, I did not. That would have been—" He thought for the word for a moment—"Inappropriate."

"I have seen the body. His face was twisted into a look of horror. He looked as if he died of fright."

He had the mentality of those rich in their own right who served the even richer: There was nothing real or personal about it, merely correct or otherwise. Mr. Wing said, "I can make no comment about that."

"Did you speak to anyone else who might have been in the rest room at the same time or earlier?"

"To my knowledge no one was in the rest room at the same time. Earlier, I also cannot say. Mr. Lim, the aged gentleman who found the body, obviously entered a little later than Mr. Tam did because Mr. Tam was apparently already dead."

"What about the rest-room attendant?"

"There is no rest-room attendant in the private rest room. There is one in the first-class rest room, but immediately that was opened to the gentlemen of the private banquet room he was sent home." He saw Feiffer's face. "Millionaires do not carry money. I would not embarrass one of our gentlemen by having him make excuses to a mere rest-room attendant for not having a few coins to tip him." He glanced around the room for a moment and wondered how long he should let Feiffer even look at it. "The rich are not like ordinary people. Their words and actions are not the words and actions of ordinary people. Their words and actions, everything about them, is money. They are watched, studied, speculated upon, written about, analysed, lied about, dunned by entrepreneurs, driven mad by investors, fawned upon by sycophants, planned and plotted against, sometimes not only by their own employees and board members and shareholders, but often even by their own families, many of whom are employees and board members and shareholders." It was the little speech he gave to anyone rich and powerful contemplating using his establishment: it showed he understood their problems. "They are spied upon, eavesdropped, electronically bugged, phone-tapped; their every move, hint or whisper, change of expression or tone of voice minutely scrutinized by every member of the investing public and the stock market itself for any little hint that something could be about to happen to a point where they will do almost anything simply to have a little privacy."

"And talk amongst themselves?"

"Yes."

"About what?"

Mr. Wing said proudly, "I have no idea at all. Once the door to this room closes, I am on the outside conducting my own affairs."

"And the twelve cooks and eight kitchen hands?"

He permitted himself a faint smile. He knew the rich. That

he knew them had made him rich too. Mr. Wing said, "And the thirty waiters."

"And the thirty waiters, all employed by you."

Mr. Wing said, "Are all deaf and dumb." He was so proud of how far he had come he could not resist smiling again. "And—and it has reached a point in my dealings with the rich that their security staff no longer check but take my word for it—cannot lip-read."

He was a happy man growing fat and prosperous in his little niche in life. Everything in the room worthy of an emperor's palace was his, shared with no one.

He wondered, as he often did, what his vile-smelling fourth-deckhand grandfather hauling in his filthy wet nets would have thought of him now.

Mr. Wing, with nothing to hide, said with the faintest imperious flick of his fingers out towards the corridor running parallel with the upper deck to dismiss the question from his mind as not the sort of thing a man in his position and with his connections should permit himself to even think anymore, "Come. The place where Mr. Tam died—the private rest room—is down this way."

In the Detectives' Room, still sound asleep, the demon, as if he had done his duty, sat down in one of the two chairs in front of O'Yee's desk and squirmed about for a moment, wriggling to get himself comfortable.

Maybe he wasn't used to sitting in chairs. Maybe he was used to hanging upside-down from the roofs of caves.

No, it wasn't that.

It was his axe.

Reaching behind him, still with his eyes closed and making little bubbling breathing noises, the demon took it out at light-ning speed and drove it into the top of O'Yee's desk with a whack that brought dust and plaster down from the ceiling, and then, contented, let his head fall back and began snoring.

Inside the scrupulously clean, mirrored rest room, Mr. Wing said in a matter-of-fact tone of voice, "He was found there, by the last washstand, half slumped against the wall looking out towards the door, but I know no more than that, and you will get no information from the family of either the dead man, Mr. Tam, or from the family of the man who found him, Mr. Lim. By now, they will have closed not only the doors to their mansions on The Peak, but also their ranks, and anything that needs to be said will be said at the appropriate time by one of their lawyers or business spokesmen—and as for participating in a public police investigation with its inference of foul play—"

There was no police investigation. Feiffer said evenly, "There is no investigation. This is merely a routine follow-up enquiry of a report of a dead body."

"By a detective chief inspector?"

"Where the cause of death is unclear." What had happened in there was nothing. What had happened in there was that an old man had died of a heart attack. It was a long, glittering well-lit room with cubicles and urinals and sinks and expensive soaps and deodorants and hand towels where nothing could happen, where the field of vision from any one point in the room took in every other part, with one door in and out and no ventilation grilles or air-conditioning or exhaust-fan ducts big enough to admit anything bigger than a house cat, and where, as he looked, old paint still covered all the screw heads the cat would have to have taken out to even get at the grilles and exhaust-fan passages. "You said this rest room was also available to the first-class diners. If you were about your own affairs, I assume you would have been moving about in that area. To your knowledge, did anyone from first class use this rest room at about the time Mr. Tam died?"

"No."

"Did anyone from first class use it at all?"

"No."

"Would they have been permitted to?"

They were not the rich, but they were still the first class. Mr. Wing said with a shrug, "One would have hardly attempted to stop them if they so desired."

"And did one?"

"What?"

"Did you or any of your staff attempt to stop or even consider stopping someone from first class coming in here at approximately the time Mr. Tam died?"

Mr. Wing said tightly, "It was not a murder. The poor gentleman was well into his eighties. His heart merely stopped beating!"

"Why?"

"I have absolutely no idea at all! Ask a doctor!"

"I have asked a doctor, and the doctor tells me that only a postmortem would tell and the family have refused permission to allow one to be done."

He paused. He was still the grandson of a fisherman and he still knew when to let the line out a little before pulling it in. "But surely in the case of a suspicious death the family has no say in it?"

"It is not officially a suspicious death."

"I see. Then what is it?"

"I don't know. I'm not sure."

"Then . . ."

He looked again, but it was all glittering light and mirrors.

Harry, he saw something, something awful . . . and whatever it was that he saw killed him! He had heard the words before, a long time ago, but he could not remember where or when, but he could not get them out of his mind. What she had seen—maybe—had been a panther. And the man before Mr. Tam, the first one to die with the look of horror on his face: what had he seen?

Feiffer said as Mr. Wing turned to lead him out, "Tell me, do you know a man named Yuan Fook Chee, age about eighty-one, also known as Frederick Yuan?"

"The late head of International Rice?" Mr. Wing shook his head. "No. I gather, a very private man and not a member of the Millionaires' Club."

"What about a man called Ronnie Wong, age thirty-five—"

"The late market analyst of Star Insurance? No. Only by repute."

"I see."

Mr. Wing smiled his polite smile.

Harry, he saw something, something awful . . . and whatever it was that he saw killed him!

He looked around the room again, and all he could see and all Mr. Tam would have seen, was his own reflection.

He had no idea why he asked, but for the same reason he kept hearing Rebecca Pickering's words over and over in his mind— and that was no reason at all—he asked Mr. Wing's back, as the man turned away to get the door, "Tell me something, Mr. Wing, do you believe in ghosts?"

It stopped him. He turned. He was a man who had never once visited his dead deckhand grandfather's grave or even acknowledged his existence.

Mr. Wing said with sudden anger on his face, touching at his wrist and the snow-white cuff and gold Rolex there, "No! No, I don't! Why? *Do you?*"

5.

In the sewer, the Creature from the Wall of Slime said—in the same tone of voice the giant Queen-creature used in *Aliens* when it said, "Ggggnahh—!!!"—*"You touched the bomb!"*

The blow from the hammer had sent the bomb spinning off to one side and it rested, blue-black and huge and horrible, against the side wall.

Emerging from behind the veil of ooze on the back wall with a sound like the six-foot-diameter suction cup of a plumber's friend being pulled out of a three-foot-diameter cesspit, Auden said so the man would know the reason he was going to be torn limb from limb and then eaten, *"I told you not to touch the bomb back there, and you touched the bomb!"*

He put an oozy finger in his mouth where the fuse had been to check whether his teeth were still all there.

They were.

Auden, dripping disgusting exudation, taking a single step forward and then being snapped back like an elastic band, said in a snarl, *"When I get over there I'm going to kill you!"*

He was going to use his hands.

Not so easy.

He looked down at what had once been his body and was now a larva case of mucus and couldn't see them. Auden said, *"So help me God, I'm going to get over there and kick you in the head so hard you'll need a goddamned road map to even know which way is up!"*

To kick you needed a foot. He had no feet. Still straining against two feet of solid glue holding him to the wall, all he could see below his waist was three feet of solid sewer sludge and more glue. Auden, pushing, shoving, straining, trying to get loose, said, *"Ggggnahh——! Ggggnahh!!"*

. . . Well, so that was all there was to it. One decent whack with the hammer and the fuse had come off in his hand and that was all there was to it. Standing to one side of the now-harmless bomb, looking down at the fuse in his hand in the harsh light of both reality and his flashlight, Spencer said like a disappointed child, "Aw, gee . . ." The fuse, a mushroom-shaped object with old, rotten wires running from a cracked and broken black Bakelite panel under the stem, was so old that, as he turned it over, the stem containing the gaine broke off and spilled the picric-acid accelerant charge out onto his palm. The charge was so old it had turned to dust. Spencer said, "Just a simple seven-second-delay fuse to give the bomb time to penetrate a building before it went off and a single fly-wheel clockwork concussion-initiated backup in case the batteries didn't work."

And they hadn't. Spencer said, "It wouldn't have gone off anyway whatever I did: the batteries are all long dead. The ticking we heard was the last of the power discharging itself into the earth." He looked again at the fuse and spun off one of the bronze O-rings around the Bakelite. "And the clockwork initiator would have never gone off either: it's all crushed and out of true and broken."

He sounded so disappointed. Spencer, oblivious to all but the unfairness of it all, said sadly, "Really, really I'd hoped for just a little better than this."

One mighty bound and he would be free!

Well, at least, one tremendous wrench.

A decent shove?

A good foothold on the rear wall and . . .

Auden, caught fast, said with his teeth clenched, "Grrrah, grrrah! . . ."

He was talking not to Auden but to God. Spencer, lit up in the yellow glow of the flashlight like some mad monk holding in his palm what he had been led to believe was a sliver of the treasured True Cross and had turned out to be nothing more than part of a discarded Popsicle stick, said on the edge of losing his faith, "Maybe I was being a bit optimistic hoping that it might be all sweat and terror and heart-stopping suspense, but at least it could have been a little more mentally up-market than just whacking the thing with a bloody hammer!" He wasn't a man to abuse the Divinity, but, really there were times . . . Spencer said petulantly, "What the hell did I spend all my life here in the East learning about self-knowledge and inner strength for, if the one time I get to use it all and think I have to delve into my deepest Self for courage and forbearance and fortitude beyond those of mortal men all I have to do really is delve into my bloody toolbox for a bloody *hammer?*"

In the wall, Mucus Man, making an inch and losing six, said with the exertion sending him red in the face, "Grrr . . . *grrrr!*"

That's what he thought too. Spencer, just wanting to throw the fuse away like the rotten second-rate toy it was, said angrily, "It just isn't fair!"

One mighty *glurrp!* and he was free! He came off the wall like a postage stamp and he was free! Auden, released at last, free to roam the sewers and kill at will, said with his lungs suddenly full of fresh, clean sewer air, "Ah-*hah!*" His feet and legs were standing painlessly in two feet of sludge. They were painless because he couldn't feel them anymore. Taking a step forward by the simple method of throwing his hip forward and hoping something below it moved, Auden said with the effort, "Uh-*huh!*"

Something below his hip moved. It was the sludge. It moved in and devoured his hip and when he put his hand down into it to dig his hip out, it devoured that too. For the briefest of moments before all the feeling in his hand went, he felt the feeling of the sludge. It was a feeling like quicksand. Auden, sinking into it, going down like a paper boat in a whirlpool, said with a picture in his mind from all the old quicksand movies he had seen when he was a kid, of nothing but a bony entreating hand sticking out of a pool of the stuff, "Oh—*no!* . . ."

Sadly philosophic, Spencer said softly, "All chimera. All just shadow play in the dark corners of the electrical circuits of the mind . . . 'The gods are the Ones who determine the time and course of life and death; Man merely exists to engage in the Struggle between those times of life and death, so the Struggle is all that is important . . .' " It was an ancient Sanskrit adage.

Spencer said to those ancient Sanskritters, "Wrong!" Oh, he was so unhappy. "The only struggle there is between life and death is remembering to bring along a fucking *hammer!* And *Tao,* the Chinese road to knowledge: what knowledge? The only thing you need to know to get along in this life is how to give something a decent whack if it gets in your way!" All was Dust. Spencer said bitterly, "No, that old pagan, Omar Khayyám, had it right: '*A jug of wine, a book of verse, And thou, singing beside me in the wilderness—*' "

In the wilderness, someone, not thou, but Auden, was singing at that exact moment. His song went, "*Ohh! . . . Ooohhh—!*"

Spencer roared, " '*And wilderness is Paradise enow!*' " And that's all there is to life! That's all there is: just fucking boozing and screwing and hammering!" Spencer shouted, "Damn it! It wouldn't have hurt, just once, to let me see what I was made of!"

He was made of quicksand food. Auden, making a superhuman effort, getting one foot free, said with every atom in his body straining, "*Gggnnnooom!*"

He hated the bomb. Slapping at it with the flat of his hand, Spencer said to chide it, "Rotten, stupid, feebleminded bomb! . . ."

And then the other foot. And then the first foot again, and then . . . And then, he could *walk!* And then, with a sound like an octopus sucker coming off a wet wall, his right hand came out, and then his arm, and then with a *blurp!* his other hand, and then his hip, and then— Auden the Ooze Man, taking one stumbling, stiff-legged step at a time, his hands outstretched to kill, said happily, "*Aaaahhh . . .*"

He gave the bomb, not a little slap, but a good, solid backhander right across the body. Spencer said, "Lousy, brainless, dumb, useless, rotten *bomb!*" Against stupidity even the gods railed in vain. Spencer, giving it a jolly-good crack about the chops, said with the anger of an intelligent man fallen into the hands of the moronic masses, "Dumb, stupid, single-fused, idiotic, cretinous *bomb*—what use are you to anyone?" He gave it another good whack and it moved a little. Spencer, getting really mad, roared, "Take that! And that! And that!"

"*Aaaahhh . . .*" One small step for a man at a time, Auden got to the nose of the bomb and laid a mighty oozing mitt upon it to steady himself.

Not too steady. Laying a kick on the bomb that almost broke his foot and made the bomb shake and quiver along its entire length, Spencer shrieked, "I thought through you I might learn the meaning of life, but all I learned is that everything is a fucking joke and all there is in eternity is oblivion and I hate you for it!"

Not too steady at all. The bomb, vibrating through its entire length, came off the wall, hit something about six foot tall standing unsteadily with its oozing mitt out to steady itself, and, for a long moment, pivoted in midair looking for somewhere to go.

As far as he was concerned, it could go straight to hell! Spencer, giving it another kick, shrieked, "Take *that!*" and the bomb, taking it, swung through sixty degrees, mowed down the six-foot oozing thing with its oozing mitt resting on it, and rolled over.

He didn't care. Caring was for people with souls. People had no souls. All was illusion. Spencer, kicking it again, yelled, "And that!"

And it rolled through three hundred and sixty degrees and he saw in its belly something he had only ever seen before in pictures in books and in Glenn Ford movies where old Glenn, his gaze steely and his hands steady, his forehead glistening sweat, reached into the deepest innards of the bomb and—

He saw an entire compartment full of fuses and detonators and wires and wires and trembler switches and mercury motion-sensor tubes and wires and—and everything anyone could ever possibly hope for!

It was not a dumb bomb at all. It was the Ultimate Bomb. It was a cleverly disguised anti–bomb-disposals-team bomb designed, not to destroy buildings, but to blast into a million little pieces the first brave Bomb-Disposals man who came to defuse it.

Brave Bomb Disposals Bill said in a hushed, contrite voice, "Oh, oh, thank you . . . Oh, thank you . . . Oh, thank you very much!"

He looked around for Auden to tell him the good news, but he already knew.

Behind the bomb, now sitting almost flat in the water with all its diabolical innards exposed in the open compartment, he saw Auden's hand, like a hand sticking up from quicksand, waving at him over and over to show how happy he was just to be part of the pure, unalloyed, deeply philosophically satisfying joy of it all.

2. *All weapons and dangerous objects, including guns, knives, swords, clubs, whips, chains, bludgeons . . . shall be gathered up, crated in wooden boxes, and sent to headquarters by common carrier to— for reasons of security—the fictitious personage of (Address) "Mr. George Gunn" . . .*

Guns, knives, swords, clubs, whips, chains, bludgeons—did it say axes? Maybe it hadn't said axes.

It had said axes. And hatchets. In the Detectives' Room, gaping at the awful object half buried in the top of his desk, O'Yee said in a gasp, "Oh, God—!"

. . . [they] . . . nothing common did, or mean,
Upon that mem-or-able scene—

O'Yee said in a whisper, "Oh, God, oh God, oh God, oh God, oh God! . . ."

The Demon was comfortable now, sound asleep with its claws resting gently in its lap, its mouth wide open to display its full set of sharpened teeth. (O'Yee, seeing the teeth, said, "Oh, God!")

O'Yee said, —but nothing came out.

Grab the axe. Grab the axe and wrench it out so fast the little bastard didn't even have time to blink and then, if he did blink, whip the axe back and with a blow that would have brought a hiss of wonderment and astonishment at the perfection of his art from his ancient Chinese ancestors and a boozy belch benediction from his Irish, take his head off at the neck so fast he'd be still halfway through the blink when his head landed on the floor.

Yeah. Right.

Or just shoot him.

Or just—

O'Yee said in a whisper to himself, "Take the axe." At least, that was what he thought he said.

What he actually said was, "Oh, God, oh, God . . ."

He reached out to take the axe.

O'Yee, reaching out, said in case he had forgotten to call on the Almighty in his time of need, "Oh, God, oh God, *oh, God—*"

"OH, GOD!" Down in the sewer, Spencer heard the happy shout of joy from the other side of the bomb where Auden was, and, looking around for the man, said in his ecstasy, "Yes! Isn't it wonderful! An anti-BD bomb! Have you any idea at all just how rare they are?"

He was so happy.

On the other side of the bomb, Auden was so happy too. He was so happy he could not even speak, but merely, happily waved his hand up in the air over and over, burbling, almost, one might say, hysterically.

It had taken Feiffer less than five minutes to drive from the Hong Bay waterfront to The Peak that was the highest point on the island of Hong Kong.

It had taken some of the people who lived up there, in their walled-off and heavily guarded mansion houses, a lifetime.

Sitting in his car a little back from the driveway entrance to Mr. Tam's estate at the end of General Tsiang Avenue, all Feiffer could see of it—all anyone was allowed to see of it who had no right to see more—was a long, curving high white wall with security cameras mounted every fifty feet, a sidewalk and roadway outside so clean it must have been swept and washed at least twice a day, not by the city but by private contractors, and, set back a little behind the twin iron gates that closed the property off to the street, a sentry post with two huge Sikh guards with shotguns, and beyond that, where a line of carefully transplanted fully grown trees lined the drive to the house, the corner of some other sort of building with more security cameras mounted on it.

The Sikhs, enormous, red-faced, military-style uniformed men with moustaches and full beards and turbans who looked and were meant to look exactly like the evil devils in the Chinese panoply of gods, were there with their ferocious appearance and single-shot shotguns to keep the common herd away; whatever was inside the little building farther up the driveway was there for serious threats, and they, undoubtedly, had fully automatic Uzis and God-only-knew what else and men trained to use them.

Sitting there gazing at the gate, as, no doubt, the people in the building ran his license plate and photographed and ID'ed him from every angle, Feiffer wound down the window of his car, lit a cigarette, and thought about the man who had owned all of it and now lay dead on a steel tray in the hospital morgue with his face twisted in horror and his eyes scratched out by his own fingernails.

In almost thirty years of being a policeman—he thought suddenly, "Is it really that long?"—he had seen a lot of death, violent and otherwise, some even worse to look at than Mr. Tam's, and he thought he had grown used to it, come to recognize it for what it was—just death in one form or another—and become familiar with its smells and its coldness and its—he thought for a moment for the word—and its ordinariness.

But this time, sitting there, watching the smoke from his cigarette hang in the still quiet air in the deserted and twice-daily swept and washed-clean street, he felt something he had not become used to, something he had not felt or sensed for a very long time about death and the dead.

It was the *hush* of death, the silence you could feel from behind those walls where once Mr. Tam had lived, the invisible grayness and coldness and hurt and loss of death, and it was a different death from any of the others he had seen or been involved in: a death that, as he thought about it and the man he had never known in life, made him blink back a feeling of sadness and grief.

Harry, he saw something, something awful . . . and whatever it was that he saw killed him . . .

Behind those walls, in the house at the end of the driveway, he knew the family was talking in whispers, in sighs, in silences, meeting in rooms in little groups and—

And it all meant something to him, but he could not think what.

And in some of the rooms, or sitting on the bottom steps of staircases, or walking out in the grounds gazing at the trees, there were members of the family and friends alone with their thoughts and mourning and regretting not saying to their grandfather, or father, or brother, or whoever Tam had been to them in life, what they now thought about him in death.

The silent, unseen house was full of sadness and incomprehension, and even if he had had any sort of legal excuse that would have gotten him past the hard, armed men in the building inside the driveway—and he did not—he would not have been able to bring himself to intrude.

And he had no idea why in almost thirty years of death and the dead—and never once before—he felt that way.

He thought idly that perhaps it was the death of an old man and the death of the Colony of Hong Kong dying at the same time, but it wasn't. It wasn't the end of something: families like Tam's—the eternal Chinese—went on eternally and, like his own family in the East now for three generations, survived everything. In his own case, his grandfather, a sea captain running opium from India to the China ports in the late-nineteenth century, had survived war and piracy and even, the one time Feiffer had met him when he was a boy, civilization. His father, a police inspector in the Shanghai International Police in the thirties and forties, had survived the Japanese and then internment, and then, after he had gone back after the war, he had survived the Communists and a new beginning with a wife and young child in Hong Kong.

And then, suddenly, his father had died, cut down by a massive heart attack at age fifty, and the house they rented out in the New Territories was suddenly full of whispers and silences and a *hush* and Feiffer and his younger brother had sat on the bottom step of the big lacquered Chinese staircase that led up to their parents' bedroom where his father lay and tried to comprehend the grayness and the loneliness that had filled the house.

He had been eight, and his brother three: too young to be allowed to see their father in death, and they had both sat there listening to the whispers and obediently, as their father would have wanted them to do, moving to one side to let people go up and down the staircase about the business of death.

Only when the coffin was brought down were they gently but firmly moved away and sent to one of the side rooms off the entrance hall to gaze out a window at the trees in the garden until the coffin and the undertaker's hearse that would transport it and their father away forever was gone.

It was a long time away and in a different place, but everywhere about the place that had once been Tam's, and even in the street where he was, he felt the hush, and he could not think why he felt it, or what there was that was familiar about it.

In the car, Feiffer said softly to himself, "This is crazy!"

He thought of using the car phone to call his wife at the hospital just to talk to her, but if he did that whatever he said would probably get back to Rebecca Pickering and she had her own ghosts and phantoms to deal with without taking on any more of his.

He had asked the man on the boat, *"Tell me something, Mr. Wing, do you believe in ghosts? . . ."* and had had no idea then or any idea now why he had said it.

He thought to call O'Yee back in the Station, but he was in the midst of dealing with some mad epistle from the Colonial Office and had probably already been driven half mad by red tape and paper clips and would not be fit to talk to about anything.

And there was no one else, and with no legal warrant to enter Tam's house and nothing on any of the three death certificates,

Tam's or Yuan's, or the earlier one, Wong's, but the words *natural causes*, nothing more to do about it.

There was nothing to do and nowhere else to go.

Stubbing out the remains of the cigarette in the ashtray in the dash and then winding up the car window, Feiffer started the car to go back to the Station and, making a U-turn, turned on the emergency channel on his car radio to get himself back into the real world and see if anything was happening he should know about.

Something was happening he should know about.

On the radio, there was the voice of one of the paramedics from an Advanced Life Support Vehicle reporting a dead body in a temple in Wanchai Street just off Hanford Road, Hong Bay.

He was calm, merely listing the details in an even but slightly quivering voice, but someone in the background behind him wasn't.

In the background behind him, someone was shrieking over and over and over again in utter, total, and uncontrollable horror.

It was stuck. He couldn't move it. It wasn't an axe driven into a desk, it was Excalibur buried in a boulder. Sprawled halfway across his desk, hanging on to the haft with both hands and pulling and getting nowhere, O'Yee jammed both his knees into the drawers on either side to get a better purchase and, this time, didn't pull but *wrenched*.

Wrenching got him nowhere, so he *hefted*.

He hauled.

He *"hrrrgggahhh-ed!"*

It didn't give. It didn't move a millimeter.

He hoisted.

Nothing.

He hefted.

El Zippo. Nada. Zilch.

He hoisted, hauled, hefted, hrrrggghhh-ed, and with a final mighty effort, almost herniated.

O'Yee, letting go of the axe and sliding off the desk to the floor, said in agony, "Ow! Ow! Ow!"

He nothing common did, or mean . . . Like hell he didn't. On his hands and knees, reaching for his Colt Airweight in its shoulder holster, O'Yee shouted in dire warning, "You! You there! Fangface! Wake up and give me the fucking axe or I'll—"

It must have worked. There was a sort of crunching sound from the other side of the desk and when he crawled back up to look, the demon, still asleep, had the axe in his hand and was getting to his feet.

O'Yee said, "Yeah! Right! See! I'm in charge around here! Get up on your damn feet and give me the axe now!"

And he did. Got up on his feet, anyway. And, as an identical nut-brown man appeared at the door wearing an identical gray T-shirt and slacks and no shoes, without opening his eyes even for an instant, but still happily sleeping and making little burbling noises, he took the next chair at the desk to make room for his new friend and drove the axe back in in a new spot on the desk with a bang.

His new friend carried not a cannibal's beheading axe—nothing so brutal or vulgar—but a long, razor-sharp flesh-filleting knife.

Sitting down next to his old friend, identical twins in every way, still soundly asleep, he held the awful instrument up in the air for a moment, turned it so it glittered in the light, and then drove his knife into the desk next to the first sleeper's axe.

Then, with two happy sighs, the two creatures from hell let their heads fall gently onto their chests and continued sleeping.

In the sewer, Spencer, on the first leg of his Voyage of Self-discovery through Detonation, forgetting about the waving hand, stopped to sniff the air.

The air was full of methane.

Brave Bomb Disposals Bill, all his senses heightened and tingling with anticipation, said as if someone had asked him about it, "Ah, methane: an odorless colorless inflammable gaseous hydrocarbon otherwise known as marsh gas. Ah, marsh gas: a colorless, odorless inflammable gaseous hydrocarbon otherwise known as methane." You couldn't fool him. "Ah, methane: a colorless, odorless, flammable marsh color that—" High as a kite, Spencer said to Auden who he could hear sloshing around on the other side of the bomb just checking to see that everything was ready over there for the Great Defusal, "Ah, methane— Ah,—"

There was something huge and black and horrible and dripping rammed halfway across the sewer.

It was a bomb.

With his brain reeling, Spencer asked the other black and horrible and dripping thing appearing by degrees from behind it, "Ah, Phil! Ready to go?"

Spencer said with a grin as he went reeling happily towards Auden and Auden came reeling happily towards him, "I just can't wait to make a start! Can you?"

On the car radio, the screaming behind the paramedic's voice went on and on and on, so loud it drowned out every second word the man said.

There were words in the screaming, but they were in a language Feiffer did not know.

Perhaps they were not even words. As the paramedic said something in Chinese to the despatcher that sounded like "devil faced," perhaps all they were, over and over and over again, were shrieks of utter, panic-stricken, animal-like terror.

He looked on the other side of his desk and there were two sleeping demons, identical in every respect.

And beyond the desk, a few feet inside the door of the Detectives' Room, on their way in, two more.

These two carried swords.

And beyond that, two more, with what looked like clubs.

O'Yee, recoiling in horror, thought he said, "Oh, my God!" but he didn't. What he said, and it came out as a very strangled version of the sound, was, *"Akk!"*

O'Yee, rooted to the spot, said as if it meant something, "Akk! Akk! *Akk!*" but if it did, no one heard it above the shatteringly loud sawmill-like sound of all the six sleepers, moving and in repose, all snoring at top volume, all together, in perfect, identical, stentorian, somnambulistic, six-part, horrible harmony.

Then, on the radio, as the paramedic completed his message to Base and signed off, the screaming stopped, and all there was on the radio as Feiffer turned at the end of the street was a silence and—he felt it, heard it, knew it was there—a sudden long, awful, eerie, lost and uncomprehending . . . *hush.*

6.

In the Temple of a Thousand Buddhas on Wanchai Street, the body of the old man lay full length where it had fallen in front of a shrine to the White Monkey God, the bringer of Buddhism from India to China and the protector of all classes of people from hobgoblins and evil influences and the unknown things that moved in the still of the night.

It lay in semidarkness in the far corner of the great altar room of the wooden black-lacquered and camphorwood-smelling place where effigies of the Buddha covered every shelf and niche and alcove, lit only by the glow of candles to the Monkey God in the shrine itself and the pencil-thin beam of Victor Chen's pocket flashlight. Everywhere, overpoweringly, there was the smell of incense and burned ashes: the residue of paper prayers and entreaties and pleas burned in the pottery offering pots in front of each of the Buddhas and the panoply of minor gods like the White Monkey that served them.

It was the body of an old, completely bald Chinese man with both his eyes clawed out by his long fingernails and a face

locked in the contortion of a gargoyle. Still caught in the fingernails where his hands lay stiff and twisted like talons on the
lapels of his expensive suit was the jelly of his eyeballs and, as
Feiffer saw it lit up in the moving beam and then glanced away
from it quickly, what looked like part of a cornea and pupil.

Victor Chen was the regional director of the Emergency
Medical Service, a quiet, diminutive man in his early thirties
known for his calmness in crisis and a face that showed no emotion, ever.

He showed no emotion now. Looking down at the body in
the beam of the flashlight and reacting to the sight of it not at
all, Chen said in what as usual came out as a calm, professional
assessment, "Anonymous call: probably a worshipper who came
in and found him and then fled." He shone the beam directly
onto the cheeks and lit up all the blood from gash wounds.
"Probably afraid to get involved in what looked like a murder.
My people responded within thirty seconds of the call and arrived here in a dispatch-timed two and half minutes, but he'd already been dead for at least half an hour, so he had been dead
twenty minutes by the time the anonymous caller found him."
Victor Chen, still looking down at the body and moving the
beam over the awful face, said to explain it, "They called me because they didn't know whether they should leave the body *in situ*
and call in the coroner and the police as a possible homicide, or
simply treat it for what it appeared to be: a massive heart attack,
and transport it to the nearest hospital for a DOA pronounce-
ment." He looked up. Chen said suddenly, not sure himself,
"They didn't know what to do with it because of what the hell
it looked like!"

He looked, lying there on the lacquered black floor, exactly
the way Kenneth Tam had looked on the steel tray in the morgue
at St. Paul deChartres Hospital. He was almost Tam's clone: a

tiny twisted man almost the same age with the same long manicured rich-man's fingernails and, in his case, a lightweight gray
suit and silk shirt that would have cost more than Feiffer and
Chen put together made in six months.

He looked, with his eyes gone and his mouth open in horror
and his hands clenched into bloody claws, like a creature cast out
of hell.

He would have already checked. Feiffer asked Chen, "Who is
he?"

He still showed no emotion. "According to his ID in his wallet in his inside pocket, one Lee Tse Wa, aka John Lee, age seventy-
eight, company director, with an address on Leighton Hill. And
about a million-dollars' worth of gold and platinum credit cards
in his wallet and a receipt from a taxi company for the trip from
his home to here timed approximately an hour before the anonymous call came in that he was dead." Chen said, "I didn't know
him personally, but I've read about him in the papers and seen
his picture from time to time on the financial pages: he was the
head of that huge building on Beach Road overlooking Hong
Bay in the Hop Pei Cove area, the International Cloth Buyers
Building. He was some sort of goddamned multimillionaire!"

Feiffer said softly, "Like the one your people found on *The
Pearl Princess*, Tam, and the one before that, Yuan, and the one
eight weeks ago, Ronnie Wong."

He didn't think he knew. Chen said in what sounded like relief, "Yes!" And then something happened inside him and his
face changed, became slack. "Harry, I've never seen anything like
it before. I don't know what it is. And my people don't know
what it is and it's beginning to upset them. Not one of them was
even given a PM because the families apparently came down to
the hospital with a legion of lawyers who threatened to sue anyone who even mentioned it and had the corpses taken away so

fast you'd have thought they were victims of the Black Death and my people are worried about possible repercussions now about anything they might do. And it's frightening them. They're all just ordinary working men with families and they're worried about doing something that might land them in court." He jerked his thumb out in the direction of the street where the two ALSV crews that had responded to the call were still waiting by their parked vehicles. "I've told them just to park out there in their vehicles and wait until I can give them some sort of official determination as to what they should do and I— And until I can get some sort of official determination of what *I* should do." He turned his gaze to Feiffer. "Harry, is it a murder, or at least a suspicious death, or not?"

He had no idea at all. Everything that he had had officially determined for him, first by Pickering and then by Wing, said it was not. Feiffer said, "I don't know. What is it medically?"

"Medically, it's a massive heart attack and, judging by the twisted left side of the face, probably a stroke thrown in for good measure, and probably—if anyone gets to be allowed to open him up, and they won't be—" Suddenly, he lost it. "Harry, he clawed his own eyes out!" He almost said, *He saw something . . .* "He clawed his own eyes out while he was still alive! And he's the fourth, not the first, but the fourth in eight weeks!"

There was nothing he could say. He had no official position in it and no authority and nothing to go on. Shaking his head, Feiffer said, "I'm sorry, Victor, I don't know. I don't know what to advise you to do."

"My people can't take a lot of this, Harry. They're good people, caring people. They're people trained to act quickly in an emergency and take action without reference to anyone, and they can't function if they keep running across things that look like this that are untouchable because they might do something that lands them in court. It destroys their professionalism and then they're no good to anyone!" It was always important not to display any emotion. "And it gets to them and they stop thinking like trained, professional people there to do a specific task without reference to their own personal problems or feelings or emotions and they start acting like civilians, and they get frightened!"

"I know. I heard one of your people on the radio, screaming."

It irritated him. Chen said tightly, "Did you?" Chen said with his mouth pursing and unpursing, "He was a good man before this. He was one of the best emergency CPR people I've ever had in the service, and now he's fucking finished! And now, having been through this four times, all he's good for is to be a fucking orderly in a geriatric hospital somewhere and push a fucking gurney around so he can take old ladies out onto the verandah for their morning sun! My people aren't here to deal with things that look like they fell out of a fucking nightmare they don't dare touch and who get spirited away with no explanation as if they're fucking extraterrestrials, they're here to save lives, to bring people back from the brink of death through their training and skill, and, as part of it—and an important part of it—sometime, sooner or later, in some way or another, feel good about themselves when either the person they've saved or the family comes to thank them with goddamned tears of gratitude in their eyes!"

"Was he the same one who lost it with Kenneth Tam and refused to go back in the ambulance with the body?"

"How did you know that?"

"Rebecca Pickering at St. Paul deChartres mentioned it to me."

"Yes. Yes, he is."

"Where is he now?"

Chen asked tightly, warily, "Why?"

"I just wondered why it upset him even before he knew what was going to happen when the body got to the hospital."

Everyone had something to lose. In the Temple of a Thousand Buddhas on Wanchai Street, Victor Chen asked in the same tone Wilfred Wing had asked on *The Pearl Princess*, "Why? Is this part of an official investigation or not?"

Feiffer said firmly, "Not. I just wondered why he—"

He jerked his head in the direction of a dark, incense-filled corridor leading off the main altar room. Victor Chen said, "He's down there. I sent him off by himself so he could try to calm down a little. He's with the priest down there trying to—"

Feiffer said, "What priest?"

"The one who runs the place. The—"

"You didn't tell me there was anyone else around when all this took place! Are you telling me while this happened there was a goddamned *priest* in here?"

"Yes." He needed an official determination of what to do next. The only official there was who could determine it was him. Victor Chen said, "Yes, there was a priest in here!" It was like everything else, dark and arcane and somehow, happening far, far out of his view and out of his control. He looked down at the body in the pencil-thin beam of his flashlight and shuddered, not out of fear, but out of anger. "Didn't I tell you that? Didn't I? Yes, there was a goddamned priest in here! So you go talk to him! Find out what happened." And then he lost it completely and his whole face twisted in hard, bitter, frustrated anger and rage. "Oh, but one thing—just like every other thing in this whole miserable, evil, sorry picture—make sure you take into account when you talk to him that the man is utterly, completely, and permanently *blind!*"

In the sewer, sloshing happily down towards Auden and the bomb, Spencer said with his brain full of marsh gas, "Dear old chap . . . good old fellow . . . dear old fellow good chap . . . fellow old chap good dear . . ."

Rough diamond though he was, he'd always liked old Auden.

Rough diamond though it was, he'd always liked the old bomb.

Spencer, muttering, "Slosh, slosh, slosh . . ." as he went through the effluvia slosh, slosh, slosh, said with affection and love dripping from his every pore, "Dear old good . . . chap fellow old . . ."

He thought he would give the pair of them a couple of jolly-good pats on the back.

Wires. There were two big brightly colored wires in his way running across the width of the sewer.

Rough diamonds though they were, he had always liked wires.

He took another happy slosh forward to give them a jolly-good pat too.

He was half Chinese: he could think. And half Irish: he could think good. Facing the phalanx of happily snoring killers at his desk, O'Yee thought all he had to do was very quietly get up, go to the door of the Station, and call the uniformed men cordoning off the street for the bomb to come down and arrest them.

He thought Uniformed probably wouldn't come.

He thought it didn't matter anyway because his chances of getting to the door without being axed, filleted, slashed, and clubbed to death were nil.

He thought, thinking hard, that all he had to do was call the

Riot Squad to come down and arrest them. He thought the Riot Squad would come.

He thought of their number.

Their number was 284–2840, Extension 111.

All he had to do to begin was dial the first number.

He couldn't remember what the first number was!

It was 2.

Staring hard at the snorers, he lifted up the receiver of his phone and touched the first number, 2.

It was a very quiet touch-tone telephone and the snorers did not stir.

He punched up 8.

So far so good. His Irish brain, cackling away with triumph said to congratulate him, "Well done, yourself, and may you be in heaven half an hour before the devil knows you're dead!"

His Chinese brain said to his Irish brain, "Shut up!"

He punched up 4.

He was almost halfway there. Both brains together said, "Heh! Heh! Heh! This is going to work! . . ."

He punched up . . . 2.

The corridor through to the rear of the temple was so low Feiffer had to stoop down to get through. Dark, and heavy with the smell of incense, it led, not into another part of the temple itself, but abruptly out into the daylight and a tiny but wonderfully designed and planted tree-and-rock garden.

The paramedic was at the far lefthand corner of the place sitting on a black-veined stone bench carved in the shape of a lion, bent over with his head in his hands, still sobbing.

A little back from him, ancient and shaven-headed and dressed in saffron robes, a Buddhist priest stood with his hands clasped loosely in front of him, consoling him, perhaps speaking words so soft Feiffer could not hear them.

There was something strange about the priest, but with his eyes smarting from the incense, for a moment Feiffer could not quite work out what it was.

It was the way the priest stood. Barefooted, it seemed he was not standing on the ground at all.

It seemed for an instant as he turned his blind gaze to Feiffer and moved his body slowly to face him that, an inch above the ground, he *hovered* in midair.

In the sewer, Spencer, the methane mate of all mankind and organic material, slapping at the wires, shrieked in good fellowship, "Jolly good, fine, hardworking, unappreciated, bright colored old *wires!*"

Only two numbers and an extension away from success, he punched up *8.*

His Chinese brain said, "Well done—*ho ho!*": which meant in Chinese, "Very good!"

His Irish brain said, *"Ho, ho, ho!"*: which meant in Irish, "Ho, ho, ho!"

At his desk, the six sleepers continued sleeping.

He tapped up *4,* and then, from deep in the bowels of the sub-basement, there was a spluttering sound as if someone swiped at a live electrical wire and made it spark, then a clang as if a bomb moved, then a sort of strangled shriek as if someone underwater saw a bomb moving their way, then another shriek— a big one—as the bomb did move their way and then a clang and a shriek and a splash as the someone shrieking got mowed down by the bomb and sank beneath three feet of mire, and then—

And then the sleepers, all at once, stirred.

He punched up *0!*

As simultaneously—splutter, clang, shriek, then shriek again, then clang, then shriek again, then splash, *flash!*—all at once, all the telephone and fax lines in the Station went completely dead.

A tiny, birdlike man apparently in his late sixties, but entirely possibly much, much older, he wasn't some sort of dilettante temporary priest from the outside world doing his one- or two-year monastic stint to purge his soul and atone for his past sins before he went on to commit future ones—he was the real thing: a near-perfected Zen Buddhist holy man who had probably been in saffron robes since he was six years old, a man, judging from the unreflecting matte pupils of his eyes, blind from birth who had spent a lifetime looking, not outward, but inward.

Still attached by the finest and most tenuous of threads to the world, he was not hovering in midair—it was an illusion. As he came towards Feiffer, placing one bare foot carefully and slowly in front of the other like a ballet dancer practising in slow motion, he walked on the balls of his feet so gently it was like the gentle caress of a hand across the surface of still water.

As he walked, with no expression on his face at all, his step left no ripples on the surface of the raked-sand path he trod on, and made no sound or disturbance or impression.

With his hands held lightly cupped together in front of him, the fingers and palms barely making contact, he was not a member of the real world at all, not a priest, but the guardian of the temple, protecting it at the rim of the spirit world where he dwelt, from the evil and black influences on the other side.

Waiting until he halted a few feet in front of him, Feiffer said softly in Chinese, "Detective Chief Inspector Feiffer from Yellow-thread Street Police Station." He did not address the man by rank or title because so close to becoming Nothing and No One, he had none. "Thank you for your care of the distraught man over there." In his life, the man didn't listen for human voices but sounds creatures with human voices didn't hear and he had to concentrate on the words. "A man is dead in the temple and before he can be removed to the care of his family, it is important for us to know how and why he died."

As soon as he had said it, he knew it was the wrong thing to say. People died because the Wheel of Life turned and they ceased to be what they were and became something else. *How* was immaterial.

Feiffer said, "We need to know for his family if anyone was with him when he died—whether he gave some message to that person that might help to console them."

He looked hard at the priest's face and saw nothing. There was an old Chinese adage that before the truly good man the unworthy and unperfected slunk away in shame. Feiffer said, "I'm sorry to interrupt you on your path, but—" He saw a faint, gentle smile at the corner of the man's mouth and knew he was doing something he should not do. Feiffer said awkwardly, full of a feeling of awkwardness, "I'm very sorry to intrude."

He listened, concentrating hard. Behind him from the stone bench where the paramedic was, there was a sob and, attuned to it, hearing it a second before Feiffer did or even a second before it actually happened, the priest turned to the man and raised his hand a fraction to pacify something—not the sobbing man, but the sob.

He was tiny, nothing but skin and bones, like a sparrow. To one side of the corridor there was a wooden pallet where he sometimes slept and a cracked pottery bowl for the times when he ate something, and nothing else.

Turning back to Feiffer, still with the gentle smile on his face, the priest said in a surprisingly strong voice, "I heard a man come into the temple and go to the shrine of the White Monkey God and light a taper."

"An old man?"

"Yes."

He had heard it from out here. He had heard the shuffling footsteps of age that to him in his vast, silent inward cosmos must have sounded like hammer blows, and then he had heard the match striking, and then—Feiffer looked hard at his face and knew—he had felt the light of the candle as a tiny pinprick of light on the edge of the universe.

"And then?"

And then, because he would have been able to hear every word of the man's prayer as it passed by him on the edge of that universe to the spirit world but the prayer was private, he had not listened. "And then, nothing." He smiled at the word.

Feiffer glanced for a moment at the paramedic, still with his head hidden in his hands on the stone bench, weeping. "And then? After a while?" He wanted to know if the priest had felt the coldness of Death pass quickly by him and brush at him with his flowing robes.

He shrugged and opened his hands to show they, like all the things of the world men's hands grasped at, were empty. "And then—nothing."

"And you felt—?"

There was a silence, and in that silence the priest looked into Feiffer's soul and penetrated all its secrets. "I sensed a change and for an instant the world was out of balance, and then, somewhere, life began for someone or something else and the balance restored itself." He meant, somewhere out there in the darkness where *his* soul lived, he had hung precariously as something died to keep the world in balance by the force of his own prayers until the moment the Wheel turned and gave the old life of the dead thing to something else in a glorious instant of continuation and hope. "I felt the loss of a person of some good acts, many venal ones, and many deeds and acts of greed and cruelty to others."

Feiffer said, "His name was Mr. Lee. He was seventy-eight years old. All his life he had been engaged in the pursuit of money and power, and now, I assume, finding him here, he was engaged in the restoration of his soul and preparation for his next life."

"He came here often. I often heard his step."

"Did he come alone?"

"At first, no. At first, he came by car." He moved his hand gently in the direction of Wanchai Street—"with two others, one of whom waited in the car for him, and the other—with a heavy, heavy footfall—who accompanied him inside, came each time through the corridor, gazed for a moment at the garden and whoever was in it, then went back inside to be with his master."

He had been the CEO and probably major shareholder in the Asian Textile Traders conglomerate, one of the largest exporters of Chinese silk and cloth in the world. The two men with him had been his driver and his bodyguard.

The priest said as if it had been known from the start, "And then, after a while, he came only with a man who waited for him in the car and stayed longer, and then"—he meant, as his soul matured—"and then, finally, he came alone and had walked a long way to come here and was a better man."

"Did he come alone today?"

"Yes."

"And was he alone all the time he was here?"

He fell silent.

"Did you go into the temple while he was here?"

"No."

"Did someone else enter the temple while he was here?"

He turned his head slightly to look at the paramedic and did not speak.

He saw something, something awful . . . and whatever it was that he saw killed him, and in that instant he was afraid to ask and, like the priest, fell silent.

In the garden, there was only the stillness and tranquillity and contemplation and the soft, muted sounds of the uniformed man on the stone bench weeping.

Feiffer said at last, "Did *something* else enter the temple?" All he wanted to do was turn and go. He had asked Wilfred Wing on his boat, "Do you believe in ghosts?" and the man, lying to him, had said firmly, *"No!"* Feiffer asked, not wanting to know, "Did something—"

The priest said with a nod, "Yes."

"What was it?"

"I don't know."

"Was it another man?"

He remained silent.

"Was it a sound? A whisper? A *presence?*"

"It was a presence."

"Did you hear it?"

He had not. He had sensed it. "No."

"What did the paramedic tell you?" and saw from the priest's face that he did not know what a paramedic was, "—the weeping man on the bench?"

"The soul of the weeping man on the bench is deeply troubled."

"Did he tell you that?"

"It was clear to me."

"Did he tell you that in words?"

He shook his head. "No."

"What did he tell you in words?"

"Nothing." The priest said with a gentle shrug and a smile, "I cannot understand his language."

"Did you hear anything, anything at all, in the temple after the presence entered?"

"Yes."

He glanced at the paramedic and wondered why the priest had not been able to understand what he had said. "What? What did you hear?"

"A sound. A sound like a *blossoming*, and then"—and he clutched his hand into a fist as if something had suddenly fallen from it and he had been unable to catch it before it fell—"And then the soul of the man who had come to atone for his past life fled and was gone into the cosmos to be reborn."

"And then—?"

"And then—nothing." He had been at his post on the rim of darkness praying for the soul and the return of the world to the equilibrium the lost soul had disturbed—"And then I heard no more, and when I returned, there was no more to be heard."

"Did you hear the blossoming in the temple or in the place you had gone to?"

"I heard it in the temple at the shrine of the Monkey God where the old man stood worshipping."

"A blossoming of what?"

He thought hard, going back on all the sounds he had heard in all his life. "I cannot say."

"It was a sound? Not a sensation, but a *sound?*"

"It was a sound."

He looked over at the paramedic, but the man would not look up, and anything he might know had happened after the Advanced Life Support Team he was part of had arrived, and he would know nothing of what had happened before. Feiffer asked, "From all your life as a priest, can you think of anything you have ever heard, or heard of, that made that sound before, or anything that made a sound anything like it?"

"No."

It was hopeless. It was all nothing and nothingness. "From the time before you were a priest? From when you were a child?"

Such a long, long time ago. As if he rose that long-ago part of his existence up, like a conductor gently bringing up the volume of a part of an orchestra so far in the symphony silent, with his eyes closed, the priest stroked at his chest in gentle wavelike motions to summon it.

He was thinking of that part of his life. Feiffer saw him smile gently and happily at the memory of it. Feiffer said again, "A blossoming."

"Yes."

"Like something remembered from—"

Suddenly, he smiled with a wonderful smile of wistfulness and joy. "From when I was a small boy at New Year and gifts were exchanged in wonderful packages of bright-red colored paper and all the house was—" The priest said, smiling with gratitude for being reminded of something so wonderful and precious. "A blossoming..." He brought his head up and looked at Feiffer with his dead, unseeing eyes and saw everything in the man that he needed to know about him. "It was the sound of paper: the blossoming. It was the sound of red tissue paper, suddenly, like a gift, full of wonderful, secret, unseen things, opening all by itself—" He turned back to the direction of the paramedic to tell him and then remembered he did not have the man's language at his command, and turned back to Feiffer for help. The priest said to explain, "He speaks Tagalog, the language of the Philippines, and English, and I—"

He saw something, something awful . . . and whatever it was that he saw killed him! Feiffer said in a gasp, "What?" and in that instant, the paramedic looked up and Feiffer saw his face and the expression on it he had seen before, long ago and far, far from here.

The paramedic was not Chinese at all, but Philippino, and in the garden of the Temple of a Thousand Buddhas, suddenly chilled to the bone, Feiffer said in a gasp, "Oh, dear Christ!" and knew what it was that had entered the temple after the old man, Lee, and killed him, and what had entered the rest room on *The Pearl Princess* before or after Mr. Tam and killed him, and what, before that, had found Mr. Yuan and killed him, and, five weeks before that, had found Ronnie Wong and killed him.

He knew why the paramedic had not ridden back to the hospital with Mr. Tam's body and why now he would not go back into the temple and wept uncontrollably, shaking with fear.

He knew why he, himself, standing in that silent, serene place, suddenly, uncontrollably felt all the muscles in his stomach tighten in fear.

All the deaths were what the Philippinos and they alone, in their horror, had known over the centuries was the worst death there was to die.

It was the death they called in the native language of the country, Tagalog, *bangungot*—"Nightmare Syndrome."

7.

"Bangungot: nightmare syndrome . . ."

In Wanchai Street, Feiffer had managed to find a reasonably quiet phone to call from on the dock of a deserted warehouse far enough away from the temple so that the paramedics from the two ALSVs still parked outside in the street could not see him without having to leave their vehicles and make their curiosity obvious.

On the other end of the line, Lieutenant Felix Elizalde of the Metro Manila Police, asked, "Do you want the standard definition?" He was a mestizo, half Philippino and half Spanish, a man who, each evening, dropped whatever he was doing and went almost religiously to the shoreline of Rizal Park in the center of the city to smoke a cigar and drink coffee and watch the sun go down. He had a soft, Spanish, almost poetic lilt to his voice.

"In the first instance, yes."

He was speaking at two in the afternoon his time from police headquarters in Manila City. Elizalde said, "The standard definition is that it's a rare disease said to be peculiar to young

Philippino males, usually bachelors, between the ages of twenty-five and forty. They go to sleep one night and are found dead the following morning, apparently after suffering a violent nightmare."

Standing there on the deserted dock, watching as Victor Chen came out of the temple gate with his arm around the still-weeping man and put him in the back of his car to wait for him, Feiffer thought it was a long time since he had taken the time to sit in Rizal Park with Elizalde and smoke a cigar as the sun went down, an even longer time since he had taken the time to sit and smoke a cigar with anyone, or even taken the time to think about doing it.

Elizalde said, "There are two schools of thought as to the cause: the first and most scientific-sounding, but equally as unlikely as the unscientific-sounding one, is that it's caused by eating a heavy meal just before bedtime, particularly *bagoong* and *patis*—" He waited. "Or in English, for the forgetful—"

Feiffer said, "Fermented shrimp in brine with relish."

"Ah." Then Elizalde said a little sadly, "It's a long time since you've been here, Harry."

"Yes." At the temple gate, Victor Chen paused for a moment, then motioned for the first ALSV crew to come in with a stretcher to get the body.

Elizalde said, "The disease kills approximately one person each month, so the odds of a particular meal that's eaten by almost all the population of the Philippines at least twice a week being responsible is fairly thin. Generally, it's put down to what it appears to be: a massive heart attack or stroke or combination of the two caused by a previously undiagnosed existing condition."

"And the autopsy results say what?"

"The autopsy results say that the attack was so catastrophic it would have wiped out any evidence of a previously undiagnosed condition, but that doesn't mean it wasn't there."

At the temple, the ALSV crew went in through the gate to do their work on the dead man in there and closed the gate behind them.

In his house in the New Territories, as he and his younger brother sat at the bottom of the big staircase and watched, two men in suits, who he knew were undertakers, went up the stairs to their parents' bedroom to do things to the dead man in there who had been his father.

Feiffer asked, "And the unscientific explanation?"

Elizalde said, "The unscientific explanation is that it's a form of sorcery called *kulam* and it's the work of a *mangkulam* who has the power to summon up a demon that sits on your chest at night, a creature of such dreadful appearance that the very sight of him when you wake is enough to stop the heart with terror and explode every blood vessel in the brain."

He saw something, something awful . . . and whatever it was that he saw killed him . . .

Standing there with one hand on the receiver and the other pressed hard up against the other side of his head, ostensibly to drown out the sound from the street, Feiffer could not stop himself from shaking. "And what do you believe, Felix?"

There was a silence, then Elizalde said softly, "I believe, Harry, that you think you have a case of *bangungot* up there in Hong Kong." His voice was even and merely informational— "Again, the standard, scientific view is that it is peculiar to the Philippines and, like good wine, doesn't travel well."

"And?"

Elizalde said, "I don't have the actual report, but it's known that there were several instances of it in Hawaii between the years 1942 and 1945."

"Philippinos?"

"Yes."

"How many?"

"Sixty-seven. A flurry of about thirty the first year, and then the next a dozen or fourteen, and the rest the year later."

"And then?"

"And then nothing."

"So the *mangkulam*, if there is one, got out of the Philippines just before the Japanese invaded and stayed in Hawaii until war's end, when he went back."

Elizalde said noncommittally, "Possibly."

God alone knew what they thought in the temple as they gently lifted the hideous creature who had been Mr. Lee onto a stretcher and covered him with a sheet to take him away. All he could think of as he sat there at the bottom of the staircase with his brother was that now he would never be allowed into his father's private room again and be allowed to sit in his big leather office chair and look at all the photos and badges and guns on the wall from the days when his father had been in the Shanghai Police and listen as his father taught him about China and the Chinese and how, when he was older and the situation in China had calmed, they would go back together to Shanghai and the Great Wall and the mountains of the north so high they had snow on them all year and at a distance hung in the sky like icicles.

Elizalde said, "*Mangkulams* are almost always local people— traditionally, nothing much more than village medicine men, and since almost all of their supposed magic powers are derived from a sort of anthropomorphic merging with the spirits of the land around them it's hardly likely they'd either contemplate or survive a quick flit in a plane thousands of miles to a completely different environment." Elizalde said, "And since they tend to dress in breechclout and cape, they wouldn't have gone unnoticed too long, especially in wartime Hawaii."

Feiffer said equally informationally, "I have four dead men in the last eight weeks. They all died of massive apparently natural

causes so violent they caused what appears to be a complete destruction of almost every internal organ in the body. They died
alone and were found with a look of almost animal horror still
frozen on their faces."

Elizalde asked, "Philippinos?"

Feiffer said, "Chinese."

"Young?"

"Their ages varied from thirty-five to almost eighty-five
years."

From the other end of the line, there was a silence.

Feiffer said with his hand gripping the receiver of the phone so
hard the knuckles went white, "And they all died, not while they
were asleep, but while they were all awake, and, Felix, before they
died, in each instance, they tried to claw their own eyes out with
their fingernails!" *And when they brought his father out it was in a coffin
he had not even seen anyone take in, and he never saw his father's face again.*

Standing there on the empty dock, feeling like a small, lost
child, so alone, Feiffer said into the suddenly silent, empty void
of the phone, "Felix? . . . Felix, are you still there?"

It sounded as if he had moved to another phone or closed the
door to his office. His voice was different. Elizalde said for the
second time, "It's a long time since you and Nicola were here,
Harry—much, much too long."

"It's a long time since you've been in Hong Kong, Felix."

"Yes." They were words, but they were not meant to commu-
nicate anything: the meaning and the communication was in the
silence between the words. Elizalde said, "Yes, yes, it is. Maybe I
should come up and sample the joys of the last surviving exam-
ple of British nineteenth-century colonialism while I still can."

"Yes, maybe you should."

Elizalde said, "It's dying there a little at a time, Harry, isn't it?"

"Yes, I'm afraid it is."

"Yes." Elizalde said again, "Yes." Then there was another silence. Then Elizalde said in a tone Feiffer had never heard him use before, one full of fear and whispers and the face of terror itself, "That's why he's there."

"Who?"

Elizalde said, "The *Dalagangan*—the great priest, not some local half-naked savage *mangkulam* drunk on rice wine and ignorance scaring people to death with threat and superstition, but the real thing—the thing that is *bangungot* itself: the demon in human form—a living man who, so far as anyone can judge, cannot die, and so far as the records that exist show, has lived in his present form for a minimum of, at least, one hundred and fifty years . . ."

In Wanchai Street, the ALSV crew brought Mr. Lee's body out on a stretcher, covered in a sheet held down at the head and feet by what looked like improvised body straps. As they went to the back of the ambulance and waited for the door to be opened from the inside, they were silent and did not look at the body.

Silences, *hushes*, half-heard words and silences . . .

At his father's funeral, all his father's old friends from the Shanghai International Police had come to pay their respects, the men he had seen in the old photographs on the wall, men in their dress uniforms and plumed parade helmets from every country that had been part of the international force that had policed the tiny violent territory in the center of Shanghai, and men from the Hong Kong force and Macao his father had dealt with in his job as an investigator with the Securities and Exchange Commission, and others, men and women, European and Chinese, with their eyes full of tears who, like him, had merely loved him.

And in that moment, looking out into the street, he could not watch as the crew put Mr. Lee's body in the back of the ambulance and shut the door on it, and took the phone away from his ear and closed his eyes.

Elizalde's voice came back to him from a distance, as if he had been talking a long time. He was from a different world to Feiffer—the world of Spanish-Philippino culture and Catholicism and a deep, personal mysticism that combined the two—and it was not the *what* of life that exercised his mind, but the *why* of it.

Elizalde said with his voice fading, thinking about it in his office now as he had thought about it so many times before in the last fading moments of a beautiful sunset across the bay at Rizal Park, "... there are only six basic categories of magic of any type, genuine or otherwise, that can occur in the physical world, whatever the cause, Harry: Production, in which something appears or multiplies; Transformation, in which something changes in color, shape, or size; Transposition, in which something moves from one place to another; Penetration, in which one solid object passes through another; Mentalism, which includes thought-reading and predictions; and Disappearance, in which something vanishes from sight . . ."

He had been in Hawaii during the war. Feiffer said tightly, "Where else has he been, Felix? Apart from Hawaii? This Dalagangan?"

They were still there, the ALSV crew, inside the ambulance, not moving, waiting for Victor Chen to come out of the temple and tell them what to do next.

Maybe he had answered him and he had not heard. Feiffer said into the phone, "Felix?"

There was a pause as if he thought about it a moment, then what sounded like a sigh. Elizalde said, "After Hawaii in 1942 to 1945, we have reason to believe he was in India briefly in either 1948 or '49—"

"Just at the time the British were leaving and power was being transferred to the Indians—"

"Yes. And then, again, in 1949—"

Feiffer said, "China. In the last few days of the Communist Revolution—"

"Yes. And then, in the Malaya Emergency of the mid-nineteen fifties, we believe he was in Kuala Lumpur for a while and then, at the height of the terrorist campaign, in Singapore." Elizalde said a little apologetically, "But any records we have are sporadic and no more detailed than that. We know when he leaves and sometimes even have a rough idea where he may be going, but by the time we contact the authorities wherever he's been, invariably, power has changed hands and everything is in chaos and there are no records." Elizalde said, "We do know for certain, however, that he was in Hong Kong in 1966 at the time of the Cultural Revolution and the—"

Feiffer said, finishing his sentence, "And the riots here. And the daily threats by the Chinese Red Army that they were about to come in in force to restore order." He waited for Victor Chen to come out and order the paramedics to take the dead man away as he had waited for his father's funeral among strangers to be over so he could go home and be alone. Feiffer asked, "Am I right?"

"Yes, you are." Elizalde said, "And, we think, in the seventies—"

"How *old* is he?"

"We don't know." Nothing was clear. It was all chaos and mist and half-information and rumors. Elizalde said, "No one knows. After a hundred years of Spanish colonialism, Japanese colonialism, and then American colonialism, we just don't have any reliable records about anything. In the late nineteenth century, the missionaries even got the local people to change their names to Spanish ones and gave them new birthdates to coincide with the Saints' Christian names they gave them at baptism, so for half a century or so—" Elizalde said, "And then, during the Occupation, the Japanese burned every Catholic or Western document they could lay their hands on, so even those records went. And then, when we were liberated by the Americans . . ." Elizalde said with grim humor, "That's why we Philippinos are famous for our delicate sense of *amor proprie*, or self-esteem: because we have no idea who we are we are touchy to any suggestion, real or otherwise, that we are nobody, and, in that other famous manifestation of the maintenance of personal ego and identity, at the faintest slight, run amok and kill everybody in sight." Elizalde said, "Physically, he appears to be about eighty years old, but there are rumors that he was active at least in the nineteen-twenties, so he may be much, much older."

He was about to say, "That's crazy!" but Elizalde had his own sense of *amor proprie*, well-disguised or not, and he did not. Feiffer asked, "What does he do in these places he goes to? He doesn't just go there and kill a few people and then leave for no good reason!"

"We don't know. For the reasons I've already explained. By the time we know where he's been the place is usually in such a state of flux there's no central authority we can ask, and usually, in a situation like that when an entire country is in upheaval, the unexplained deaths of a few people who probably died of natural causes anyway is the least of anyone's considerations."

"Where does his money come from?"

"We don't know."

"Does he *have* money?"

"He appears to. It appears to come from legitimate investments and land he owns here."

"Does he have money from any of the places he was supposedly in over the years?"

"According to our taxation investigators, no." Elizalde said educationally, "Harry, a lot of the Philippino economy is a cash economy. If you had money from somewhere else and you brought it in in some easily disposable form like diamonds or gold or even large-denomination bills, you'd have very little trouble converting it into property and even less paying for anything you wanted in the gold and diamonds you had in the first place. And then, of course, in a country fueled by bribery and influence—"

"Is that what you think happens?"

"*I don't know what happens!* What I'm telling you is what the rumors say."

"And do the rumors say who hires him to go to these places and kill people?"

He must have hit a nerve. There was a silence. Then it lengthened. Then Elizalde said in a tone of voice he had not used before, "He is not a *mangkulam*. He is the Dalagangan. The man of awesome powers." His voice sounded suddenly a little breathless, as if he did not even want to say the words—"No one hires a Dalagangan."

"So he just turns up here out of nowhere, summoned by no one, kills one young market analyst, three old millionaires—"

He was hurt, or angry, or both. Elizalde said tightly, "He is summoned by the times!"

"And then, for equally no apparent reason, leaves again and—
and does what? Kills a few more people at home and blames it all
on eating goddamned shrimp cocktail and relish?" Victor Chen
was never going to come out and order the ambulance to leave.
They were never going to finish the service in the English church
on Great Shanghai Street and take the awful polished coffin away
out of the aisle so he would not have to look at it anymore. Gripping at the phone, losing control, Feiffer shouted down the line,
"Is that it? Is that the whole story? Is that the whole fucking explanation of why I have four dead men who look like hell with
their eyes gone? Is that why I can't do anything about it? Because
it's all just rumor and hearsay and the whole goddamned history
of Asia wrapped up in one neat, inscrutable package? Is that the
best you can do, Felix? After almost thirty years as a fucking cop
listening to every bit of bullshit the human mind is capable of
dredging up, is that the best you can do by way of explanation?"
He saw him. He saw Victor Chen come out of the gate and, still
carrying the cellular phone he had used to arrange it all, motion
to the two Advanced Life Support Vehicles to go. "Do you even
know his goddamned *name?*"

The voice that came back was like ice. Elizalde said, "His name
is Jesus Sixtus Caina, the name the Spanish missionaries may have
given him. By appearance at the present time, he is approximately
eighty years old, tall"— Elizalde said with heavy sarcasm, "We
have no exact height measurement, but since we Philippinos are all
little people both in stature and mental development, you may assume that means he probably stands anywhere from five foot nine
to six feet, very gaunt and thin, with very long, beautifully formed
hands and long, manicured fingernails."

"Is there a photo?"

"No, there is not."

"Have you ever seen him yourself?"

"No, I have not." And then, across the street, at last, they went and took the dead man away and something tight across Feiffer's back relaxed all at once and he had to grab hold of the phone on the wall to stop from staggering; and then, at last, he was away from the church and the coffin and was back in his house, but the house was all full of people, and he heard one of them, an American who had served with his father in the International Police in Shanghai who had come all the way from the Philippines to be at the funeral say in a loud voice, "Bang! Gun got him!" and he thought as his mother hushed the man and then sent him and his brother away up the stairs to their room that his father had shot himself with one of the guns on the wall and he could not understand why or what he had done wrong and— And then, finally, even Victor Chen started the engine of his car and went away, and he could not . . . and he would never see the snow on the mountains in northern China that hung like icicles in midair and he would never . . .

Elizalde said angrily, "I'm sorry to disappoint you, Harry. We just do the best we can. I've had a man on him for at least the past two months, he hasn't come up with anything either, but then, maybe what happened to him will make you feel a bit better and maybe more or less raise us just a little in your esteem—*because we've completely lost contact with him and we think he's fucking dead, which is a great pity because, like you, once upon a time he was a friend of mine and I had a great and loving affection for him!*"

He could not catch his breath. On the phone, covering his eyes with his hand, Feiffer said in a whisper, "Oh, God . . ."

He saw something, something awful . . . and whatever it was that he saw killed him . . . Bang! Gun got him!

He could barely speak, and when he did his voice was so low Elizalde could not hear him and he had to repeat the question.

"Felix, do you know where he was in 1956? At the end of June? June the twenty-third?"

He had to think for a moment. "Your part of the world, somewhere in the South China Sea area."

"In Hong Kong?"

"I don't know. Probably. Were there—?"

"There were riots all that month and bombings engineered by the Communist faction here to bring the Mao government over the border."

"Then he was there." Elizalde said, "Why? Why especially that date? Why do you ask about that date in particular?"

His voice was so low Elizalde could not hear it, but he heard what was in it.

Elizalde, his voice full of concern, said anxiously, "Harry? Harry, are you all right?"

It was not Bang! Gun got—it was *Bangungot*.

On the phone on the deserted dock, sitting in his room alone and weeping, Feiffer said in a terrible, lost voice, "Oh, God, Felix . . . oh, God . . ."

It was not the what or how of life that mattered as he sat each evening there at the shoreline of Rizal Park watching the last rays of the sun, it was the why of it and the few constant things that abided through it like duty and honor and friendship and forgiveness that mattered. And they mattered to him very much. Elizalde said with his heart hurting for the man, "Harry, what is it? What's wrong?"

"Oh, God . . . oh, God, Felix . . ."

Shaking like a leaf, barely able to hold on to the phone, barely able to get the words out, Feiffer said in a whisper, in a *hush*, "Oh, God, Felix, I think he was the man who—almost forty years ago—killed my father!"

8.

In the sewer, coming towards Spencer with his hands held up like hammers, Auden said (he thought), *"What do you mean, all of the great secrets of Life can be decoded and deciphered and understood in the one single great act of defusing an undefusable bomb?"* but what he actually said was, "WHADDABOMBMEANINGACT OFSINGLEGREATLIFEDECIPHERINGDECODING . . . *FUCKING KILL YOU!!! . . .*

All he had to do was decide the method.

Coming towards Spencer, he decided stomping.

Stomping would be nice.

At least, he thought he came towards Spencer. What he actually did was haul a horrible slime-filled black boot an inch out of slime, look down at it with horror as it filled with even more slime and then, as it reached slime saturation, sink again, and anchor him there.

Or mashing. If he could just get to him and mash . . .

He couldn't get to him and mash. In the slime there was a flash as one of the live telephone wires touched the top of the primeval ooze, then a bubble, then a flurry, and in the great soup of the sewer, in only the second recorded instance since the Dawn of Time, new life was created out of nothing and began to swim towards the surface.

It swam towards the light and the sunlight and the air and evolution and Auden.

Mistake. Pulverizing whatever the filthy swimming object was that had waited in the wings a million years for this one moment with one blow of his fist, Auden shrieked at the still-smiling Spencer, "I'm going to kill you! I'm going to murder you! I'm going to tear you into little pieces!" Then he was going to go upstairs, get on the phone to Hetherington-Smith or Feather-in-the-Snit or whatever his fucking name was, get him to get his ass down to defuse the bomb, and then stomp, mash, grind, and tear him to pieces as well.

On the other side of the bomb, Spencer stopped grinning. High on methane gas and objects of mass destruction with his brain working very, very slowly, Spencer said as if in slow motion with his brows wrinkled to comprehend, "You don't want me to defuse the bomb anymore?"

No, he didn't want him to defuse the bomb anymore. Auden, with a strange strained look on his face as if both his feet were stuck in ooze and he couldn't get them free, said, "No, I don't want you to defuse the bomb anymore." He thought if he could just get a firm hold on the bomb, lean a little over it and haul, maybe both boots would come out at once ... or maybe, if he strained to the limit and got his feet right *out* of the boots, maybe he could ... Death at a distance: that was what evolution was all about. Upstairs, his beautiful, evolved to the nth degree, lightly oiled, fully loaded Colt Python .357 Magnum sat in the top

drawer of his desk just awaiting the call. Up there . . . up there . . .
Straining, wanting it, wanting it, Auden said, *"Grrr—!"*

He was hurt. And shocked. Spencer said through his haze of
marsh gas, "You don't think I can do it!"

He got a boot out. Something moved down there in the mire
and the boot came loose and he pulled it up and he could *walk!*

He walked a single step, then there was a sound like something disgusting disappearing down the drain hole of a very
old septic system and the other boot came out and he could
walk like a man!

Spencer said incredulously, shocked even more, "You don't
trust me!"

He could sink like a man. Taking a single step into what
under the slime suddenly opened up into the Mindanao Deep
and disappearing in a single giant bubble, Auden said in fervent
agreement, "Yerr-rerr—!!"

Well, that hurt. That was the unkindest cut of all. Spencer,
having to look away in his humiliation, said with his mouth
trembling, "Oh." He had thought Auden was his friend. Touching at his tear ducts, Spencer said sadly, "Oh. Gee."

Somewhere under the bomb, in blurred and grainy black and
white, the Monster From The Black Lagoon swam in silent,
bubbleless and increasingly more desperate circles looking for
the surface of the slime.

Spencer said through his brainful of gas, "Then what is all
the struggle and learning of life if it is naught and it comes to
this? What availeth a man if he gain the whole world and lose
his—" It was all so clear to him now—" 'To strive, to fight, and
not to yield,' does it mean *nothing?*"

It meant nothing.

" 'Never surrender. Never, never, never. Never.' Was Churchill *wrong?*"

He was wrong.

"Is it all just a *lie* foisted on the working classes to ensure they do the bidding of the masters and die before the canons at Balaclava with a smile on their faces?"

Under the bomb, there was a big bubble.

On the other side of the bubble, Spencer babbled, *"Now all the youth of England are on fire, / And silken dalliance in the wardrobe lies; / Now thrive the armourers, and honour's thought / Reigns solely in the breast of every man: / They sell the pasture now to buy the horse, / . . . For now sits Expectation in the air / And hides a sword from hilts unto the point / With crowns imperial, crowns and coronets, / Promis'd to—"* Spencer, echoing in Sewer Central like Olivier on Shaftesbury Avenue, shrieked, "All this is chimera? All this is nothing but empty air and declamation? A tale told by an idiot signifying *nothing? 'If we are marked to die, we are enow / To do our country loss; and if to live, / The fewer men, the greater share of honour . . . ' "*

Near the tail of the bomb, the bubble burst and for an instant something that looked like it had tendrils growing out of the sides of its head surfaced, gasped in a desperate breath of air, and then sank again.

Crying bootless to heaven, Spencer shrieked, "I grew up on the stuff of great challenges! This stuff is the stuff of me!" Spencer, no longer shrieking, but roaring Churchillianly, declaimed, " *'Never . . . in the field of human conflict . . . has so much been owed by so many to so . . . Men will say . . . This! . . . was their finest hour! . . . ' "* His entire life flashed before him. It was a sort of schoolboy's life. Spencer yelled, "Is everything I was ever taught to believe about honor and glory and achievement and—and— wrong?" Spencer yelled, "I've spent my entire life waiting for the one great moment in which to shine"—and in which, presumably, to demonstrate his perfect grammar under fire—"And now, when the moment arrives, you tell me what I really am in men's eyes: someone not to be trusted, a fool, a jester, a mere diversion on the real road of worldly affairs—a *dupe!*"

The Creature slowly, drippingly, painstakingly, surfaced.

Spencer, high as a kite on the gas, roared, "The wise man is not taken in by all the promises that life can rise above the mundane into the heavens; the wise man merely sits in front of his television with his beer in his hand and thinks no nobler thoughts than what piece of puerile palliative for the masses is coming on next. Is that right? Is that right?" He could have sat down in the slime and wept. Spencer said, brokenhearted, "*'Nothing so much became him in his life as his leaving of it.'*" Spencer said, shaking his head, "Is everything just a lie? A tale told by an idiot, full of sound and fury, signifying *nothing?*" Spencer, reaching in under his coveralls and pulling out his Detective Special and cocking it, said sadly, "Then die, Caesar . . ."

He had a gun! He-had-a-*Gun!* The Creature, getting shakily to its hind legs on the near side of the bomb and reaching out for it, said, "Huhh-*rerrr!!*"

He saw him. Spencer, putting the gun to his head to make an end of it all, yelled, "Don't try to stop me!"

Stop him? *Stop* him? He wanted to *help!* Auden, slodging through the sewer at top slodge to get his finger on the trigger too to be part of it, thundered, "Ahhh—RAHHHH!!!"

He had one last thing to say before he saw himself off and blew his poor, befuddled brains out. From the depths, from the very bottom of his being, Spencer, baring his soul, shrieked, "God! God! *God, how much I hate people like Captain the Honorable Roger bloody Hetherington-Smith!*"

✳ ✳ ✳

On the subject of being better off dead . . .

Two floors up in the Detectives' Room, surrounded by the phalanx of sleeping cannibals, O'Yee tried to count his blessings.

The only blessing was that Emily and the kids were in San Francisco visiting her parents for a month and they wouldn't have to ID his chopped-up remains after the cannibals had axed, stabbed, filleted, and clubbed him to death and then, after they had munched all his tender bits, gnawed at his bones and used what was left for a few postprandial games of knuckle-jacks on the Station floor.

Irec Algr Amasc Afmm Icba Atta Emma Zip . . .

Trying hard, he tried to think what to try next. His son Patrick had been a sleepwalker when he was little, for two or three months or so when he was five, and, gazing hard at the sleepers, he tried to think back on what the doctors had told Emily to do about it and what she, in turn, had told him.

Something about not touching him or disturbing him as he walked, but gently, quietly walking alongside him and saying his name in a tender tone, and then, even more tenderly—

O'Yee said tenderly to Sleeper Number One, the one with the axe, "Hello? . . ."

They were all armed to the goddamned teeth. He looked and even their teeth, sharpened to razor-sharp points, were armed to the teeth. O'Yee said, a little louder, "Hi, there!"

O'Yee said loudly, "Hey!"

Irec Algr Amasc Afmm Icba Atta Emma Zip.

God alone knew what that meant!

O'Yee, leaning forward at his desk to show them he wasn't a man to be trifled with too long, said firmly, "Hey! Wake up!"

Not even the breathing varied.

He was in a deserted Station in the middle of Hong Kong with six cannibals sleeping at his desk on one floor and two morons on another working away at a bomb and blowing every phone and fax in the Station one after another. O'Yee said as an order, "I'm a sworn police officer in my legal jurisdiction and I'm giving a legal order to one or all of you to wake up and explain yourselves!"

O'Yee said, "You can't get away with it, you know. The Royal Hong Kong Police always get their man!" O'Yee said, "Okay? Now, I'm going to count to three and then—"

O'Yee said, "One!"

O'Yee said, "Two!"

O'Yee said, "Three!"

O'Yee said, "Look, I'm trying to be reasonable here. I don't want to have to use force, but if you force me to use force then I'll be forced—" He was blathering. O'Yee said as a command, "Wake the hell up, will you, and tell me what's going on!"

O'Yee said as a warning, "My son used to be a sleepwalker— and I remember that my wife was told by the doctor that shaking a sleepwalker awake was an extremely dangerous thing to do because if the poor soul was really asleep—*and not just faking*— it could make them start screaming and thrashing and, quite possibly, do permanent and irreparable damage and—" He was blathering. O'Yee said, "But if pushed to the limit, I won't shrink from—" O'Yee, getting to his feet with his hand firmly around the grip of his gun, said, "I won't shrink from doing it!"

Sleeper Number One didn't look like a screamer or a thrasher to him.

"Okay?"

Not a creature was stirring, not even a throwout from hell.

"All right then." Reaching out for the sleeping man's shoulder with his free hand, O'Yee said as his very last warning, "Well, you asked for it. Don't blame me if you suffer some sort of short-term psychological trauma from it—"

He didn't look like a brick falling on his head could cause him any psychological trauma, short-term or otherwise.

O'Yee said pleadingly, "Come on, will you? Wake up!"

He didn't look like a screamer to him.

He gave the man, at first, the gentlest of gentle little shakes.

Above the sound of a bloodcurdling scream from somewhere up in the Detectives' Room, The Creature From Under The Black Bomb, halted in mid-slodge, said through a mouthful of mire, "Aye? What do you mean you hate people like Captain the Honorable Roger bloody Hetherington-Smith? You *are* people like Captain the Honorable Roger bloody Hetherington-Smith! You're his goddamned clone! I'm the one who hates people like Captain the Honorable Roger bloody Hetherington-Smith, not you!"

He had just a few more words to say before he blasted himself off his perch and left the vale of tears. Spencer, smiling through the methane and madness, said sadly to his own private dark lady of the sonnets, " *Ah, Love, let us now quit this sorry scheme of things and . . .'* "

Auden said as an order, "Shut up and put the fucking gun down! What the hell do you mean, you hate him? How can you hate him? You think just like him! You even talk just like him! You *are* him! You even went to the same damned schools he did!"

" *If were done, when was done, t'was best it was done quickly . . .'* " But he uncocked the gun for a moment. Spencer said, "I went on scholarship!"

"To where?"

"It doesn't matter to where!"

"Yes, it does matter to where!"

"No, it doesn't!"

"It was Eton, wasn't it? Or Harrow? Or Rugby, or one of those!" Through his screwed-up scaly orbs he watched Spencer's reaction. Auden said in triumph, "My God, it was Eton, wasn't it?" It couldn't have been worse. Auden said as a terrible accusation, "You-went-to-*Eton*, didn't you? Along with all the aristos like Hetherington-Smith: all the Honorables, all the sons of dukes and earls and—"

Spencer said tightly, "An Honorable isn't the son of a duke or an earl. An Honorable is only the son of a baron."

Auden shrieked, "Whaddya mean: you hate people like him? You're one of them!"

"I was never one of them!"

"You were always one of them!" The Dripping Heap From The Deep said in a terrible roar, "You went to Eton! Didn't you?"

It was all out now. Dropping his head and almost taking the top of his ear off with the front sight of the Detective Special still jammed up against the side of his head, Spencer said in awful admission to the Unpardonable Sin, the biographical detail that dared not speak its name, "Yes! *Yes!* I went to *Eton!*"

Auden said with an ugly tone in his voice, "I went to Jack the Ripper High, Limehouse."

"I went to Eton all those years in a coat too big for me that didn't quite match the pants because my mother was too poor to afford the proper official school one!" Spencer said desperately, "I was never part of anything! I was never part of *them*— of the ruling classes! I was always the boy in the funny coat who was embarrassed all the time. I was the one who had to believe in the notion of glory and achievement by a single man taking the tide at the flood because, by God, I didn't have any of the natural advantages of family or position or birth or money that any of the other boys had! I was the one who swallowed the notion of a lone individual changing the course of history and striving with the gods because—let me tell you—I couldn't strive much with anyone else . . . and because I didn't have the right-colored uniform coat no one would even be seen with me!" Spencer, suddenly gasping in another lungful of methane and recocking the gun to End It All, said sadly, "And now, when the great moment is before me: when I *can* become someone, what happens? It's all taken away from me again!"

In his experience, no one ever took anything away from the old boys of Eton; in his experience, one way or another, the old boys of Eton took everything you had away from you. Auden roared, "Who's taking it away from you?"

Spencer roared back, "You are!"

He didn't want to take anything away from him. All he wanted to do was kill him. "So? So what?" In the good old days of Etonry, one of the lads, thus miffed by a mere peasant, would have one of his loyal retainers slice said peasant into quarters and feed the quarters to the hogs. Auden thundered, "So what? So what? Since when has anyone like you ever cared about anything anyone like me wanted to do?"

There was a long silence.

Auden yelled, "Well?"

There was another silence, then Spencer said softly, "You're my friend. You're the only real friend I've ever had."

"So what?"

He drew a breath. Spencer, mad as a meat axe on the methane, said with the gun suddenly hanging loosely by his side, "You're the only real friend I've ever had—" Spencer said suddenly declamatorily, " '*We few, we little few / We band of brothers*'—And, succeed or not, death or glory, when it's all over and when flights of angels sing me to my rest, I want you there with me in death as you always were in life—"

Auden said, "Oh, my God—!"

He was dripping ooze everywhere. He brushed it off with an ooze-dripping hand. Auden said, "Oh, my God! . . ."

He took a single careful sludge forward.

Scratching at his head, going goop-goop-goop, Auden said suddenly softly to explain to the Ratbag with the Revolver, "All very well and good, Bill, but, you see, the problem is, Bill, that I don't know anything about *bombs*. At least you've read a book on it." Auden said softly, still coming forward, moving gingerly, hand over hand along the length of the bomb, "I don't read much, you see." He shrugged in embarrassment and something black and vile and oozing that blew bubbles in the air as it fell dropped off his shoulder and sank beneath the surface of the slime with a hiss. "Maybe I watch too much television and I—but I—"

He had read a book, once, in school. He couldn't remember the name of it, but it seemed just the right book to quote then.

Auden, getting to the axis of the bomb, touching at it gently to stop it from swivelling, said at the top of his voice, " '*What light by yonder window shines?!*' "

Spencer said, "Exactly!"

In the sewer, Death Wish Spencer lowered the gun.

It had been the perfect, the exact, *les mots justes*, of just what to say.

Auden said something else. Taking another step forward, getting an inch past the axis of the bomb to where only a good Herculean push on the infernal device from Spencer could possibly mow him down, Auden, going for the lowered gun, roared, "You maniac! You goddamned overeducated, away with the fucking fairies, raving fucking *maniac!* ARE YOU COMPLETELY AND UTTERLY OUT OF YOUR GODDAMNED *MIND?*"

Yes, he was. He gave the bomb a damned good push.

He was actually in midair, with his hands out, actually in midstrangle. So close . . . and yet so . . .

He thought as the bomb rumbled and the laws of gravity took him inexorably back down to it, he sighed.

Auden said sadly, "Oh, no! . . . ."

And then, as he hit the surface of the water again with a splash, the bomb—again—mowed him down.

When you shook a somnambulistic demon hard on the shoulder to wake him he didn't scream and thrash—he screamed and thrashed and fought and punched and flailed and kicked and shoulder-charged and, as he and O'Yee went backward over O'Yee's chair and crashed into the front of Auden's desk and blasted all the drawers on either side of it out and open, he howled like all the horrors of hell were hot on his heels and punched and flailed and kicked even harder.

And then, as both he and O'Yee came off the desk locked together in an awful embrace and collided with the other five stillsleeping sleepers, the other five still-sleeping sleepers screamed and thrashed and fought and punched and flailed and kicked and shoulder-charged, all still sound asleep.

And then, as suddenly as they had begun, they stopped and, one by one, filed back to their chairs to go on sleeping.

On the floor, with his brain clicking back to the last thing it had any clear recollection of, O'Yee yelled, "*Two—!*" and reached in under his coat for his gun.

The gun was gone.

It was a half-Chinese–half-Irish brain: it could work under the worst conditions. O'Yee, getting to his feet and then falling down again and then rolling over to the debris of Auden's desk, yelled, *"Two and a half—!"* and reached into what had been the topmost drawer for Auden's Colt Python.

There was no Colt Python: that was gone too.

Spencer's desk. In the second drawer of Spencer's desk there was a little Browning .25 Spencer had bought his girlfriend for a gift and his girlfriend hadn't wanted, even as a gift.

Getting to the second drawer and wrenching it open, O'Yee yelled, *"Two and three-quarters—!"*

No gun.

O'Yee's brain, catching on slowly, said, *"Oh-oh . . ."*

O'Yee's brain said, *"Oh."*

Considering every aspect of the situation, considering all the options, putting everything into perspective and finding its own little place in the scheme of things, it tried to think of what to do next.

It was a good brain: a best-of-two-worlds kind of brain.

Coming up with the solution, working at top speed with its usual well-oiled efficiency, it went, all at once, *"Fizzz! . . ."* and went out to lunch.

Maybe the Eton story was all true. Maybe not. Maybe the closest he had ever gotten to Eton was on the train from London back to his family's house in Stratford. But as he trolled happily in the slime for his lovely tools, what was true was that he hummed, "Lovely Boating Weather . . ." and that, as he turned his flashlight on and hunched over the open access plate to the bomb, his eyes shone with an eerie reflected light and did not quite seem to be in the right locations in their sockets.

And was the jacket story true, or was that something Auden

had once told him in great confidence about *his* childhood and forgotten?

Spencer, still humming, still trolling, said as if it was a matter of no importance at all, nothing more than an afterthought,
"Oh, by the way, one thing, Phil: Um, fairly important. When it
comes to cutting the electric wires and all that, if you don't mind
too much, I'd appreciate it if you'd . . ." Spencer said, "Phil—?"

He looked around and couldn't see Auden anywhere.

He must have been around somewhere: he could hear him
breathing.

No matter. He was happy being the Lone British Officer for
a little bit longer.

He heard a bubble, and Spencer said cheerfully to it as it burst
in the air somewhere a few feet from the still-open manhole
opening back to the sub-basement, "Well, anyway, I'll just make
a start, shall I?"

Still humming, with a smile like a Cheshire cat slowly crossing his face, Spencer glanced at the bits of bubble falling back
into the sludge and closed his right eye for a moment in an evil
wink.

Or was it an evil wink? Or merely a momentary mote of
methane? Or a sudden twitch of pure terror?

Or none of the above?

Hard to tell.

Spencer, talking to the bits of bubble and the faint disturbance deep in the sludge beneath it, said only, in a whisper,
"Jolly, jolly *good!*"

He was sorry Elizalde had lost a man, particularly since it was
someone Feiffer knew: one of Elizalde's detective sergeants he

had met in police headquarters the last time he had been in Manila.

But he could not bring himself to think of it now.

It was cold on the dock, in the midst of one of the loudest, busiest streets in Hong Kong, silent and still and awful, and with his voice still trembling, Feiffer asked as a final question, "Felix, one last thing: a sound. A sudden 'blossoming.' The sound of something like tissue paper suddenly 'blossoming.' Does that mean anything to you at all in relation to all this?"

"Did someone tell you that?"

"Yes."

"Someone reliable?"

"Yes, very."

From the other end of the line, there was a silence.

Elizalde, thinking about it, said, "No."

Then there was another silence.

Elizalde, feeling his friend's pain, said sadly, disappointed in himself to have let him down, "No, I'm sorry, Harry, it doesn't mean anything to me at all. Nothing. Nothing at all."

9.

Growing dark. The last few moments before night. In the huge public car park on the corner of Beach Road and Canton Street, the last few vestiges of the twentieth century in the place—the last of the day-parkers—maneuvered out of their spaces onto Hanford Road and Tiger Snake Road into the traffic, and for a brief moment the place where they had been was dark and timeless, and then, in a flurry of running men fighting for the best position for their stalls and booths and kiosks and racks and display cases, the entire area was lit by free-burning flambeaus and torches and glowing charcoal braziers and the last of the twentieth century turned back into the lagoons of light and smells and sounds and color of the China of antiquity.

After dark, the car park became the Poor Man's Nightclub: a seething village square full of food stalls and market tables and theater and balloons and musicians and lanterns and paper dragons and noise and magic.

Moment by moment, as the very last of the cars went away in the darkness, the lights from the torches and braziers spread out across the expanse of tarmac and turned it bright yellow, their smoke, like the smoke from ancient villages, reaching up into the trees, filling the air with the smell of burning wood and charcoal and cooking pork and beef and fish and spices and sauces.

The smells and the flames and the smoke were the things of the earth: they were the things from which he drew all his power. At the far end of the car park, sitting slightly bent over to one side with one thin leg crossed over the other on a bench facing Canton Street, the Dalagangan, a frail, ancient man wearing a lightweight inexpensive gray suit, closed his eyes as if he had nodded off to sleep and, emptying his mind of all its thoughts, for a moment, became part of it.

With his head fallen on his chest, he was nothing more than an old, old man dreaming of other days.

As he dreamed, everywhere in front of him the light spread and, finally, reaching him as the stalls multiplied like cells, rose up onto his face and turned it, in the light and shadows, into the face of a polychrome painted wooden statue, painted with deep lines and hollows, and tufts of wispy, silken black hair, and where the hair receded, smooth patches of shining bald scalp.

Behind him, as the last of the day died and became night, all the buildings along Tiger Snake Road turned on all their lights at once and backlit him like a painted actor in a Chinese opera awaiting his call in the wings to play his part on the brazier- and flambeau-lit stage.

Then, as he opened his eyes and glanced in the direction of Canton Street, all the street lights came on, and the lights of all the cars jamming the street, and then all the lights in the buildings around them came on, and the entire street was a lagoon of brilliant white light.

In the light, there were people everywhere—business-suited

men and well-dressed women, laborers and shopkeepers, coolies and beggars, children and shrieking babies in arms, all hurrying home or to their place of work or merely out in the night, and for a moment, still with no thoughts in his mind, the Dalagangan, with the unhurried interest of an old man, watched them and listened to their sounds.

He seemed ancient, infirm: as he reached inside his coat and took out a single Marlboro filter cigarette, his long, bony hand, made bonier by the undulating yellow lights, shook, and he had to put the cigarette carefully in his mouth with two hands and hold it there for a moment in his lips to stop from dropping it.

With the single cigarette, he had taken out a tiny box of Double Prosperity matches, and, letting go of the cigarette, he held the box carefully in his left hand and, with the thumb of his right, pushed the box open and then took out a single match.

At his age, with so little strength left in his muscles, he had trouble lighting the match and had to strike it against the phosphorous paper on the side of the box over and over until it finally caught and, shielding the flame in his cupped hands, he could light his cigarette.

He was not Chinese: in the little corona of light from the match, his skin was darker, a browner color than the color of Chinese skin and he had lined differently and he had darker, rounder brown eyes—to anyone watching him, probably someone from somewhere farther south: a Philippino perhaps, or a Malay, or Indonesian, but, in any event, harmless.

If anyone was watching . . .

He glanced around, but no one was, and, taking the cigarette out of his mouth and letting it burn away between his fingers, he closed his eyes again and seemed to doze, still holding the box of matches in his right hand as if he had forgotten to put them back in his pocket.

And then, as if something in his dreams made his hand twitch, they were gone, and in his open hand lit up bright yellow by all the lights, there was nothing.

And then his hand twitched again and the matches were back there again, and in the light the palm of his hand was not the gnarled, arthritic hand of an ancient, old man, but the smooth strong hand of a man in his twenties, rippling with muscles.

And then he closed his hand and suddenly the box of matches was between his thumb and index finger, and then, as he barely flexed, it rolled, end over end, onto his forefinger, and then, as he made a barely perceptible movement of his hand and closed it into a light fist, it rolled over onto his ring finger and, as if in midair, hovered there for a moment before he flexed again and caught it with his little finger and, again, barely moving, took it in under his palm and made it disappear.

A creature of the elements, he drew all his power from the things of the earth: from fire and smoke and light and the smell of burning charcoal and wood—with his eyes still closed, drawing those things in now, using only the hand that held it in his palm, he pushed open the box of matches with his thumb and, with his index and forefinger, withdrew a single match and placed it between his little finger and ring finger.

Then, still holding it there, still with his eyes closed, he withdrew another match and placed it alongside the first, then another, and then another, and then another. Then, withdrawing two more at once, put them between the ring finger and forefinger and held them there.

. . . there are only six basic categories of magic of any type, genuine or otherwise, that can occur in the physical world, whatever the cause: Production, in which something appears or multiplies; Transformation, in which something changes in color, shape, or size; Transposition, in which something

moves from one place to another; Penetration, in which one solid object passes through another; and Mentalism, which includes thought-reading and pre-dictions . . .

It was none of those. It was merely something he did to keep his hands supple for his real magic.

In the light, in the darkness, in the darkness becoming light and then undulating back to darkness again, in his apparent sleep, he drew his right hand across his eyes and opened them, and in the place of magic and illumination and all the smoke and smells of the earth, the eyes were suddenly no longer the round-pupiled brown eyes of a man but the elliptically-black pupiled, bright-veined green eyes of a lizard.

Then he stroked the hand back and when he opened his eyes again, they again were the eyes of an old, old man sitting on a bench at the end of the day awaiting the night.

Between the fingers of his left hand, he had a total of seven matches poking through, all exactly level, all the right way up.

And then he flicked his hand and they were gone and all he had in his open palm was the full box of matches.

And, as it seemed he moved his hand not at all, the box was gone and his hand was empty.

Everywhere, in all the streets around the place, there were people and noise and cars and lights.

He was an old, old man on a bench, dreaming his dreams of what once was, the cigarette in his right hand all burned away to ash, listening with his eyes staring off into the distance, to what only he could hear.

He heard heartbeats. He heard them everywhere.

Crossing over Canton Street to Tiger Snake Road to get through to Hanford Road there was a short, dark-suited south-ern Chinese businessman carrying a briefcase hurrying to get to an appointment somewhere, and, there, just behind him, picked up in the midst of a crowd of people, he heard what he had been waiting all this time to hear.

He heard a heart beating differently than all the rest.

At a distance of a hundred and fifty feet, part of his magic, near to its central core, he heard a heart racing inside its chest cavity in a mixture of fear and excitement and trepidation.

Getting to his feet, bent over from the spine as a man his age would be, with his head cocked slightly to one side, with his eyes flickering back and forth through the crowd, the Dalagangan waited, watching the people crossing the road until he could see exactly who it was.

At dusk, his father had gone out through the French windows of his office to smoke a cigarette in the cool evening air and died.

He had died on the stone steps out there, three unpainted concrete steps that were never the same again to Feiffer and he could never either see or stand on again without tears welling in his eyes.

The steps led out onto a path into a tiny flower garden his mother had planted, all the stems hung with little labels written in her copperplate hand listing the variety and the date planted and the number of blooms produced each year—after he died and she let the garden turn to weeds, like little plastic-covered paper epitaphs hung on colored sticks at a Chinese funeral listing what the dead man was in life and exhorting the gods to judge him kindly in death.

He had been standing there on the dock, for it seemed, a very long time. In Hanford Street, all the lights were on and it was night.

And then his mother's aunt—the stupidest creature who ever

lived—a pudding-faced, overdressed loud woman coincidentally on vacation with them in Hong Kong from somewhere in the north of England—had come to comfort him and his brother and told them in her ringing voice as if it were a piece of deep and arcane wisdom, *"Well, you know, dear, only the good die young . . ."* and sitting there at the bottom of the staircase with his arms around his brother, not knowing what to say to him, he had said to her, eight years old, in Chinese so she would not know what the words meant, only the tone, *"Go to hell! Just go to hell!"* and instantly regretted it, and in the confusion of death, been glad that his father was dead and had not been able to hear it, and then, because his father was dead, put his head on his chest and sobbed.

Someone else said that the moment his father died, a sudden gust of wind had come out and scattered all the papers on his desk through the open window and that it was his soul leaving his body, but he had not believed that either and thought it had only been a gust of wind.

He had thought—

He thought, for the sake of his sanity, he should get the hell off the dock and go into the city where there was life and light and noise and people.

His car was parked at the end of Wanchai Street, at the corner of Icehouse Street where there would be traffic and noise and crowds and anonymity, but as he went down the three stone steps from the dock onto Wanchai Street, for some reason he could not bring himself to go to it, and, instead, going quickly in the other direction, turned the corner onto Hanford Road and began walking south.

☆   ☆   ☆

At the end of Tiger Snake Road the man in the suit carrying a briefcase hesitated for a moment and then turned north onto Hanford Road.

It was a long, wide street, full of shops and arcades and businesses on the ground floors, and on the floors above, hotels and restaurants and expensive boutiques: one of the main arteries of Hong Bay that ran north to meet Yellowthread Street and the direct expressway and rail and bus lines to Central.

The street was full of people, but, even bent over with age, even, it appeared, moving so slowly he shuffled, the Dalagangan passed through them easily and quickly.

Listening, he heard all their voices and their breathing and their heartbeats. Listening, he heard the sound of the one heartbeat among them that raced out of time and, looking up into the crowd of people in front of him, identified it.

In front of him, laden down with parcels and packages, there was a family of five—husband, wife, and three little girls—and, in front of them, half blocking the way, to the frustration of the children trying to get through to look at the shops before their parents caught up and hurried them along, two heavily built northern Chinese wearing shorts and torn T-shirts arguing about something and flailing their arms about. They were rickshaw drivers and carriers: the Dalagangan glanced down at their naked legs and saw they were knotted with muscles.

So did the small middle-aged Chinese dressed in a windjacket with the words Hong Kong Golf Club embroidered in English on its back, whose wife the flailing arms of the rickshaw men kept hitting, and, shaking his hand in the air, informed his cursing wife with a dismissive motion of his hand that, no, he was not going to do anything about the two arguing men and get himself beaten to a pulp.

Ahead of him again, there was a knot of half-a-dozen young

men, all about eighteen, on their way home from college, making it clear to each other with sign language and nods of their heads and smirks exactly what they would like to do to the beautifully groomed long-haired Chinese girl in the short skirt and bright white blouse clipping along ahead of them on high heels to what was probably her next appointment on a long list of job interviews.

Ahead of her, moving at the same pace as the businessman carrying the briefcase, twenty feet in front of him, there was a man in his mid-thirties wearing coveralls marked Hong Kong Telephone Company that did not quite seem to fit carrying a small brown satchel under his arm who kept looking back and then forward and then across to the other side of the road as if he thought someone was following him.

The rest were merely extras. The Dalagangan swivelled his head in an arc and listened to all their heartbeats and they were nothings and their existence was of no consequence to him.

At the head of the spear-shaped group of people the Dalagangan had singled out, the businessman paused for a moment to glance down at a piece of paper in his hand and was swallowed up by the rest of the crowd moving past him—all except the telephone man, who dropped back, stopped dead, and, as if trying to find some reason to be there unmoving in the street, looked up into the air.

For a moment, alone in the gap between the tail of the crowd and the next crowd coming up behind the Dalagangan, the telephone-company man looked directly into the Dalagangan's face.

The telephone-company man was not a telephone-company man at all: under his ill-fitting coveralls, he wore an expensive hand-tailored silk shirt.

The Dalagangan looked down at his shoes. The Dalagangan

was a Philippino, from one of the largest exporting countries of cheap and middle-price-range shoes in the world.

The shoes the telephone-company man wore were best-quality Bostonians, bought in America, two hundred dollars the pair, bought anywhere else, twice that.

For a moment, as if he were unsure of something, the telephone man hesitated, then, suddenly making up his mind, turned before he was himself swallowed in the next tide of people, doubled his step, and caught up with the family and the dodging, weaving, vainly entreating window-shopping children.

Back at the head of the crowd, without breaking his step, the man in the suit carrying the briefcase looked down at the scrap of paper to check his bearings.

Behind him, the heart that was following the man jumped as if it was suddenly afraid the man would turn around and see it. Then the heart slowed down a beat, then speeded up, then, moving quickly along behind the businessman, ever watching, ever alert, beat in a hard, steady rhythm that matched the pace of the businessman's footsteps.

The Dalagangan was an old, old man, but he had no trouble keeping up with the crowd as it continued north on Hanford Road and passed over Stamford Street.

Stamford Street was the diamond merchants' street, and as the Dalagangan crossed it, he glanced down at all the shopfronts there and, at the same time, listened for a moment to his own heartbeat.

In all the heartbeats he heard, it was the slowest and calmest, beating at the same steady, even pace it had beat—in the absence of any records—at least eighty years and would continue to beat at it—probably—forever.

Mounting the kerb to continue on Hanford Road, the Dalagangan touched at the place on his chest where his heart was and something there made a rustling noise, like paper.

His hand, as it came away from his heart was stiff, with all the fingers outstretched, and he looked down at them for a moment, then flexed them open again, and then closed them again and then let the hand fall limply to his side.

He heard, just ahead of him, a heart miss a beat in excitement, then beat hard and fast.

It was the telephone company man. Turning suddenly in mid-stride, the telephone company man, with his heart beating hard and fast and with urgent portent, came directly towards him.

He had taken his keys out of his pocket, and as Feiffer walked south on Hanford Road through the throngs and knots of people, he turned them over and over in his hand.

It was early night: the street was full of businessmen and families and students and laborers on their way home or to their night jobs, the air full of all the smells and smoke from the Poor Man's Nightclub in the car park at the end of the street near the harbor.

And his father was dead forever, and the first thing you forgot when someone was dead was what their voice sounded like, and then, what their touch felt like, and then what love felt like being with them, and then—

And then you forgot even what they had looked like when you knew them, and started to believe that the face in all the old photographs you looked at was the face you remembered, when it was not. And then—

Stamford Street was just a little ahead of him to the left and as he passed by a businessman carrying a briefcase and a blur of people behind him, for an instant he thought he recognized someone, but by the time he turned around, they were gone.

And he would never go with his father to the north of China where the snowcapped mountains hung like icicles in the sky, and he would never—

In the street, screwing his eyes shut, Feiffer said in a gasp, "This is crazy! It's all too long ago! This is *crazy!*" and, starting to put the keys back in his pocket, half turned to go back the way he had come.

And then the telephone man passed by the Dalagangan, and, glancing quickly around to again make sure no one in the street recognized him in his disguise, dashed into the traffic and got into the passenger side of a car driven by the young, over-madeup woman driver who was his mistress and ducked down below the level of the windshield to hide.

In the street, Feiffer saw him.

The man dressed as a Hong Kong Telephone Company man was one of the directors of the Hong Kong–Shanghai Bank, off for a evening of fun and adultery.

In the street, Feiffer said softly, "I'll be damned—!" and tried to remember the man's name but could not, only that he was married with children, and as the crowd enveloped him and he was pushed and shoved, alternately, by a muttering man in a golf jacket and his cursing wife, and then flailed at by two arguing men in shorts, he turned to go back the way he had come.

And then something touched him that was like a whisper and froze him where he stood.

It was like the sudden touch of the hem of a cloak, dark and heavy and at the same time ethereal, full of ice and cold and extinction, and it was Death.

✽   ✽   ✽

At the end of the crowd, as he passed by a tall, fair-haired European hesitating in the street and accidentally brushed against him, the Dalagangan still heard the sound of the heart beating in fear and excitement behind the businessman with the briefcase and narrowed his eyes to get a clear picture of the person whose heart he was hearing.

It was too long: as the businessman carrying the briefcase reached the intersection of Market Lane and crossed over, the Dalagangan decided the heart had been beating too fast too long for it to be anything else than the thing he suspected and, drawing in a shallow breath, flexing his hands by his sides to keep the fingers supple, began to prepare himself.

In the street, Feiffer said in desperation, lost beyond finding, "Oh, shit! Oh, *shit*—!" and turning quickly into Stamford Street, separating the keys in his hand as he went to find the right one, went to the door of number 456 marked Hong Bay Storage and Archive Repository where all his parents' papers and effects were stored and went in.

The next side street was Market Lane, and then, another block farther north, the Jade Steps, an ancient flight of stone stairs that led across to Canton Street above Jade Lane and the windowless stone walls of the old warehouse buildings on either side of it.

Walking, listening, breathing in long shallow breaths, all the sounds of the street and the traffic and the people ebbing away, hearing now only the single heart beating in fear and excitement and trepidation ahead of him, the Dalagangan, like a dragon stoking the fire inside its belly, began to fill himself with his magic.

✻   ✻   ✻

In the basement of the repository, Feiffer opened the black-painted steel door to the storage room and smelled everywhere the smell of his father's cigarettes and had to reach out and catch the edge of the door to keep his balance.

Feiffer said softly, "English Ovals." He had no idea where his father had gotten them because he had never seen them anywhere again in all the years since he had died and when, from time to time, he had mentioned them to someone, it was a brand no one had ever heard of.

They were the smell, not of the storage room, but of his father's office.

They were the smell of his parents' furniture, antique carved-camphorwood chests and tables piled neatly one on top of the other in the storage room, and of his mother's collection of jade bought one precious piece at a time in Shanghai and now wrapped piece by piece in silk and protected by plastic bags in an old leather suitcase by the side wall, and of his father's ivory chess set, and his old Shanghai Police uniform, cleaned and mothballed and hung on a rack in plastic, and of a profusion of bags and cases and boxes and objects he had almost forgotten they had owned.

FEIFFER.

It was not his name, but his father's name, stencilled on a rusting army footlocker way back at the rear of the room under the legs of a beautiful carved Tang dynasty chair his parents had had as their greatest treasure in the front entrance hall of the house in the New Territories.

It was where what was left of the things his father had thought important in his life were kept.

Mainly, overwhelmingly, it was where the smell of his father's cigarettes and all the things his father had been, still lingered as if he still lived.

*   *   *

In the storage room, dragging the box carefully out from under the wonderfully carved chair, which he realized suddenly was no longer his parents' chair, but his, Feiffer opened the lid and looked inside.

In the street, as he walked, the Dalagangan began to become the thing of awesome power, and began without anybody around him seeing or noticing anything, to transform.

At the corner of Market Lane, the man in the golf jacket and his wife both turned off and, with the wife making one last comment to her husband about the arguing rickshaw men, were gone and their space behind the students watching the girl immediately taken up by the family with the three little girls.

At his sides, the Dalagangan's hands flexed in readiness and filled with strength. Then the strength went up his arms and reached his shoulders, and with his nostrils flaring as his lungs sucked in air to pump blood through all his veins and arteries, he pushed out at his dorsal muscles and opened his back. Still bent over, with his spine straightening, he drew a single breath and all the muscles in his face tightened and poured their strength and power down into all the muscles in his neck.

He looked and, ahead of him, one of the students—an acne-covered boy of about eighteen wearing an American windjacket with the legend "Red Dog Beer. Be Your Own Dog" on it—half turned, collided with one of the little girls scampering in her mother's hold to get free to look at the shops and, for a moment, glancing at the little girl's father, tried to decide just how much of his own dog he was and what sort of dog it was.

He decided it was a nice well-bred dog from a respectable Chinese family with little sisters of his own.

The young man, reaching down to touch the girl gently on the shoulder, apologized to the family for his clumsiness and smiled a nice smile.

Thirty feet ahead of the crowd, the businessman carrying the briefcase got lucky with a break in the traffic and, without breaking his stride, crossed over Market Lane and continued north.

And then—

And then, in that instant, as he listened to the sound of his own heart and it slowed and slowed and then seemed to stop in midbeat, there was a tremendous roaring in his ears and he transformed, and everything slowed, and then, with a sound in his head like a piece of thick canvas being suddenly and violently ripped apart, everything around him went into monochromatic x-ray picture and was reversed black and white, white on black, and was absolutely, utterly silent, and as he moved behind the crowd he moved as if he were a giant in a dream, above them, looking down on them and all the things around them, and then all the things around them—the street, the traffic, the buildings—faded, became blurred, and he was in tunnel vision and all he saw was the little knot of moving people on a single raft of light with nothing around them but an endless ocean of darkness.

He needed to see nothing around them. He knew what each and every one of them would do.

He looked, and far, far away on another little circle of light, the man carrying the briefcase reached the corner of the Jade Steps.

He looked back to the raft, and, as if they stepped off it into oblivion, one by one, all the students went away to the left to cross the street to get into Wanchai Street and were gone.

He looked and all that was left on the moving, bright raft of light was the family of five and, ahead of them, the young girl in the white blouse and dark skirt.

He listened to the heart beating in excitement.

With all his senses heightened, he felt his fingertips tingle and he touched them together to the center button of his shirt and felt their electricity surge into his stomach and diaphragm, and as if his fingers could not contain the power, his left hand spasmed and from nowhere produced the little box of matches, then, in another spasm, made it disappear again. Inside his coat, some-where under it, something rustled as if it, like a flower, began to come alive and blossom, and then, as the box of matches ap-peared again, rustled again, filling with life.

On the human plane, he was an old, old man on Hanford Road shuffling along behind a knot of people going in the di-rection of the Jade Steps.

On the plane inside where all the things of his magic were, he was God, looking down on the ants.

Far, far ahead, moving in slow motion, the businessman reached the corner of the Jade Steps and, even though he knew exactly where he had to go next, looked down at the scrap of paper in his palm to make sure.

Behind him, on the raft of light following him in the ocean of blackness, the girl in the white blouse suddenly looked over to the right to where an arcade of shops and boutiques cut through to Canton Street and, glancing down at her watch as if she wondered if she had enough time to look at some of the shops in there, nodded to herself and, with her high heels click-ing, turned right and disappeared off the light of the raft into the curtain of darkness surrounding it and was gone.

Then, on the raft, the husband and father of the woman and three little girls, a squat well-built northern Chinese wearing a loose-fitting lightweight brown suit, pointed at something out in the darkness—a vacant cab or a bus—and with a quick wave sent his family out of the light and was alone.

Now hearing nothing else, the Dalagangan could still hear the heartbeat. As the businessman turned in his little pool of moving light to mount the steps to get through to Canton Street, he heard it speed up, become rapid, and then in the same instant as the husband, now a creature in his own right, increased his pace, become briefly arhythmic, and then, working to fill all of its body's muscles with oxygen, become firm and settled and regular.

Flight-or-fight syndrome. He heard the heartbeat fill all the muscles of its body with coiled-up strength ready for whatever was to come next.

The smell inside the box was not the smell of his father's cigarettes, but only the smell of age and extinction and neglect.

In an unsuccessful attempt to keep out the damp, after she had gathered everything up that had been his father's and no one else's and put them in the box, his mother had covered them with a sheet of oilcloth, but over the years the metal of the box itself had rusted and the cloth was covered in mildew, and as Feiffer pulled it away, it fell to pieces in his hands.

It was all he had left of his father. After his mother had died, his younger brother who had not a tiny apartment in Hong Kong but a house with a garage and storage space in Hawaii, by mutual consent had taken everything else for safekeeping.

He had taken all the things of his parents' lives together: some twenty-three years of marriage, and all that was in the box were the things of the final day of his father's life.

In a manila envelope, there were photographs that had been in the top drawer of his father's desk: fading, sepia pictures of

the Bund in Shanghai in the thirties, and of groups of policemen with his father among them, and, at the bottom of the pile,
a tiny, overexposed shot taken with an old Kodak Box Brownie
of what looked like elements of the Japanese Army drilling on
the other side of the barbed-wire line that separated the old International Settlement from the rest of Occupied China.

On the backs of the photographs there were no inscriptions
or dates at all, or if there had been they had been written in pen-
cil and long ago smudged off.

Kneeling in front of the box with the single light in the storage room directly above him, Feiffer drew a breath and wanted
to be somewhere else.

Under the envelope, there was a small, unmarked manila box
containing his father's pistol: an old Colt .32 automatic with the
legend "Shanghai Municipal Police" engraved on its slide and a
rack number, 731, in red paint on the grip.

He pulled back the slide and, as it had been on the day his father had died, it was still loaded.

And, under that, set into a rectangle of marble as a paper-
weight, his father's badge, Shanghai Municipal Police, number
5385, with the rank Detective Chief Superintendent embossed
on it in gold.

And to one side of that, in another manila box, his silver
identification badge from what he had been when he died: Chief
Investigator, Securities and Exchange Commission, Hong Kong.

It was what his mother had thought a firstborn son would
want: nothing but martial metal and violence.

He moved some of the rotting oilcloth aside and, in a velvet-
covered jeweller's box, were the artifacts from another period of
his father's life: the war—a Burma Star for service, and, next to

it in the wrong order for anyone to whom such things were important, the Military Cross for valor.

In all the times he had sat in his father's office talking to him and listening to him and being with him, his father had never once mentioned the war or shown him the medals.

With a growing sick feeling in his stomach, Feiffer closed the jeweller's box and put it carefully back in the box.

There was a folder full of papers jammed up against the side of the box, lists and lists of companies and businesses in Hong Kong in the fifties, all with now-antique names like the Hong Kong–Malay Rubber Plantation Company and the China-India Tea Export Association and the Hong Bay Home Ice and Refrigeration Supply Company, all out of order, all written in his bold hand in the permanent black ink he always used, some ticked, some not, some with exs and question marks against them, none of it explained.

And against the folder so long it had stuck to it, the slender blue presentation case containing his father's pen: a beautiful old marbleized red-and-green Waterman Patrician fountain pen from the late 1920s that he must have kept and hidden and treasured through war and battle and upheaval and God only knew what else he had been through in his life.

It was engraved on the silver clip, simply "From E"—his mother—and he supposed that too, now, was his, and for a moment wanted to take it out of the box and put it in his pocket, but as he reached for it, he could not bring himself to do it and closed the lid of the case and put it carefully back next to the files.

He saw something, something awful . . . and whatever it was that he saw killed him.

And all he wanted to do, as he knelt there under the light like a small boy rifling through the drawers in his parents' bedroom while they were out, was go.

And, except for the black celluloid folding double-frame photograph holder his father had had on his desk showing his mother as a young and beautiful woman and a shot of the entire family outside their house in the New Territories when Feiffer had been six or seven, that was it, all there was.

It was all so long ago—even the photograph, posed and stilted, everyone smiling, was from a time that seemed a century ago, from the past, from a place now of impenetrable whispers and secrets and silences.

And hushes.

And as he looked, there was nothing, nothing at all to tell him who the man who had been his father was, or had been, or had wanted to be, or wanted in his life, or wanted most in his life.

As he closed the photograph holder and held it in his hand for an instant, there was a crackle as if the celluloid hinges had broken or had not closed properly, and as Feiffer opened it again to reset the two frames, he felt something move the family photograph and, using his fingernails, pulled it out from where it had been hidden in there.

It was a tiny black-ink drawing, done, he knew the moment he saw it, by his father using his Waterman pen—a drawing with no signature or explanation on it of a mountain somewhere in northern China with snow on it, so stark and plain and beautiful alone in the absence of anything around it that it seemed to hang like an icicle in the sky.

And on the back, in his father's hand with an exclamation point at the end of it, was written "Harry. Born August 13, 1948!"

And kneeling there, putting it carefully on top of the folder in the box and looking down at it under the light, he could not control himself any longer and put his hands to his face and wept.

The businessman carrying the briefcase was not the Dalagangan's target: the Dalagangan's target was the person following the man with the briefcase.

Reaching the Jade Steps, the family man who had sent his family away by taxi paused for a moment and looked upward to where the businessman had gone, then, deciding, mounted the first step and was gone from the Dalagangan's view.

It was of no consequence—in the last three days the Dalagangan had walked the route up Hanford Road to the Jade Steps over and over again and he knew every twist and turn of it, every shop on each side of the road, every side street and lane and arcade. He knew, for instance, that the arcade the girl had taken to get through to Canton Street was closed off for repairs and that sooner or later he would hear her high heels clicking behind him at top speed as she came back and ran to make up the time she had lost, and he knew, as the man in the brown suit went up the steps, that there were fifty-seven stairs to climb, twenty-three to the top of the curved, medieval-style structure, and then another twenty-eight at a slightly less acute angle down through to Canton Street.

The Jade Steps were where, at night, all the bird and cricket sellers came with their wickerwork cages—he knew as the businessman and the man in the brown suit climbed the stairs in the yellow glow of all the kerosene lamps lighting up each of the bird and cricket stalls, the air would be full of the chirruping of crickets and the cries of birds and the shouts and entreaties and importuning of the sellers to buy a tiny creature from their cage and set it free into the air as a Good Act to ensure a place in heaven in the afterlife.

He knew that alongside the Jade Steps, running below it at ground level, Jade Lane, a darkened, vile-smelling trash dump of a narrow way between the buildings on either side of the steps was a place no one in their right mind would go unless they were in a desperate hurry to get through to Canton Street.

In the night, compressed tight, all the muscles in his body surging with strength, all the world around him in x-ray picture, everything around him humming, the sound of the heartbeat he listened for pounding in his ears, the Dalagangan reached the black hole that was Jade Lane and went in.

In the lane, there was a faint yellow light spilling down from the burning kerosene lamps on the steps, terminating where the lamps did above at the crest of the steps, in the very center of the lane in a pool of undulating yellowness that flickered and moved like the reflection of fire.

There, with only the faintest rustling as he prepared himself, the Dalagangan waited.

He waited for the sound of the heartbeat as, now faster and more desperate than ever, it came closer and closer.

He waited, listening.

He knew, up on the steps, all the man in the brown suit had come to do was buy a bird and set it free to pardon himself for some sin he had committed in the past, or maybe now, free of his wife and children for a few hours, intended to commit in the future.

He knew the heart racing in fear and excitement he had listened to all the way up Hanford Road was the girl's, and as he listened he heard the sound of the girl's high heels as she ran at top speed into the lane to get through to Canton Street before the man carrying the brown soft-leather briefcase did and she lost him.

He heard her. He heard her heart pounding as she ran. He

heard her heels on the hard stone of the lane and then he heard her breath.

And then, a moment before she saw him, he saw her coming straight at him into his darkness.

Up above the lane, on the Jade Steps, all the birds and crickets were sounding at top voice, the sellers, having a quiet night with only one customer, all shrieking at the man in the brown suit at once to buy their wares, and in the melee no one heard from somewhere below in the lane, a rustle, and then a single, awful cry of terror and then, coming so fast it seemed to come at the same time, a sound, somehow louder than it should have been—like tissue paper blossoming.

He could not bring himself to take the drawing with him, and, putting it back carefully in its secret place, Feiffer laid the remnants of the oilcloth over the things in the box and closed the lid.

Then, after a long moment, he stood up, turned off the single light illuminating the storage room, and closed the metal door on it all and, using his key, locked it.

By the time Feiffer got back to where he had parked his car on Wanchai Street via a bar on Great Shanghai Street, it was an hour and a half later, and pitch black, and by the sound of urgency in his voice, Victor Chen had been trying to call him on the car radio for some time.

He had no idea Feiffer was so close. On the radio, ready to give directions, Victor Chen said, "We've got another one, in a place called Jade Lane, under the Jade Steps off—"

"I know where it is."

"Same M.O. exactly, with both the eyes ripped out by self-infliction. Female Chinese, age about thirty, with—" Chen said suddenly, losing all his professionalism, "Harry, it's Helen Lau from the Investigative Section of the Securities and Exchange Commission at the stock market!" Night. In Wanchai Street, with all the lights of the warehouses and docks off, it was pitch black and silent. Victor Chen said, "I knew her! I think you did too!"

"Yes." Feiffer said with no emotion in his voice, "My father worked there with her father . . . a long while ago"—it was so long it had been before she had even been born—"he was the best man at her parents' wedding."

"I'm sorry, Harry."

There was a silence.

Victor Chen said quietly, suddenly professional again, "If there's anything I can do to—"

"No."

"If you'd rather not see the body until we—"

"Thanks."

"Then I can—"

"Thanks."

Night. Outside the windows of the car, the only light he could see was the faint yellow glow of a single paper lantern burning like a distant fire somewhere in the Temple of a Thousand Buddhas. Feiffer said softly, "Thanks very much."

He thought he just needed a minute.

In the darkness inside his car, he switched the radio off and in the silence, lost beyond finding, tried to remember where he was and which way he had to go to get home.

Night. All over Hong Kong, the night was full of light and sound and motion.

Night.

All over Hong Kong, the night was full of death, and heartbreak.

10.

Whatever it all was, it wasn't the end of the world.

The world, if it didn't have telephones and faxes, still had police radios in the Radio Room and walkie-talkies and cellular phones, and, if all else failed, brave Chinese-American cops who could shriek out to cowardly Chinese cops cordoning off a road to get on their radios, cellular phones, and walkie-talkies to get the Riot Squad and the SWAT teams down here with every weapon known to man short of a tactical nuclear missile.

In the Detectives' Room, O'Yee said, "Right!" He stood up.

In the Detectives' Room, all still asleep, the Six Creatures From Hell also stood up.

O'Yee said, "Wrong." He sat down again.

He thought he might spend the night sitting peacefully at his desk deciphering the meaning of *Irec Algr Amasc Afmm Icba Atta Emma Zip.*

The Six Snoozing, Armed To The Teeth Creatures From Hell thought that was a very good idea.

It was such a good idea that, hardly moving at all, Creature

Number One, breathing lightly and easily as he slept the sleep of the innocent, leant dreamily over the desk and gave him another note to go with the first.

In the sewer, something surfaced from the sludge.

It was Auden's head.

Auden's head was three feet below the open manhole access to the sub-basement and the rest of the Station and O'Yee and the phone to Hetherington-Smith and his Colt Python and O'Yee's Colt Airweight and Hetherington-Smith's Browning and slats of wood he could rip off the walls for clubs and nails he could wrench out with his teeth for spikes and window glass he would smash for daggers and electric cord he could use for garottes and for—

But with nothing to stand on and nothing to grab hold of, there was no way he could get out.

In full throat, Spencer, working away at the bomb, trilled, *"Lovely boating weather! . . . "*

He couldn't get out!

"Never mind the—"

He-couldn't-get-out!

Spencer, happy as a sand boy, said into his imaginary microphone to the Waiting Empire, "I-am-now-reaching-in-for-the-mercury-trembler-switch . . ."

He got out.

The second note, even clearer than the first, read simply "H. COYPAWS?"

Well, one might well ask.

O'Yee said with a nod, "Right!"

He tried to make his last thoughts nice ones of his wife and children.

*   *   *

"I-have-now-got-my-hand-completely-around-the . . . hmmm . . .very-lightly-balanced-trembler-switch . . ."

He got out fast.

His last thought of his wife and children visiting their in-laws in San Francisco was that it was time to join them.

He didn't think he might happily spend the rest of the night deciphering note number two. He thought he might try to make it to the door out into the Charge Room and freedom.

He looked at the axes and knives imbedded in his desk top.

He wouldn't make it to the door out into the Charge Room and freedom.

He thought he might make it to the rear door down to the cells and the sub-basement.

He looked at the clubs and cudgels imbedded in the belts of the clubbers and cudgellers.

He wouldn't make it to the rear door down to the cells and the sub-basement.

And apart from anything else, the rear door down to the cells and the sub-basement was bolted from the inside, so he couldn't make it there anyway, and if he couldn't make it there he couldn't make it anywhere.

H. COYPAWS? Still holding the note in his hand, O'Yee demanded, "What does it mean?" Seated in a slumber-party semi-circle around the front of his desk, the six sleeping homunculi, as one, cocked their heads to one side.

They were listening to something he could not hear.

Behind his desk, trying to think what to do next, O'Yee thought that if what they were listening for was the sound of his brain coming up with a decision about what to do next, they listened in vain.

If it was the sound of his pulse and his heartbeat going berserk, the noise must have been deafening.

O'Yee, shouting at them to get their attention, demanded, "*H. COYPAWS?* Is it an anagram, or a—" His brain tried to think. "It's an anagram, isn't it? It's an anagram for—"

His brain made a sort of rusty grinding noise.

"*SWAP YOCH!* Isn't it?"

No, it wasn't.

O'Yee said, "Um . . . um . . . *WAY CHOPS!*"

Nothing.

"*C. POSH WAY!*"

"*O. P. WACHY!*"

"*Y. H. SWOCAP!*"

"*A. W. . . . PSYCHO!*"

"*C. A.—*"

Ready to go, ready to make the final futile supreme effort to get to the door even if it killed him, or they did, O'Yee roared at the top of his voice at the six silent sleeping savages listening to whatever it was they listened to, "What is it? What is it? *What in the name of God are you all listening to?*"

Deep in the bowels of the earth, the methane-madman said into his imaginary microphone to the Empire, "I-am-now-touching-the-glass-mercury-phial-itself-and-being-very-careful-not-to-let-it-make-the-electrical-contact-that-will-set-off-the-main-charge-in-the-body-of-the-bomb . . ."

Halfway across the slime of the sub-basement floor, Yech-Man, slipping and sliding in slime, said in a gasp, "Oh, Jesus—!"

In case the jolly old Empire wasn't quite catching it all, he raised his voice. Demented beyond repair, Spencer yelled, "The-mercury-looks-remarkably-fresh-and-when-I-agitate-the-phial-a-little-from-the-contact-end-it-rolls-very-freely-and-easily-down-the-tube-towards-it . . . "

Sprinting across the sub-basement floor for the stairs, Auden put his foot on something so awful it reared up out of the ooze in front of him and did a somersault over his head and came down splashing.

Auden, losing his balance and coming down after it, yelled, "AAAAHHH!"

Whatever it was came out of the water again, looked for somewhere to hide, decided it was in the center of Auden's face, and landed there with a plop, and then, with a blurpp! got mashed to oblivion with a single blow.

"I-have-moved-the-phial-a-fraction-so-I-cannot-see-into-the-body-of-the-bomb—"

The voice, like the voice of God, was everywhere.

"Inside-the-bomb-there-is-a-very-large, several-ton-charge-of-TNT—"

He got to his feet. He didn't stay there. Auden, going down again on the floor as the mashed creature wrapped itself around both his boots at once in its death throes, yelled, "*Oh, Jesus!*"

". . . that-fairly-obviously-has-completely-deteriorated-over-the-years . . ."

On his knees, dripping slime mixed in with yech and blurpp, Auden said in relief, "Oh, thank God!"

"—to-its-major-constituent-part-of-several-hundred-if-not-several-thousand-gallons-of-nitroglycerine . . ."

So much for God. He got to his feet.

". . . moving-gently-back-and-forth-around-the-place! . . ."

He not only got to his feet, he got airborne.

Spencer gurgled away happily, "Funny stuff nitro . . . ouch! Funny how it burns your fingers when you put your hand in it and slosh it around—"

✶　✶　✶

O'Yee said, *"Y. C. POWSAY!"*

O'Yee said, *"W. S. WHO CAP!"*

O'Yee said, *"YAMP SHOW—"*

O'Yee said in triumph, *"CHOY SPAW! SPAW CHOY! SPAW CHOY CHOY SPAW CHOP—CHOP SPAW . . ."*

O'Yee said not so triumphantly, *"HOP SWACY! SWACY HOP!"*

His brain went bang. O'Yee said, *"HOP SWACY HOP POWSAY WHO CAP CHOP SPAW!"*

O'Yee screamed in awful, hopeless desperation, "WHAT IS IT? WHAT DOES IT *MEAN*? WHO *ARE* YOU PEOPLE? *WHAT THE HELL ARE YOU ALL DOING HERE?"*

Upstairs in the Detectives' Room, there was a heaven of lovely weapons.

Downstairs on the first step to the stairs that led up to the cell basement, there was a hell of ooze, slime, effluvia, and stench.

Most of the hell of ooze, slime, effluvia, and stench was Auden.

Upstairs in heaven there was a Detectives' Room full of deadly weapons and he could use one of them, or all of them, to—

"I-am-now-reaching-in-with-my-burned-fingers . . ."

He got up the first step to the second step.

—*to kill him!*

"—to-the-trembler-balance-mechanism-itself—"

He got up the second step to the third step.

". . . and-it's—*Uh-Oh! . . .*"

He got up from the third step to the ninth step. Auden, The Thing From Planet Toxic, oozing, dripping, seeping, sliding, slipping, six foot two and a half inches and two hundred pounds of human being covered in another three and a half inches and fifty-seven pounds of glutinous gunk reaching out for the railing at the ninth stair to keep from falling, yelled, "Don't touch the trembler balance mechanism!"

He shouldn't have reached out for the railing at the ninth stair. There was no railing at the ninth stair. There was no railing anywhere. There was just a drop twelve feet back into the two feet of slime swirling and boiling on the sub-basement floor.

On the floor, swirling and boiling with the slime, Auden shrieked, "*I'll kill you, Spencer! So help me God, I'll*—" Crawling, he got a painful foot and a half towards the open manhole access back to the sewer.

"That's better! I-now-have-my-hand-back-around-the-trembler-balance-mechanism-and-I'm-starting-to-jiggle-it-back-and-forth-a-bit—"

Becoming airborne, he got thirty-seven and a half feet back to the ninth stair and made it to the tenth.

"—the-mercury-inside-the-glass-phial-is-rolling-a-lot, but . . . I-think-if-I-just . . ."

The eleventh, twelfth, thirteenth, fourteenth, and eighteenth.

". . . then-I-might-be-able-to . . ."

And then, somehow, he was through to the basement cells and he could no longer hear the voice echoing everywhere off the sub-basement walls.

He could hear it, instead, booming out of all the opened toilet pipes in all the cells like the voice of the celestial conductor on the Terminal Line announcing all change for Armageddon.

Spencer's voice thundered like God speaking to Moses, "WHOO! THAT-WAS-CLOSE—!"

If he could have talked, Auden would have said something to someone: a plea perhaps, or a little entreaty, a confidential chat, a promise from someone that after he was dead if Spencer wasn't dead that they would make him dead.

Spencer said in triumph, "GOT-IT!" then down in Mad Central, remembered where he was, or where his mind thought he was, or where the methane told him he was, or where— Spencer said, "I-have-got-the-little-devil-in-my-hand-and-I-have-now-defused-the-trembler-switch-entirely!"

Spencer, his every syllable being broadcast over Radio Cess Pipe, said audibly, "Whew! . . ."

Spencer said just to show that, after all, heroes were human too, "Whew! I think I might just stop for a moment and have a cigarette to celebrate . . ."

He was at the first step up to the back door of the Detectives' Room, but just to show that, after all, he was human too, Auden paused to shriek down a single word.

That word was, *"METHANE GAS!"*

Actually, it was two words, but he didn't get the second one out before, simulantaneously, there was the scrape of a cigarette lighter, the *boomff!* of the wick catching, and then, as the wick caught and the gas caught and every cubic centimeter of the stuff along a hundred yards of sewer in both directions exploded in a flash of blue light and a detonation that made the entire Station shake, all the lights in the cell basement and everything else in the entire Station went out.

Ninth step.

Then all the lights flickered back on again.

Third step.

Then went out again.

And then, as they came on again, coming out in a terrible surge of moving, seething, boiling muck, all the accumulated revoltia of a hundred years of human defecation heretofore hardened in all the open toilet pipes of all the cells roared up like an oil strike, hovered in midair in an evil, bubbling black cloud, and then, at just about ninth step level, came at Auden like a tornado and mowed him down like a matchstick.

First step.

Less than the first step. Several feet below the surface of the first step, floating happily away on a sea of slime.

"Ah-ha! Ah-ha!" Through all the now-clear-as-a-bell toilet pipes, the Voice Of Lunacy said happily, "Well, well, well. Now-I-think-I-might-just-have-a-little-look-a-little-bit-deeper-inside-to-see-if-I-can't-just-find-a-naughty-little-trip-wire-hiding-in-there-too . . ."

He had known Helen Lau since she was a child, but now, as he drove, not towards the place where her body was, but away from it towards Central, Feiffer could not even remember what she looked like or what he had ever talked to her about and whether she had ever been to his apartment or known his wife, or—

All he could remember about her was how proud she had been of her long red fingernails.

And then he remembered that once, at the apartment, his wife had sat manicuring them for her and talking about men and romance and—

And that had not been yesterday, or even a year ago, but when she had been ten or eleven or—and all she had been was a little girl with big, shining bright eyes, and—

And reaching the corner of Hanford Road and Yellowthread Street to turn left towards the expressway into the center of the city, Feiffer had to pull over to the side of the street and, very slowly, and with the taste of salt on his lips and in his mouth, very slowly smoke a cigarette before he could go on.

Try again. Try hard. Try very hard.

O'Yee, trying very hard, sounding the letters out one by one, said, "H. C. O. Y. . . ."

And in that instant, his voice changed.

"H? C? O!"

O'Yee said in horror, *"H! C! O!"*

Around him, they were all sleeping, listening.

"H!"

With a period.

"C!" with no space between it and the next letter, *"O."* And between it and the next letter, *"Y,"* no punctuation either, and, specifically, no . . .

He looked at the note and could not believe what he was seeing.

H. C. O. Y. PA. WS.

In the Detectives' Room, surrounded by six sleeping demons, as the lights flickered yet again and turned all their faces yellow and satanic and evil, O'Yee said in a gasp, "Oh, my God!"

H. COYPAWS?

And knew exactly, without the smallest shadow of doubt, what it meant.

Up the down staircase. Down the up staircase. It didn't make any difference to him. Poisoned, drowned, mucked, mulched, oozed, battered, and beslimed Black Grunge Beast Man from the Galaxy Blecht! seething up the stairs like a huge human slug, didn't know where he was anyway.

Somewhere, booming in his head, there was a voice.

The Voice, chortling away merrily, said as if it came from inside the pores of the walls themselves, "Naughty little tripwire . . . naughty, naughty little tripwire . . ."

"Huh!" The Beast On The Stairs agreed with that. The Beast, down to his last two brain cells, said with one of them, "Huh!" and then with the other, "Huh! Huh!" Out there at the dawn of time where his mind was, it was cold and dark in the cave, and the Beast, pummeling the mass of goo where his chest had been, said to make the cold and the dark go away, "Huh! Huh! *Huh!*"

"Naughty little—" and then there was a flash and Spencer said through all the toilet pipes simultaneously, "Fuck!" and all the lights went out.

Cold and dark went out. Beast Man said, "Huh!!"

It was the main Station electrical conduit. Flashing off the top of the bomb and hitting the slime in a shower of sparks, it sent a charge of power through the ooze and animated life that was never meant to be animated, then, with another flash, killed it, and turned the lights back on again.

In the sewer, through the pipes, Spencer, bereft of eyebrows, said in pain, "Hell!"

Beast Man climb mountain. Beast Man chant. Beast Man chant song he know not meaning of, but like heap.

Beast Man chant, and this was his glottal song: "Gun-gun-gungungungun-gun—*Gun!* Get gun!"

And as if the words touched a part of his embryonic human soul and swelled it, Auden roared, "GUN—GUN!" and made it up two more stairs towards the bolted door to the Detectives' room.

He made another step and his little song became a melody.

His little song, "Gun," became, "Gun-get gun!"

And then swelled into a part-work. Auden roared, "Get gun, get—club!"

And then a concerto, "Get gun, get club, get—knife!"

And then a symphony, "Get gun, get club, get knife, get garrotte!"

Flowing up the stairs like a plague, Auden, singing his little song, roared, "Huh! Huh! *Kill!*"

It was the entire history of the civilization in one flight. Auden, up from the depths, the discoverer of music and culture, reaching like Himmler for his revolver, yelled, "Huh! HUH! Huh! *KILL!*"

"I-am-now-deep-inside-the-body-of-the-bomb-with-my-fingers-just-touching-what-seems-to-be-another-trembler-switch-a-little-more-delicate-than-the-first-connected-to-what-appears-to-be-a-very-lightly-cocked-clockwork-striker-aimed-directly-into-the-main-charge-of-what-is-now-nitroglycerine, and-I-am—"

At the top of the stairs, the Beast Man reached out to pull the bolt on the back of the door leading into the Detectives' Room, and then, in a single instant, with but a single word from the toilet pipes, was transformed back in whole, intact, with all his brain cells alive and working and sparking at once.

That word, as Spencer did something with the striker aimed directly at a thousand pounds of sloshing nitro—and he heard it clearly through all the pipes as if it came to him on stereo—was, ". . . *Ooops!* . . ."

H. COYPAWS? It was *H:* Harry; *Coy* Christopher O'Yee; *PA:* Phillip Auden; *WS:* William Spencer!

The six sleeping savages were a killing team.

Or were they?

Then why the note? And why *Irec Algr Amasc Afmm Icba Atta Emma Zip?*

And what did the question mark after *H. COYPAWS* mean? And the period after Feiffer's name? And why wasn't it—the way it was with all the other names—*H.F.?* Why just *H? And why the hell not C.O'Y.P.A.WS.?* And why not—?

Or was it a period after Feiffer's name and then the question mark after the rest of the names? And if it was—then—

In the Detectives' Room, O'Yee shouted at the out-cold assassins, "What is this? Some sort of goddamned *quiz?*"

They had every gun, knife, club, and axe in the place.

And they slept. Or, at least—

And listened to things he could not hear.

O'Yee shouted, "Why won't you open your eyes? Why are you here? Who are you waiting for?" The six of them were all huddled together in a semicircle of protection. "What are you all afraid of?" He got not one twitch of acknowledgement. *"What is it you're all afraid of seeing?"*

There was a crash from down in the sewer, and, with a flash, all the lights went out, and then another crash as the bolt on the rear door to the Detectives' Room came back, and then a shriek as if someone were being electrocuted in slime and then another crash and a fizz, and all the lights came back on, and there, standing at the open doorway stood The Thing.

And in the instant, as one, all the six sleeping killers opened their eyes and stared.

The Thing, dripping ooze, had what looked like very old broccoli where its face should have been. The Thing, seeping slime, had no feet: just two huge clods of mulch.

The Thing, in a voice that shook the rafters, roared, "Give me a gun! Give me a club! Give me a knife! Give me a garrotte!" and simultaneously, there was a shriek of horror from Creature Number One, and as O'Yee got to the door and slammed it in Auden's face, screaming, "Bolt it! Bolt it! And defuse the fucking bomb quick!" all the Creatures, all shrieking in horror in awful unison, all reaching in behind their backs for guns or clubs, or wrenching edged and wicked weaponry out of O'Yee's desk, gave him everything they had.

II.

They were the same people his father had worked for. On the eighteenth floor of the New Government Financial Tower off Des Voeux Road, the Investigative Section of the Securities and Exchange Commission, the stock-market watchdogs and policemen, had half the entire area, delineated by a thick, gray-metal windowless wall with a plain black plaque to one side of the single door into it marked in white, *Inv. Sect. S&EC.*

At that time of the night, the rest of the floor—some sort of payroll section of one of the government departments—was nothing but an empty sea of deserted desks and terminals, all bright and white and sterile under the forever-burning neon lights on the ceiling.

Feiffer had had to show his identification to the security people on the ground floor to get in, and by the time they cleared him, the chief investigative officer for the section, Sam Sutton, judging by the way he leant against the open door with his arms folded across his chest, had been waiting up there for him a long time.

He was a short, dark-haired man in his mid-thirties still wearing his suit coat and with his tie still knotted—he had just come back from identifying the body when Security had called him in his office. He was an American with a soft Midwestern accent that had become even softer after a car bomb attack six years ago had killed his wife and baby son and put him in the hospital for six months with a broken spine and taken fifty percent of his hearing in his right ear and completely deafened him in the left. With his already soft voice and quiet manner, the habit he had gotten into of leaning slightly forward and directing the hearing aid in his right ear in the direction of the person he was speaking or listening to had made him almost courtly.

The blast had also done something to his eyes, and behind his glasses, he seemed to be constantly blinking back a private thought no one who had not been through what he had been through could understand.

He had just come back from identifying Helen Lau's body, and, cocking his head slightly in Feiffer's direction and extending his hand, maybe that was the thought he blinked back now.

It was there, the hush: the silence in the place and in the gaps between the words that was all about death. It was palpable and had a taste.

He sighed a little: he knew Feiffer had known the dead girl for a long time. Sutton, extending his hand and leaning forward slightly to put his good ear in his direction, said softly, "Hello, Harry, sad, sad day."

After the paramedics had found the girl's identification and gun and called Victor Chen, Chen had called him to come and collect them. They lay now on yet another security-station desk just inside the open door near an open firearms and confidential-papers safe marked in both English and Chinese in large white warning letters and characters, AUTHORIZED ACCESS ONLY. Sutton, not inviting Feiffer any farther into the section, but standing at the desk gazing down at the gun and the folded leather ID badge, said softly in case Feiffer didn't know, "She was only thirty-two years old." He did not say that that was too young to die; when he had turned on the ignition of his car in the street outside his apartment and been blasted out through the windshield onto the road deaf and dying and saturated with blood he had only been twenty-nine years old himself and his wife twenty-six and their son ten weeks, and he no longer had any casual connection in his mind between death and the age at which death should come. Sutton, assuming Feiffer had merely heard about it and wanted to know what had happened, said, "Heart attack and/or a stroke of some kind." Six months of pain and drugs and doctors had also convinced him that, with everything that could possibly go wrong with it, the body was an engine that should, in theory, not even work properly for any length of time at all. Sutton said, "Her last medical didn't show anything, but, well, you never can tell."

Chen hadn't told him anything about the others, about Wong, or Yuan, or Tam, or Lee. He thought Feiffer had come merely to commiserate, and to suggest that it came merely as a consequence of seeing them, Feiffer nodded at the gun and badge on the table and asked, "Was she on the job when it happened? Where did it happen?"

There was a large picture window behind the security desk looking out across the harbor to all the lights of Kowloon and then past that into the darkness of the nine dragon hump mountains Kowloon was named for. So high up, behind the thick, soundproof and probably bulletproof window, all the lights and life passed like a dumb show in the night.

Sam Sutton said, "Yes, she was working." He thought about it for a moment and decided it was information he could share.

"She was following someone we'd targeted for investigation. She was found dead in Jade Lane just below the steps there. Judging by the perspiration still on her forehead and on her silk blouse, she'd been running so her target probably got ahead of her at one stage and she cut through the lane to make up the ground on him."

The gun was a little Iver Johnson .25, a copy of the Walther PPK. Still snug in its leather holster, the safety catch was still in the *safe* position and the retaining leather strap at the top of the holster still clipped over the hammer of the weapon. Under the gun was her closed leather ID wallet with a badge in it exactly like the one his father had carried until he too had died.

Sutton, turning slightly and glancing out the window at the lights, said with a shrug, "She was very good. She was a good officer. Her father worked here for a long while, did you know that? In the late sixties and through the seventies. He had my job."

"Yes, I know."

"I think he only died quite recently, didn't he?"

"Yes." His own father's time there had been a lifetime ago, too long for Sutton. Feiffer, playing his part at the wake, said softly, "He died about ten years ago. While Helen was in America at Harvard Business School doing her master's."

He had forgotten that: just how bright she was. Sutton, nodding, still gazing out the window, said softly, "Yes, I recall wondering when I hired her what the hell she was doing here when she could have been out in the business world making a fortune."

Feiffer said to explain it, "She was very close to her father. Maybe she wanted to be like him."

Sutton, thinking about it a moment and then forcing a smile and nodding, said, "Yeah, you could be right," then, as if it was suddenly too loud or too soft, put his index finger to his ear and did something with the volume control of the hearing aid. Sutton said as one of those things he had learned to say when people who knew nothing about it talked about death, "Nice girl, we're going to miss her a lot."

Pointing at the gun and the wallet on the table, Feiffer asked casually, "What was she working on, Sam?"

"Oh, nothing really. Just a fishing expedition. Just someone we'd targeted for investigation, nothing substantial, nothing." (He meant in his own world, nothing anyone would plant a bomb in your car for and blast you and your settled world to pieces for.) "Just a standard casino job, nothing of any—" He saw Feiffer's face. "The stock market is based on the same premise as a gambling casino: making money through luck or skill or a combination of both is good for everyone. The players like it because they're the ones who make the money, and the government is happy because everyone who makes money pays taxes, and, above all, the casinos are happy because casino owners and the stock market both have the same mentality: they love a few people winning big because it brings in more little people who lose in the long run. The only time they're not happy is when someone wins all the time and they don't know how they're doing it—particularly someone who, up until then, has been losing consistently."

"Is that who she was following? Someone like that?"

"Yes."

"How much has he been winning?"

"A lot." He thought it was just a casual conversation, something to talk about instead of the death of a friend. "In the past eight weeks or so, U.S., about three million dollars." Sutton said, "He seems to have the luck of the devil in predicting shake-ups in companies—mainly through the sudden deaths of someone crucial in the decision-making process. About a day before they die, he puts everything he has in their competitors' shares and when the news of the death hits the floor the competitors' shares skyrocket and he makes a fortune." Sutton said informatively, "It's called pairs trading. Are you familiar with the term?"

"It means moving investment money back and forth between two similar companies in competition with each other and guessing who'll do better at any one time with what amounts to the same product in the same marketplace, doesn't it?"

"Exactly. There's nothing illegal about it, and like the casinos, we wish him luck doing it, but we'd just like to know how he's doing it so well and so often to make sure he isn't doing anything funny."

"Was one of the deaths of the CEOs of one of these companies a man called Frederick Yuan?" It was the one Rebecca Pickering had told him about three weeks ago.

"That's right. He was the driving force behind the International Rice Export Company based over in your part of the world. The day before the death was announced by the family our friend put everything he had into their competitor, Amalgamated Long Grain Rice, and cleaned up when the investors deserted International and bought as quickly as they could into Amalgamated." Sutton, assuming in the world of nonstop information the stock market lived and died on what Feiffer had read or heard about it somewhere, said, "I didn't know you were interested in the stock market, Harry."

And the man in the Morgue, the man who had died with his eyes ripped from their sockets in the rest room of *The Pearl Princess.* Feiffer said, "And Tam Kwan Yu, Kenneth Tam—the head of All-Asia—"

Sutton said, impressed, "—Moldings and Steel Castings? Yes, he was another one. Their main competitor is a group based in Kowloon called Applied Fine Metals Molding, and up until the big All-Asia investors panicked with Tam's death and looked around for somewhere quick to put their money, they'd been hunting unsuccessfully for a restructuring loan for about six months and looked on the point of going under. Overnight, their shares rose from a dollar par—or less—to, now, about twenty-eight-fifty each."

He didn't know about the dead man in the temple, Lee. He wouldn't, and in theory neither would the Exchange, until the family announced it sometime tomorrow or the next day. Feiffer asked, "And before Yuan—"

"Yuan was the first."

"What about a man called Ronnie Wong?"

"No. Our friend didn't have anything in that. Wong was a market analyst for one of the big insurance companies here— The Star—their tame investment genius. When he died of a sudden heart attack in his apartment one night, the entire company's long-term investing strategy died with him and after the investors deserted en masse for their competitors, they had to seek bankruptcy protection to even manage to stay afloat. But if our friend made any money out of that we don't know about it here." Sutton said with admiration, "The man's a genius, but since before he became a genius he was a total fucking disaster, the Securities and Exchange Commission, like the casinos, would just like to know where his sudden genius came from." Sutton said to bring the conversation back to its original starting point, "That was the guy Helen was tailing, Mr. Suddenly, Out of the Blue, Very, Very Successful." But then, suddenly, somewhere in his mind, he lost the original starting point and came back to Helen Lau lying dead in a filthy back alley with newspapers and trash blowing around her and above, on the Jade Steps, all the birds and crickets there fallen silent. Sutton suddenly turning his one good ear away from Feiffer and gazing out the windows with his hand on his glasses, said angrily, "Shit, Harry! She was such a nice person, and so goddamned *bright*—!"

"This man we're talking about—" but Sutton could not hear him and did not turn around.

Sutton said in a whisper, "Oh, shit—!"

He touched him gently on the shoulder. Feiffer asked, "This man she was following, Sam—I think I may have seen him on Hanford Road on his way to the Jade Steps." He hadn't seen him, he had felt him as he brushed by like the cold wind of Death. "Is he a man named Jesus Sixtus Caina? A Philippino? About eighty years old?"

"No." From the look on his face, it was a name he had never heard before in his life. Sutton, shaking his head, said, "No." It was only a casino job that probably would have led nowhere anyway and now seemed to matter even less. Sutton, going over to the table and flipping open Helen Lau's ID wallet and taking out a grainy three-by-three surveillance photo and handing it over, said, still shaking his head, "No, it was this guy: the head and sole owner of what until eight weeks ago was the worst-run and least-successful mutual fund on the entire island of Hong Kong if not the planet—"

It was a poor, grainy-textured surveillance photo obviously taken from a moving car in Tiger Snake Road of a man coming out of the ground-floor office of a rundown office building very early in the morning.

It was of a short, stout Chinese in his mid-forties wearing a dark business suit and carrying, in his left hand, a cheap, soft-leather brown briefcase.

Sam Sutton said, turning away again to the window as if the whole thing was of no importance anymore to anyone, "Mr. Chang Ting Wa, aka Theodore 'Teddy' Chang of the Chang

Mutual Investment Buyers' Fund Corporation over there near you in Yellowthread Street on Tiger Snake Lane."

Now it really was a siege. Now it really was *Assault on Precinct Thirteen.*

With the Detectives' Room still ringing from the sound of gunfire and the rear door pocked and scarred and splintered from all the knives and axes, no one had come in from the street to help, and no one would come, and with all the creatures from hell jammed up hard against the front door with their eyes narrowed and glinting and all their weapons out and ready, he was alone, and it occurred to O'Yee suddenly that today, tonight, was the day he was going to die.

At the window, thinking about something he had forced himself not to think about for a long while—about death and oblivion and near-death and knowing, feeling, tasting what that oblivion felt like—Sutton said in a whisper, "Shit, Harry— what a fucking waste! What a fucking—*waste!*"

Still gazing out the window at the lights, into the past, into the single moment of the explosion when he had thought he was dead and into all the long dark nights alone in the hospital when he thought he was dying, Sutton said in awful, awful horror, "Those damned, goddamned long red fingernails of hers— when the heart attack or whatever it was hit her it was so catastrophic and hit her with such terrible pain that—" He closed his eyes to get the picture of it out of his mind, but he could not. "—that she ripped her own goddamned eyes out with them!"

It was too much. He could not make any sense of anything anymore, and with his hand shaking, put his finger to the volume control of the tiny hearing aid in his ear and turned it off, and, in his deep, sudden, self-imposed silence, did not hear Feiffer, after a single silent moment of his own gazing down at the badge and the gun and the photograph on the desk, suddenly turn and go.

In the sewer, all the gas had gone, and deep in the slime Spencer had his head on the bomb, sobbing, and Auden, still reeling a little from the fastest descent of stairs in the history of Man, could barely muster the strength to kill him.

Auden, sloshing up to him with the electrical wire from the wall sparking in the ooze and making it boil, thought he thundered, but only gargled, "What the hell's going on? Whatever happened to 'I-am-now-defusing-the-fucking-Doomsday-Device-with-my-nose-hair-clippers'? What? What's happened? What the hell are you *sobbing* about?"

He had one more stop to make before Chang and the mutual fund office in Tiger Snake Road. In the basement of the Hong Bay Storage and Archive Repository on Stamford Street, Feiffer, rummaging through the box containing his father's effects, found the incomprehensible lists of ancient, antique firms and businesses and ran his finger down all the ones marked in the margin with a cross or a tick or a question mark.

Whatever it was, the list represented the last case his father had been working on—the one he had had on his desk when he had gone out into the garden in the evening for a cigarette and died.

The Hong Kong–Malay Rubber Plantations Company. On the very first page of the four-page list, it was marginalized with a tick.

China-India Tea Export Association. On the same page, another tick and, next to it, a question mark.

Hong Bay Home Ice Supply Company. And another tick.

And on page two, another tick against another company long since defunct, but then, in the fifties at the height of its prosperity: *HK–Penang Rubber Inc.*, and another with both a tick and a question mark, *Colombo Tea Growing Estates (HK) Ltd.*, and then another, with a tick *HK Cold Storage and Refrigeration Inc.*, and then another, and, as he turned the pages, reading them, another and another.

All pairs.

The International Rice Export Company, and Amalgamated Long Grain Rice . . . Yuan Fock Chee, aka Frederick Yuan, age eighty-one . . . dead.

The All-Asia Moldings and Steel Castings Company, and Applied Fine Metals Molding Corporation . . . Tam Kwan Yu, aka Kenneth Tam . . . there with his eyes torn out in the toilet of *The Pearl Princess* . . . dead.

And the last one, Lee, in the temple on Wanchai Street, in the silence, the head of International Cloth Buyers Amalgamated . . . dead.

They were pairs, like his own. They were—

In the heavy, musty smell of the little room, Feiffer said in a whisper, "God in heaven—!"

Thirty years on—more, forty—he was working on the same case his father had worked on that last night of his life, and it stilled him, and then, as he held the sheets of paper in his hand and smelled the smell of his father's cigarettes still on them, filled him with a feeling he had never had before and could not identify—but a feeling that ran like an electric shock down his spine and stayed there, and he spoke to him in a whisper as if he was there beside him and listening.

The words were so soft they were not audible. Talking to him over all those years, Feiffer said, "This is why he killed you, isn't it? The Dalagangan. This is why he sought you out in your house and waited until all your family had gone to bed and watched you as you sat in your office and waited until you opened the French windows to go out into the garden and killed you, isn't it? This is why . . ." He looked down at his hands holding the sheets of paper and his hands holding the paper, now, were no longer the hands of a small child lost at the bottom of the staircase, but the hands of a man—hands like his father's.

His father, the Sinophile, in his one affection, had grown all the fingernails on his hands long to show in the old Chinese Imperial way that he was a scholarly man and did no physical work. "This is why . . ."

They had kept the coffin closed at the funeral because those long fingernails, in the awful violence and terror of whatever was done, had slashed and torn and clawed and when they had found him both his eyes were nothing more than bloody pulp ripped from their sockets.

In the tiny room, closing his eyes, Feiffer reached out for the box with the beautiful pen in it and closed his hand around it, and it was as if, in that moment, he reached out on the bottom of the stairs in the house in the New Territories all those years ago and felt his father's hand in his and was comforted.

The snowcapped mountains of China alone and shimmering in the starkness against the sky like glaciers . . . *Harry. Born August 13, 1948!*

Feiffer said softly, "Thank you."

He opened his eyes, but they were blurred. Feiffer said in a whisper, "Thank you very much."

FEIFFER. It was the name on the metal box containing all the things that had been his father's.

FEIFFER. It was his name. They were the things, now, that were his.

Putting the box containing the pen gently aside for a moment, the first thing he took that was his was the beautiful, stark drawing of the mountain.

All the methane had been burned with the explosion and in the sewer the air was as fresh and wholesome as sewer air, and when the voice finally came out of Spencer, it was not the voice of methane madness but of desperation.

Spencer said with his entire world destroyed, "I did it! I defused every fuse and trembler switch and booby-trap and trick clock and false timer and reversed detonator in the entire bomb and I'm Brave Bomb Disposals Bill and there's only one simple fuse left and all I have to do is snip a single last wire and the whole bomb is safe! And I'm ruined! And I'm found out *again!* and I'm still the little boy in the coat that doesn't match and I'm still on the out because whatever I do—whatever I do! Whatever I do, however hard I try, I still—*I still can't win because of who I am and all that stuff about striving and struggling and never yielding isn't true and however hard you try—*"

He was crazy. He had gone crazy. It took all the fun out of killing someone if they were crazy. They had to know what they were being killed for. Auden said, "Then go and get your damned tools and cut the last wire and have done with it!"

"I've got my tools!"

"Then cut the wire!"

"There are *two* wires! I don't know which one to cut!"

Maybe he hadn't read a book, but he had driven through a lot of red lights. Auden said, "Cut the red one. The red one is always the positive."

"I can't cut the red one because I don't know which one the red one is because I'm red-green color blind!" Spencer said desperately, "They both look red to me!" Spencer said, "You do it! Please! You don't have to cut the wire, but at least tell me which one I have to cut!"

Auden said, "No."

Spencer said at the end of his wire, "Please!"

Auden said, "No."

"Please!"

He should have been having fun. He wasn't having any fun at all. Auden said again, "No." He looked in at the two wires and saw what color they were. They were both . . . *brown?* He'd had a rough childhood of his own, and suffered at the hands of other children too, and—

Auden, mashing at his hair with his hand going gloop! gloop! gloop! said, having absolutely no fun at all, "I can't! I'm red-green color blind too! I can't tell one from the fucking other either!"

There was a silence.

Then, from deep inside the bomb, there was a heavy, healthy, hearty ticking.

In the echo chamber of the sewer, like a knell sounding over the towns and cities and fields for incompetents everywhere to assemble for their funerals, it went steadily, unstoppably towards the end: "TICK. TICK. TICK—"

Ask not for whom the bomb tolls; It tolls for thee.

In the sewer, in his own mind, a failure all his life, Spencer with his eyes gazing up at The Thing That Was Auden who, not only in his mind but in the mind of all who knew him, had been a failure all *his* life, said hopelessly, "Oh, God, oh, God . . . Oh, God, Phil, what would all those people who laughed at us all our lives . . . what would one of those—

someone like Hetherington-Smith— *What the hell would they do now?"*

Out-gunned, out-axed, out-knived and out-manned, what he was going to do now was . . . Um . . .

In the Detectives' Room, watching from behind his desk as the creatures, jammed up against the front door with all their weapons out waited for whoever it was they were waiting for, O'Yee, searching for inspiration, said in a desperate whisper, *" . . . he nothing common did, or mean . . ."* O'Yee, realizing that he had reached the utter desperation point, said in a gasp, "Oh, God!"

The coward dies a thousand deaths . . .

It was all he could think of. He couldn't think of anything Chinese or Irish.

He thought, as the awful beings waited at the door to knife and club and axe and shoot and hack to pieces whoever it was they knew would come through, all he had as a weapon was his body.

He thought, compared to the axes, knives, clubs, swords, and very, very sharp teeth, it wasn't very much.

On the third floor of the Peninsula Hotel on Kowloon, the Dalagangan glanced up and down the corridor for the last time to catch sight of the person he thought he had seen that morning coming out of his room and, not seeing him, closed his room door and put the key in his pocket.

8:28 P.M. He had slept for an hour and felt rested and ready and full of power.

Walking to the end of the corridor with no sound at all, he went down in the elevator to the ground floor and crossed the huge entrance lobby of the place under the crystal chandeliers like an old man going out at night for a little walk and, waving aside the uniformed doorman's offer of a cab or a rickshaw, crossed the street to the Star Ferry Terminal to make the twenty-minute crossing to the island of Hong Kong and his next target.

In his room in the hotel, pushed safely under the bed, was a soft brown briefcase containing fifty thousand dollars in fresh, crisp, US one-hundred-dollar bills, and, thinking about that for a moment, as the ferry swept into the terminal in a wash of foam and reversing engines, the Dalagangan permitted himself one of his precious Marlboros and, not caring who saw it as the unloading ferry filled the terminal with people, lit it with a match that seemed to appear out of nowhere in his left hand as if by magic.

8:38 P.M.

He took only a single shallow puff on the cigarette and, as he boarded the throbbing ferry, threw it away into the water and, for an instant, watched it until it was swallowed up and sank.

Sitting out on a bench on the starboard deck near the bow, he looked, in all the lights and shadows and darknesses and activity of the harbor, like nothing more than an old man enjoying the last few years of his life in contemplation of the sweeter things of life.

He was. Lighting another cigarette and gently, occasionally puffing at it, he contemplated death, and killing, and money.

He could not understand anything anymore.

In the outer office of the Investigative Section of the Securities and Exchange Commission on the eighteenth floor of the New Government Financial Tower off Des Voeux Road, Sam Sutton, age thirty-five, reached out with his fingertips to the soundproof bulletproof window in front of him and thought, not that he touched the window, but that he touched all the lights and movement of all the boats and sampans and ferries and people on the harbor, and, as he ran his hand up higher, all the lights of all the buildings on Kowloon, and, even higher still, the darkness of the nine dragon mountains behind it.

He touched nothing anymore. They had never caught the person who had set the car bomb, and he had not been able to attend the funeral of his wife and son because he had still been in a coma in the hospital, and he had never . . .

Turning to where Helen Lau's wallet and gun still lay on the desk ready to be put away in the open safe like a casket containing the remains of the dead, he thought he could no longer understand anything anymore.

And, with his hearing aid turned completely off, there was no sound anywhere and all the life and movement of the world, like all the lights and life and movement on the harbor and in the city he saw through his window, passed by in silence, and he, understanding life and death and loss and oblivion completely— and therefore not understanding it at all—was a ghost.

SHANGHAI MUNICIPAL POLICE
5385
Detective Chief Superintendent

It was his father's badge. He had it in his coat pocket next to his own.

. . . Thy rod and Thy staff, they comfort me . . .

Through all the lights and sound and people and movement, on the continent where far, far to the north there were mountains like icicles in the sky that were the only true, real, unchanging things of life and permanence and memory, at last his father's son, Feiffer drove towards Tiger Snake Road and Chang Ting Wa, aka Theodore "Teddy" Chang.

12.

It was the same man Feiffer had seen in the surveillance photo coming out of the ground-floor office on Tiger Snake Road, but it was no longer the same office. The entire building seemed to be in a state of change with all the doors and windows removed, bamboo scaffolding everywhere, and everywhere workmen and coolies carrying and hammering and painting and reflooring. He was going, moving: in what had once been his seedy one-room office, Teddy Chang, in his shirt-sleeves and sweating profusely, blinking back the sting of paint and thinner from his eyes, had everything he owned—computers, faxes, telephones, filing cabinets, a steel desk and two steel chairs, papers, readouts, wall charts of the Tokyo Topix and New York Dow Jones and British FT indexes—stacked in a pile around him in the corner of the room like a child's cubby house.

Everywhere there was noise: hammering, shouting, the sound of ancient filthy wallboard being ripped down, the howl of electric drills; and filling the air, the smell of dust and paint. There was a wall plaque on the top of Chang's possessions pile reading in English, *If It Sounds Too Good to Be True, It Probably Is Too Good to Be True!* and as Feiffer got in through the doorway over a gaping hole exposing a tangled mass of wires and electrical conduits, Teddy Chang, wiping at his glistening forehead with the back of his hand, took up the plaque and put it in a cardboard box.

Under the single flickering neon light on what was left of the ceiling, he looked like a war criminal dressed in civilian clothes about to flee the scene of his crimes and destroying all the evidence of them before the advancing enemy arrived.

The plaque was in English, so he spoke the language, but Feiffer roared at him in Chinese so all the workers and coolies would understand, "Where in the hell do you think you're going?"

He looked up, and, if he was defeated, the eyes were wrong for it. Full of anger, Teddy Chang snarled back, "Who the hell are you to ask?"

He paused a second. Feiffer said in Chinese, again for the workmen, "Detective Chief Inspector Feiffer, Hong Kong Police."

Teddy Chang said in Hong Kong Catholic-school-educated English, "Oh, Jesus!"

In Hong Kong, people worked day and night, in some few cases to prosper magnificently, but more frequently merely to survive. They were all survivors, the painters and the drillers and the hammerers and the coolies—they all had families to feed—and in an instant, all work stopped and they were gone en masse to wait outside in the street to see whether this night they were going to be paid for their work or not.

And, in his cubby house, surrounded by debris and the smell of paint and lit only by a single flickering light, all Teddy Chang could think of to say was, again "Oh, Jesus . . . Oh, Jesus Christ! . . ."

He touched at his forehead again with his hand to wipe away the sweat and when he looked up again the light in the eyes was gone and he could not stop his chin from trembling. Teddy Chang said, tensing all the muscles of his arms and shoulders as the worst thing he feared came true, "It's the pairs-trading, isn't it?" He looked around the wreck of the room as if he watched a great ship sinking.

"Yes."

He wasn't going anywhere: all the walls were being torn down so he could take over the entire ground floor. Taking a single step inside the doorway to stake his claim inside Chang's space, Feiffer said in English with no tone in his voice at all, "People are dead and—"

He said something, but it was so soft Feiffer could not catch it, and it was not "Oh, Jesus . . ." again, but maybe, like a small, sad, found-out child, "Oh . . . gee . . ."

Feiffer said evenly, "Mr. Yuan of the International Rice Export Company is dead, and Mr. Tam of the All-Asia Moldings and Steel Castings Company is dead, and Mr. Lee Tse Wa of International Cloth Buyers Amalgamated is dead, and before that—"

Teddy Chang said, "They all died of natural causes!"

"And in each and every case—"

Teddy Chang said desperately, "I got lucky! For once in my life, I got lucky! For once in my life, fortune smiled on me and I—" He glanced at the cardboard box where the plaque was, *If It Sounds Too Good to Be True, It Probably Is Too Good to Be True.* It was not inspirational, it was self-warning. His entire life had been built around, not the statement, but around its rider . . . *But Maybe, Just This One Time . . .* Teddy Chang said with his hands forming fists, "All my life I've had bad luck! All my life I've taken the wrong advice or listened to the wrong people, and now, the one time something good happens to me and I'm somebody—" He glanced around the entire floor he was having transformed to reflect his newfound success—"someone like you comes and tells me—"

Feiffer said icily, "And an agent of the Securities and Exchange Commission is also dead."

He was talking, not to Feiffer and whatever it was he represented, but to the gods. "Every time I get just a little bit up, someone comes and smashes me down again!" He was a short, middle-aged balding man who had been unsuccessful all his life. Up until this had happened to him all he had been heading for was old age and poverty. Teddy Chang said with his face going red with the anger and frustration of it all, "Why couldn't it have been true? Why not just this once? Fortunes change! Why couldn't mine? Other people's fortunes change! I read about it in the papers all the time! They get a bit of luck and suddenly they're somebody! Suddenly they're important! Suddenly they're—" He knew exactly what Feiffer wanted to know. Teddy Chang said, "He called me! Out of the blue! I didn't call him! He called me!"

Feiffer said, "When?"

"Eight weeks ago. All that week things had been looking good for me. Every day that week I'd stopped at the Jade Steps bird market on my way to work and had my fortune told by one of the rice birds up there—you know, where you pay a few cents and one of the birds in the cage picks out your fortune from a little wad of them and—" Every time he got up someone smashed him down again. Teddy Chang said, "And all the fortunes were good and I thought—"

"And you thought you might make one lucky investment that might pay back some of the losses you were making for your clients—" He saw the man's face. Feiffer said coldly, "You'd started stealing from the safe investments you'd made for them that gave you almost no profit and started investing them in wildcat shares, hadn't you?"

Teddy Chang said sadly, "All my life . . . But I didn't take him seriously at first. Not the first time, but he said that was okay with him because he didn't expect me to take him seriously the first time. All he said was, 'I have some inside information that I think can make us both some money and I'm prepared to give it to you for free'—and he told me that something was going to happen with a certain firm and that when it did there would be a flight of investment capital away from it to its major competitor."

Feiffer said, "The Star Insurance Company." He waited for a moment. "And what happened was that their long-term investment genius Ronnie Wong died suddenly, wasn't it?"

"Yes. Of a heart attack. And I suddenly realized, if I'd had my clients' and my own money in its competitor, in its exact pairing, we would have all made millions!" Teddy Chang said quietly, "The second time he called—" He could still remember the moment. "—the second time he called he said he hoped I'd made a few dollars from his little tip and if I was prepared to invest, say, a few thousand dollars of my profits for him in his next little tip, maybe I wouldn't mind if he made some too." Teddy Chang said, "He had the softest, gentlest voice. He told me to invest some money over the next few days in Amalgamated Long Grain Rice."

Feiffer said tightly, "And, lo and behold, the head of Amalgamated Long Grain Rice's major competitor—its exact pairing—suddenly and unexpectedly keels over and dies—"

He was still thinking about it. Teddy Chang said, "I couldn't believe my luck! I'd heard about it, you know, and read about it: those unbelievable times when everything you do turns to money and everything is nothing but success and prosperity and cash, but I—" He glanced at the damnable sign. "But all I put in it, because for once in my life I was trying to be careful, was a few thousand and I— But, even then, when he called back he didn't mind, he understood. He said that was what he would have done too, and then—"

Feiffer said, "And then he told you that the All-Asia Moldings and Steel Castings Company was about to suffer a major setback and you invested everything you had." Feiffer said, watching the man like a hawk, "And then—when? The next night? Kenneth Tam, the head of the firm, goes to the toilet at a meeting of the Millionaires' Club on *The Pearl Princess* floating restaurant and dies there, dropped as stone-cold dead as if he'd been shot!"

"But he wasn't *shot!* He died of natural causes! And Ronnie Wong! He wasn't shot either! And Yuan Fook Chee of International Rice—he wasn't shot or stabbed or killed either! They all died of heart attacks! Of natural causes!"

"What did he tell you his name was?"

"He didn't. He said because of his professional position he had to stay in the shadows and I should just deliver the money he made up to the Jade Steps in cash and simply leave it there in a doorway for him!" Teddy Chang, ever the Chancer, said incredulously, "Can you believe it? Can you believe the omen, the luck that was? Right to the same place where all that first week the birds had been telling me things were going to get better in my life!"

"How much have you delivered to him altogether?"

He thought about it for a moment. He was almost sure he had done nothing illegal. Maybe, he might even be able to keep the money. Teddy Chang said, "A little in excess of seventy-five thousand U.S. dollars."

"And you never once wondered who he was, or—"

It was the only good thing that had ever happened to him in his life. Sometimes at night when he lay in bed thinking about it and felt a tingle all up and down his entire body, the fact that it had happened was almost more important than the money. Teddy Chang, shaking his head hard, said, "No! No! I never did! He picked *me!* Of all the people in the world he could have picked, he picked *me!*" He was on the edge of tears. All his life he had been a failure. He was a failure no more. Teddy Chang, surrounded by all his files and clippings and computers and faxes and telephones, looking up and down the length of the opened-up floor that was going to be his, said, basking in the man's reflected glow, "I thought he was someone very important! Someone big! High up! *I thought he was someone like a really big-shot doctor who had inside information on the medical conditions of all the rich people in the Colony!*"

In the Detectives' Room, he thought of something Chinese.

O'Yee thought, "Number Fifty-four!"

It was from a playing-card-sized set of Illustrated Chinese Maxims he'd bought from a stall in the Thieves Market for fifty cents, subtitled *Getting Along Politely in the Far East—A Guide for Considerate and Well-Bred Foreign Travellers, 1901.*

It was the only one that, poised between earth and sky, behind desk and into midair, his mind could remember.

The maxim was, "Shooting one at his back is a sin that will go down to as far as his descendants."

And in case the considerate and well-bred foreign traveller had no idea what the fuck that was supposed to mean, it was explained in a little paragraph below:

Explanation: A Chinese sage once said, "The Super-man returns a courtesy for an evil; the ordinary man returns an evil for an evil; while the rogue returns an evil for a courtesy. One should never knock a person when he is down."

Irec Algr Amasc Afmm Icba Atta Emma Zip.

H. COYPAWS?

Well, it all made sense to him.

Behind his desk, his face set hard, gripping the top of the desk so hard his knuckles went white, O'Yee said in a whisper as the six silent murderers huddled inside the door listened for the approach of whoever it was they were waiting to kill, "Oh, God . . . oh, God in heaven . . ."

Still standing stock-still a little in from the doorway of Teddy Chang's office, Feiffer said with no tone in his voice at all, but simply as a matter of information, "He's not a doctor. His name is Jesus Sixtus Caina and he knew when and how Wong and Yuan and Tam were going to die because he knew when and how he was going to kill them, and he picked you because, just as he did research on them and on their companys' pairings, he did research on you and he knew you'd do exactly what he wanted. "

He was like a child, pouting. Teddy Chang, taking a step backward and shaking his head, said stubbornly, "They all died of natural causes."

He knew he knew. Feiffer asked, "And Lee Tse Wa, the head of International Cloth Buyers Amalgamated, what about him?"

There was a silence.

Feiffer said, "He's dead too. He died today in a temple on Wanchai Street, and by tomorrow or the next day when the family board members have regrouped and tried to salvage what they can of what's bound to be a sudden and massive outflow of capital by their investors in the company, anyone who's got money in their major competitor will be a very rich man indeed—*won't he?*"

He could not disguise the look in his eyes. Teddy Chang said in a whisper, "He's dead? Lee's dead? He's really dead?"

"*Yes, he's dead!*"

Teddy Chang said in a gasp, rich beyond counting, "Oh, my God! . . ."

"How much profit is there in it for him?"

He was still in awe. Teddy Chang said in a whisper, "Almost half a million. Half a million U.S. dollars." What was in it for him was even more. Teddy Chang said suddenly, "I don't think I want to talk to you anymore." Teddy Chang, full of power, said as a statement of fact, "I haven't done anything illegal! Have I?" Suddenly, he was puffed up like a toad. "Have I?"

"No." Maybe he hadn't.

"My luck has changed and suddenly I'm somebody and I don't have to talk to you at all if I don't want to—*do I?*"

"No, you don't." Gazing at the man, Feiffer smiled a thin, warmthless smile. Feiffer, shaking his head, said, "No, and neither did your predecessors: the men Caina did business with in the fifties and the sixties and probably the seventies and eighties, they didn't have to talk to anyone either—*because they're all dead!* Because your doctor friend or whoever you convinced yourself he was, over the last at-least forty years, all over Asia and the Pacific has killed at least a hundred and fifty people doing exactly what he's doing now, and at the end of it all—and I don't know how long it lasts: a week, a month, maybe even a couple of years—he kills everyone involved in it to clean it all up! And he *definitely* kills the little worm of a failure he's so carefully chosen to do his investing for him because he was already a nothing, a bum and a criminal before he chose him, and he absolutely wouldn't allow him to run around loose after it was all over telling everyone that it was the greatest thing that ever happened to him in his life *and exactly how it was all done!*" He thought of Helen Lau with all her hopes and dreams lying dead in the filth and blowing papers of Jade Lane with her eyes gone from her own fingernails. He looked at him and had no feeling for the man. "And he *definitely*—"

It was all he had. Teddy Chang, retreating back into the wall and the debris, said desperately, "My luck *changed!*" Or had it? Or was it ever, always, the same? It was all he had in his life: he had nothing else. Teddy Chang, shouting at the gods, roared with the tears of frustration running down his face, "It's *changed!* My luck has *changed!*"

"Yes, it has." He glanced at the entire-floor office suite that was going to be Chang's. Feiffer said softly, "Because now you're going to live."

He had never been able to see any way out before and he saw no way out now. Teddy Chang said through his tears, "How?"

"Because when he calls you to tell you the next investment, you're going to call me and it's all going to stop." For a moment he could not get the words out. He was not talking about any of the dead men. "Everything. Everything is going to finally stop. *Everything!*"

He took a step forward towards Chang with his hand reaching into his coat pocket and for a horrible instant Chang thought he was going to draw a gun and kill him. "*Everything!* The minute you call me and tell me who's going to be next, everything—all of it—*everything* is going to *stop!*"

COYPAWS?

It meant, Christopher O'Yee? Phillip Auden? William Spencer? *H.*

It meant, Harry. Feiffer.

COYPAWS?

If it had been him or Auden or Spencer they could have killed any one of them hours ago.

H.

It meant Harry Feiffer. It meant he was the one they were waiting for.

In the Detectives' Room, O'Yee glanced at his watch.

9:04 P.M.

He had not seen or heard from Feiffer since early in the morning and he had no idea where he was or what he was doing, and with the phones and the faxes out—

9:05 P.M.

He tried to think of his wife and children, but he could not, and all he could think of was that the one with the axe was the one he should hit first and, if he had a little luck, take the fillet-knife man at the same time, then, if he was even luckier and got hold of the axe or the fillet knife and had the utterly inhuman nerve to use them, drive first the axe and then the knife deep into the heart of the club man, and then . . .

Starting to shake, O'Yee tried to see his watch, but the face was blurred.

9:0 . . . 6?

Whatever it was, as he watched the second hand, unstoppably, uncaringly, relentlessly, ticked away another and then another and then another of the last moments of his life.

9:07 exactly.

In his car, turning onto Beach Road to make a left towards Canton Street for the run up to Yellowthread Street and the Station, all the lights on *The Pearl Princess* were ablaze in the harbor like the lights of a carnival merry-go-round, and Feiffer had to look away and press his hand hard on his father's badge in his pocket for comfort to stop himself from shaking.

Thinking about it, Auden had absolutely no idea what people like Hetherington-Smith would do now.

Spencer said brokenly, "I'm a failure! I'm a joke!"

All he knew was what he would never do now, and that was

hit a man while he was down. Auden said as a statement of fact, "You're not! You're Brave Bomb Disposals Bill!" Auden said firmly, "You're alive! You've done all that had to be done so far and there's no reason you can't do the rest! There's no reason you can't do the rest of it now!"

"*How?*"

And then, as it sometimes did, that single brain cell in Auden's head that held all his great thoughts sparked into life. Auden said, "You said it's a booby-trapped bomb—what makes you think that if you cut *either* wire—red *or* green—it'll defuse the thing? Maybe it doesn't matter that we're both red-green color blind! Maybe that's the one thing the swine who built the thing didn't count on: the wild card in life—that *both* the people defusing the bomb might be red-green color blind! Maybe the bomb is a symbol of the ultimate metaphor of life, and both the wires have to be cut together!" God, that sounded wonderful. Auden said, "Maybe—"

It *was* wonderful. Eton-educated, all that, Spencer said in awe, "Oh, my God! That's wonderful!"

Nothing stopped him now. On his feet in the ooze, his hand a clenched goop statue's hand of all the oppressed ordinary people rising up against their oppressors, Auden said in declamation, "Maybe . . . maybe they—maybe no one considers that one little thing that people like you and"—he almost said, "me," but this wasn't the time, his brain cell told him, to get things wrong, "People like you and I have that, for all their airs and graces, our masters and betters don't have and never will have and never have had is—"

His eyes were like saucers. Spencer inquired of the great man, "What? What have we got?" All his life he had wondered.

"It is not what we have, but what we are!"

"What are we?"

In the sewer, the methane was coming back. Auden, his brain happy, said illustriously, "Yes, by God, *yes!* That's it!"

"What? What's it?" All his life he had wondered. Spencer said desperately, at last maybe to hear the answer to the true, the real, the deepest secret of the meaning of life, "What are we? People like us?"

Spark. Ping! It was the sound of his single remaining brain cell giving out, or, as Auden reached out and held the telephone wire running across the sewer in his hand like a twisted thresh of grain twisted into an all-purpose both literal and figurative symbol of resistance, it was the sound of all the telephone and fax lines coming back on.

Auden said, "What are we?" Without the cell, it was a bit of a hard one. "Why, we— We are—" He didn't read much. Auden said, "We—we are—we are—*Blessed by the Gods!*" He didn't read much, but he had read that. He had read it on a wine label.

Auden said, "See? I'm right! " And then the cell came back and said, "What—Or am I" and then died again.

Auden, down in the sewer with the bomb and bone-brain, getting a little confused by all the mental activity in his head, said, as all those truly blessed by the gods said in one way or an-other every day of their lives, "Oh, to hell with it! Why not? Let's just do it and see what happens!"

There was a *ping!* and all the phones and faxes in the Detectives' Room came on, but it was too late.

In the corridor leading from the Charge Room to the door to the Detectives' Room, the six killers huddled behind the door and simultaneously heard what they had been waiting to hear.

They all heard the sound of someone coming down the cor-ridor to the Detectives' Room door.

*   *   *

In the sewer, poised over the nearest main-circuit wire, Auden said, "Okay." He had Spencer's desk scissors in his hand. "Are you ready?"

Deep inside the bomb at the other wire, Spencer had a pair of silver nail clippers. Spencer, nodding and trying to see his wire through the blur of emotion, said in a whisper, "Yes." He was a great man, too, in his own way, and he hoped at what he thought now was the hour of his death, in all his life he had never knowingly harmed another human being.

All his life he had wanted to be brave.

Now, at the brink, on the edge, dancing at last with a friend on the rim of the volcano, Brave Bomb Disposals Bill said not bravely but *magnificently,* "One-two-three . . . *cut!"*

It was Feiffer: he knew it was.

Behind his desk, summoning every atom of power in his entire being, coiling like a spring, filling his essence with the primeval power and sinews of a wild animal, O'Yee, readying himself to scream as his war cry and his death cry, *"Aarrrrggghh!"* said to his wife and children somewhere knowing they would never hear it, "I love you . . . I . . . " and, as simultaneously, down in the sewer, Auden and Spencer, as one, cut both the wires, in the last, the finest, the greatest and noblest act of his life as the door swung open, *leapt.*

13.

As the door was flung open from the inside and O'Yee, obviously in a hurry, flew by him at shoulder height, Feiffer asked politely, "Christopher? . . ."

Then as O'Yee twisted in midair, from behind the open door Creature Number One, with a terrible look on his face, advanced on Feiffer with his cohorts in a pack behind him.

The terrible look on his face was a smile. Creature Number One said with his eyes open, all his choppers bared, and his hand outstretched, "Harry!"

Still half twisted, O'Yee hit the floor of the Charge Room.

Feiffer said, "Baptiste!" then there was a crash as the rear door of the Detectives' Room was flung open and two voices as one yelled in triumph, "We defused the bomb!"

Then someone said, "What bomb?" and then someone said like Churchill, "*The* bomb!" and then the door was slammed shut and there was a sound like something heavy gooping its way across the floor, and a terrible smell.

It was not the smell of the goop: it was the smell of Yellowthread Street—all of it—as, like a radio suddenly being turned up, everyone who had flooded out suddenly flooded back in, started selling and buying and screaming and complaining and arguing and honking and tooting and revving as if nothing had happened at all.

Then two atrocious toxic apparitions seeping slime stood over him and one of them said, "We're just going upstairs to the locker room to shower and get some clean clothes on before we go home," and then, as they went, going gloop-ger-splosh-goop-goop, from somewhere, wafting back like the echo of long-forgotten, perhaps never-were days, there was a brief barbershop duet of the first bars of "Lovely Boating Weather," and then, crashing in on hobnail boots as if they had been just waiting all the time for their call to rush in and lay down their lives, all the Uniformed cops came back in, crowded around, and gazed down at him.

"Harry!" "Baptiste!" Honk. Toot. Shout. Scream. Irec. Algr. Amasc. Goop. Bomb. Boat. Gaze. It was all too much for him.

Lying full-length, totally out of it, O'Yee shouted in awful, lost desperation, "What? What? *What? What in the name of all that's holy is going on around here?"*

In the Detectives' Room, with his hand on his shoulder as if he had known him a long while, Feiffer said to O'Yee, introducing Creature Number One, "Detective Sergeant Baptiste Bontoc of the Metro Manila Police."

There wasn't an axe or a club or a gun or a nuclear warhead anywhere in sight. Bontoc, arcing his hand around the little semicircle of the other five Odes To The Awful, said, both to O'Yee and Feiffer, "And my cousins from the Bontoc tribe: Sergio and Juan, Placido, Ferdinand, and Fred."

Feiffer said with a smile, as if things must have just been

going swimmingly for them all, all afternoon and evening, "Christopher O'Yee you already know."

There was a babble of sound. Bontoc said, "Ah. COY! I had a list from Felix Elizalde but the only one I knew by sight was you, Harry." He said, as if it were the same the world over, "I didn't know who to trust."

"Felix thinks you're dead."

There was a silence, then Bontoc said with a nod of appreciation in their direction, "When I needed help the only phone call I dared make into the Philippines was to my old tribal village in the mountains."

They *were* cannibals and headhunters: it was all real. In the Detectives' Room, O'Yee said nothing.

"Everything's tapped. Nothing is secure." Bontoc said, still smiling and nodding as if they didn't speak a word of English but read faces and tones, "I asked the village head man if the village could afford to send one or two of my cousins who had a passing resemblance to me, and he sent the entire five." He smiled again, his eyes moist with emotion, "First-class air."

Bontoc said, "They knew what they were facing and they all came anyway. They're all very brave men."

So must have been the other first-class passengers. On the long eight-hour flight from Manila to Hong Kong, they must have been positively heroic.

Bontoc said to explain all to O'Yee, "It's the Dalagangan. If you open your eyes and see the Dalagangan, he kills you."

O'Yee said, "Right." He smiled too.

Bontoc said, still talking to O'Yee, "All we could think of was to come here to the Station. I thought Harry would be here. The H. COYPAWS note was in case I was killed and my cousins had to come here alone—it was to tell them to trust only Harry, because—because I didn't know you or the others. And then when

Harry wasn't here, for all I knew—" Bontoc said, "We had to pretend to be asleep so you wouldn't know what to do with us and you'd let us stay. Then, when we could hear people downstairs and all the phones went out and the lights started flickering, we took every weapon we could find in the place to protect ourselves! And then people started appearing in doorways and—" Bontoc said to make it clear, to make him understand, "He's the Dalagangan: the man of awesome powers! Death! He's been Death for a hundred and fifty years! He appears from nowhere, from out of the wind and the fire and the earth like a little, ancient, harmless old man—and then he transforms and no one who has ever seen him in his transformation has ever lived to tell about it!" Bontoc, waving his hand at the semicircle of his friends, said as if it had been the last hope of a hopeless man, "I got my cousins up here because I thought because his heart is so evil that he wouldn't have the ability to see through the surface into another man's soul and he wouldn't be able to tell us one from another or see who each of us really was!"

And he had done it: done the thing he hated most when other people did it to him—treated people who looked different and thought differently and were different as if they were a lesser race. He listened, and Bontoc had, like most Philippinos, an American accent, and then he listened harder and heard the New England in it and knew he had been to Yale. O'Yee said softly, "I'm sorry." *He nothing common did, or mean*... Everything he had done had been common and mean. O'Yee said, "I'm sorry I didn't know what to say or how to—" When you didn't notice the color and the sharpened teeth and the axe, he had a very nice face. O'Yee said bitterly ashamed, "I'm sorry I—"

He also had a very nice soul. Bontoc, smiling at O'Yee and nodding, said softly, "That's okay. I understand. Maybe I would have done the same thing myself." He turned to Feiffer. Bontoc said in a whisper, "I trailed him all the way up here via Singapore, Harry, and then across to Kuala Lumpur and then—he was doing it all just in case anyone *was* following him—then back to Singapore again and then through to Djakarta in Indonesia and then, finally, here to Hong Kong to the Peninsula Hotel on Kowloon." He waited, but Feiffer only listened and said nothing. "He's been here, now, for about nine weeks, and in that time—"

Feiffer said evenly, tightly, "In that time, he's killed at least five people, including an agent of the Securities and Exchange Commission, and it's entirely possible that he's due to kill someone sometime tonight or tomorrow."

"I lost him every time! Every time he went out from the hotel and I followed him through the streets I lost him because I was afraid to get too close in case he saw me, and he just got swallowed up in the crowds or—" Bontoc said softly, "They say he's immortal, that he's over a hundred and fifty years old, and that he can kill with a single look and that . . ." Bontoc said suddenly, *"And he's looking for me, Harry! And I think by now he may even know who I am!"* He was not simply afraid, he was terrified. "Two days ago when he came back from his breakfast, I followed him right into the lobby of the hotel, and when he collected his key, I got his room number, and I waited until he went out again and then I paid one of the bellboys to let me borrow his uniform and I went into his room to search it, but he came back earlier than I expected and he saw me coming out!" He gestured at the five identical, silent creatures gazing at him in wordless incomprehension. "And I couldn't think of what else to do or anywhere else to come but here, and when you weren't here and the whole street was cleared—"

His voice was strained. Feiffer asked, "If you've seen him you know what he looks like."

"He looks like a harmless old man in his eighties! He looks, when he does things like sit on a bench in a park somewhere or go to the shorefront and stare out over the harbor at the junks and sampans, like an old, old man dreaming of nothing more than all the wonderful old times of his youth that are gone forever!" Bontoc said with his voice suddenly rising, "His wonderful old times of his youth are of killing people all over the world for at least fifty years that we know about, and probably even longer!" He saw the look of alarm on his cousins' faces but could not control the fear in his voice. "His room was just the room of an old man with lots of clippings about stocks and shares and companies and the people who ran the companies, and nothing—nothing else!" Bontoc said, "No medicines or powders or phials or prescriptions or— He's at least eighty years old and there wasn't even a bottle of aspirin for an eighty-year-old man in the entire room! And nothing, nothing on paper—no letters or documents or plans or maps or itineraries or—or anything except one single sliver of paper hidden behind the plastic cover of the electric light switch in the bathroom!" He had almost torn the room apart to find it, and how he had it tight in his balled-up fist. Bontoc said, "I made a copy of it. But all it reads"—he handed it over and recited it from memory—"is 'Irec Algr Amasc Afmm Icba Atta Emma Zip.' "

He waited, gazing at Feiffer as if he was his last hope.

Bontoc said with a look of utter desperation on his face, "Harry, it's all there is! Have you any idea—any idea at all—what it *means?*"

In the silence, Feiffer said softly, "Yes, I know what it means."

It meant, *Irec:* the International Rice Export Company, and the murder of its driving force, Yuan Fook Chee, aka Frederick Yuan, age eighty-one.

Algr: it meant Irec's main rival and competitor, the Amalgamated Long Grain Rice Corporation.

Amasc: it meant the All-Asia Moldings and Steel Castings Company, Tam Kwan Yu, aka Kenneth Tam, age eighty-three, its CEO dead in a toilet on *The Pearl Princess* with both his eyes torn out by his own nails.

Afmm: It meant All-Asia's sole competitor in Hong Kong in the heavy-metals casting and supply business, the Applied Fine Metals Molding Corporation, Kowloon.

Icba: It meant International Cloth Buyers Amalgamated, Lee Tse Wa, aka John Lee, age seventy-eight, dead in the awful silence of the Temple of a Thousand Buddhas on Wanchai Street, and it meant International Cloth's major and only rival in the same business, Amalgamated Textile Traders Asia.

Emma: it meant Enterprise Mass Media Associates, and,

Zip: Enterprise's competitor, Zong Ipoh Programming.

Ronnie Wong and his insurance company were not on the list: they were unimportant, merely a dress rehearsal for Teddy Chang's benefit.

It meant, properly set out in columns times two:

1. IREC	:	ALGR
2. AMASC	:	AFMM
3. ICBA	:	ATTA
4. EMMA	:	ZIP

It meant Teddy Chang. It meant, with only one last brace to go, almost half-a-million U.S. dollars. It meant Helen Lau dead in the blowing papers and filth of Jade Lane. It meant *pairings.*

It meant that the next one to be attacked, the next company to be destroyed by a single, quick surgical assault on its heart, was Enterprise Mass Media Associates, the owners of half the television and electronics supply companies in Asia. It meant the sole, lifelong driving force behind it was going to go. It meant he was the next target.

It meant the old man who had found Tam's body on *The Pearl Princess* and, according to Wilfred Wing, the owner of the place, had completely lost his mind at the sight of it.

It meant, Mr. A. K. Arthur *Lim.*

It meant, since with Helen Lau's death everything had to happen quickly and be finished with, it was probably going to happen tonight.

. . . Lists and pairings, columns of letters and abbreviations and the names of companies long since gone out of existence, all ticked and question-marked and crossed with an ancient, beautiful Waterman Patrician fountain pen Feiffer still had in its box in his pocket . . .

It meant in the silence of the Detectives' Room as Bontoc waited for Feiffer to answer him that, without a shadow of a doubt, the Dalagangan, all those years ago in the little garden at the back of the house in the New Territories, was the man who had killed his father.

9:32. The Dalagangan was nothing more remarkable than an old man travelling on a bus at night from Central to the district of Hong Bay on the southern tip of Hong Kong island, turning an unlit Marlboro cigarette over and over in his left hand and looking down at it as if he didn't have a match or was trying to give up smoking or used it merely as something to play with as he rode.

The bus was marked *Star Ferry—Beach Road.* Beach Road was the last stop on the line at the waterfront in Hong Bay, and as it reached the last stop and the few remaining people on board emptied out, for a moment that and the darkness of the night reminded the Dalagangan of another last stop on the line of another bus somewhere else: the bus from Manila Central far out to Terminus Monumental to the northeast, to the City of the Dead, an entire one-square-mile Chinese Silent City the size of central London with beautifully laid out streets and gardens and marble houses and mansions full of televisions and telephones and rich furniture and brocaded curtains that housed only the departed—the greatest surviving single monumental mausoleum on earth still in use, a celebration by the Chinese of the city of the things in death they had never had in life.

He liked the gardens and the trees there, the power of them, and when he was in Manila, at night, in the darkness, even though it was not allowed and the walled perimeter of the place was patrolled by police, went there often.

9:34 P.M. Standing for a moment at the sea wall and gazing out into the blackness of the South China Sea and the twinkling yellow lights of the junks far out to sea working it for fish, and thinking about it, an image came to his mind for a moment of another garden somewhere and of a tall, European man in his shirt-sleeves standing on the bottom step outside the rear of his house in the New Territories lighting a cigarette with an old-time flint lighter and then, in the midst of the smoke, gazing up at the night sky to the north; and it came as a mild shock to the Dalagangan to remember that it had been almost forty years ago.

Then the image faded, and all he could remember—after the ecstasy of it all, the joy, the sweetness and power of it all—was the *hush*.

9:44 P.M.
On Beach Road, the Dalagangan began walking north towards all the lights of the buildings that lit up all the shoreline for as far as the eye could see in a blaze of light.

       ✳   ✳   ✳

In the Detectives' Room Feiffer asked, "How is it done, Baptiste? Felix gave me the usual stuff about *bagoong* and *patis,* and young, unmarried men being the only victims, but it isn't that, is it? That's the stuff of *kulam,* isn't it? Village stuff. And the local *mangkulam* scaring the wits out of somebody already half mad on superstition and religion—but this guy is more than that, isn't he? And whatever he does is real, isn't it?"

"Yes." He was still terrified. A Bontoc from the mountains whose ancestors had had everything their culture meant smashed apart by the Spanish missionaries and remolded into what amounted to medieval Inquisitional Catholicism, and then that mold smashed again by the exported American culture of the thirties, and then that obliterated again by the All-Asia Co-Prosperity Sphere invasion of the Japanese in the forties, he had nothing to hang on to except what he was inside.

Inside, compared to the ageless, unchanging, unvarying-through-the-centuries pure and undiluted power of the Dalagangan, he was nothing. Bontoc said, starting to shake, "Yes, it's the real thing. But I don't know how he does it. Nobody does. Anybody who does know is dead."

"Someone who heard it said that it sounded like a blossoming, like the sudden blossoming of something like—"

Bontoc said violently, "I don't know!" He saw the faces of his cousins and knew that even though they understood not a word of what was being said, they knew what was being talked about. Bontoc said, "*I don't know!* Nobody does!"

Feiffer said tightly, "It's something so awful that at the sight of it people tear their own eyes out to stop seeing it."

"I don't know what it is! I don't know!" In all the time he had followed him, he had never once had any clear notion of what he would do if he realized the Dalagangan was about to kill. Bontoc said, not caring anymore about the looks of terror on his cousins' faces, but lost deep in his own private nightmare, facing his own private terrors, "I don't know how he does it! That's why the six grown men standing here armed to the fucking teeth are too goddamned terrified to even go out into the street in case he sees us! I just don't know! Anybody who does know is *dead!*"

In the wreck of his office on Tiger Snake Road with all the workmen, unsure of their money, out in the street conferring about what to do next, Teddy Chang sat with his back to the door in a shabby steel chair from his previous life as a failure and contemplated the ripped-down walls that opened up the entire ground floor into a single, wonderfully opulent office suite that, up until an hour ago, was to have been the showpiece of his new life as a success.

On the phone, snaking out on a long black extension lead was the cheap black plastic telephone that had also been part of his previous life, and, looking down at it with the taste of dryness and salt in his mouth, Teddy Chang did not know whether, at that moment, he wanted it to ring or not.

At his desk, Feiffer opened the phone book and looked up the address for Mr. Lim on The Peak.

It was Lim: he knew it was.

In the Detectives' Room, in a silence that no one could think of a way to break, Feiffer sat at his desk gazing at the telephone waiting for Teddy Chang to call him.

9:45 P.M. In his life, in over fifty years of killing, the Dalagangan had opened a lot of doors and picked a lot of locks, and as he bent down in the side doorway of the brilliantly lit fifty-story Enterprise Mass Media Associates Building at the top of Beach Road ostensibly to light a cigarette away from the wind, he looked at the single Chinese double-key bar lock there and thought it would cause him no trouble at all.

Glancing up with the cigarette in his mouth still unlit, he read the time on the stone signal tower of the typhoon shelter in Hop Pei inlet a hundred yards away on the other side of the road.

9:46.

He had at least a full two hours to get ready.

Under the tower, lit by a single overhead argon light, he could see a telephone box, and, with all the time in the world, he tossed aside the unwanted, unlit cigarette, and, as old men did, carefully and slowly negotiated through the traffic in the street and went to the tower to make a call.

10:00 P.M. exactly.

It was Teddy Chang, making the only right decision he had ever made in his entire life, and, because he was Teddy Chang, sure it was wrong.

On the phone, his voice so soft it sounded like he did not want the words to come out at all, Teddy Chang said, a series of nouns and nothing more, "Company: ZIP—Zong Ipoh Programming, Malaysia–Hong Kong."

Then there was a silence.

Then Teddy Chang said, "The pairs competitor is EMMA— Enterprise Mass Media Associates, Hong Bay."

Teddy Chang said in a voice that held no emotion at all, "CEO and central driving figure, Mr. A. K. Arthur Lim."

And then, feeling as if he was doing it not just on the telephone but on his entire life and all his hopes and everything he might have been, he hung up.

Night and silence.

In the Detectives' Room, Feiffer said as an order to O'Yee, "Wait here."

10:02 P.M.

A *hush*.

. . . Thy rod and Thy staff, they comfort me . . .

"You and Baptiste and the others and Auden and Spencer wait here until you hear from me." Night, and the silence of the mountains that hung like icicles in the sky . . .

Nobody said anything or questioned him, but, as if they had, Feiffer roared as an order, "Just wait! Just wait until you hear from me! Okay?!"

He was his friend. He had been his friend for over twenty years. O'Yee said with a nod, "Okay." O'Yee, seeing the man's face and wanting to go over and lay his hand on his shoulder to comfort him, said gently, "Okay, Harry, whatever you say."

"Good." But for a moment he could not get his legs to work.

Glancing at the door of the Detectives' Room, Feiffer, nodding, said suddenly, again, "Good," and he went out through the door, went, not out into the city, but into the place where his mind was, back out into the garden at the back of his parents' house in the New Territories all those years ago and to what there, hidden and secret and silent among the trees and the flowers and the *hush*, stood waiting for him in the darkness.

10:05 P.M.

Inside the fire stairwell on the first floor of the Enterprise Mass Media Associates Building on Beach Road, everything around him suddenly going into X ray, the Dalagangan, on time and on schedule, began to fill himself with power.

14.

He had thought after he had Lim's name that all he would have to do was find out the man's schedule, dog his every move, and, sooner or later, probably sooner—tonight—he would have the Dalagangan cold.

It was not going to happen. In the main entrance hallway of Mr. Lim's magnificent house at the top of The Peak, Miss Lim, Lim's daughter, said firmly to Feiffer for the second time in as many minutes, "No, I can give you no information at all."

She was a plain, austere, unmarried woman in her late forties or early fifties dressed in a simple black skirt and blue silk blouse with a thin gold chain around her neck with a single sapphire on it that would have cost more than Feiffer made in a year. Framed in the hallway by a wonderful collection of jade that lined the carved teak walls on either side, and at the end of it the silent and heavily armed security dark-suited man who had accompanied Feiffer all the way in from the main entrance gate from the street, Miss Lim, folding her arms across her chest and shaking her head, said finally, "No, I cannot be of any assistance to you at all."

He had nothing: no warrant, no authority, no probable cause—nothing. All he had were five dead human beings with their eyes ripped out of their sockets by their own fingernails. Feiffer said desperately, "People you know are dead. Ronnie Wong from Star Insurance—"

She shook her head. She did not know him.

"—and Frederick Yuan of the International Rice Export Company—"

A flick of her head. She knew him, at least by reputation.

"—and Kenneth Tam of All-Asia Moldings, whose dead body your father found on *The Pearl Princess* floating restaurant. And—"

Standing in front of him like a rock, with her arms still folded across her chest, Miss Lim said with no emotion in her voice at all, "My father was very distressed by that incident. He is still very distressed by it, but Mr. Tam died of natural causes."

"And Lee Tse Wa, John Lee of International Cloth, who was found dead in the Temple of a Thousand Buddhas on Wanchai Street—did he die of natural causes too?"

Miss Lim said, "I have no idea. I did not even know Mr. Lee was dead. If he is, it has not yet been announced either by his family or his company, so I can make no comment on it at all."

"Does your father have any appointments or commitments tonight? Or any regular routine he follows that might be well known or someone might be able to find out about?"

She turned slightly to the security man and he took a single step forward.

Miss Lim said to the question, "I cannot reply to that question."

"I appreciate the problems you have with giving out any details of your father's activities. I understand that even the most remote possibility that he is either ill or incapacitated or under the threat of death would fuel a run on his company's capital, but—"

Miss Lim said in a voice like ice, "I said he was distressed finding the body of his old friend Mr. Tam. I did not say he was ill or incapacitated." She was used to being the buffer for her father, his spokesman. She was used to talking to people who listened for every tone and quiver in her voice for something, or a hint of something, anything. Miss Lim said definitively, "And you have yet to convince me that any threat against my father's life is real."

She, like the house, was a bastion, a fortress: without permission there was no way to breach it. She had had money a very long time: she was afraid of nothing and no one. Miss Lim said, "And you have yet to tell me who it is you claim is threatening my father's life and why he or she would want to."

"There are things I'm not at liberty to disclose either." At the end of hope, knowing it was the last thing he should say to someone whose every waking moment was concerned with business and profit and certainty, Feiffer said, "All I can do is ask you to take what I'm telling you on trust." He demanded before she could reply, "Does he have any reason this evening or later tonight to go out into the city alone and unprotected and unguarded? Any personal or private—"

Miss Lim said as if it had been an insult aimed directly at her, "My father is never unprotected or unguarded!"

"What about on *The Pearl Princess?*"

"He was not, as I understand it, in any danger on *The Pearl Princess.* As I understand what happened on *The Pearl Princess,* a man of some eighty-three years of age, and known not to be in the best of heath, went to the rest room probably feeling in some discomfort from the heavy meal he had just eaten, and died there of a heart attack. I have spoken to Mr. Wilfred Wing who owns *The Pearl Princess,* and that is what he says; I have spoken to the family to extend my family's sympathies and that is what they say, and in the absence of a coronial insistence on a postmortem and police at a higher level than one man coming to my father's house late at night with nothing more substantial to show than a feeling that something is wrong, I can only assume that is what the police and other authorities *at the level my family is used to dealing with* say too, and are satisfied that it was a death due to natural causes too. As were the deaths of Mr. Wong, who we did not know, and Mr. Yuan and Mr. Lee."

"I believe the deaths are part of a scheme to do with pairs trading. I believe it may all be part of a series of planned events designed to temporarily destroy investment confidence in one company in order to artificially raise the value of its rival company."

As, indeed, for all she knew, and she suspected, was this little planned event.

She reacted to the information not at all. It was not the first time everything the family had, everything her father had worked for all his life had hinged on a single word, and at a single word of hers at that.

Miss Lim, looking directly at the man without blinking, said with no room for argument, comment, or any further discussion, "The affairs of Enterprise Mass Media Associates, which is a company that now extends through seven countries in Southeast Asia and the Far East and is about to extend into the Pacific and Australia, are at the healthiest and most profitable they have been in the last ten years, and with upcoming Chinese investment in the parent company here in Hong Kong, will continue to be so up to and after the takeover in 1997, and under the continuing guidance of my father, Mr. A. K. Lim, should see even more growth next year than it has this year, and any rumors to the contrary created in order to artificially and maliciously manipulate the value of the company—"

And he was going to get nothing.

Miss Lim said, "—will be dealt with severely . . ." She meant, anyone trying to do it would be ruined—". . . both in a court of law and through the investigative division of the Securities and Exchange Commission."

He was going to get less than nothing. In the morning, there would be a note from the commissioner on his desk asking him to call him.

Miss Lim said with a sudden venom in her voice, "I don't know you, Mr. Detective Chief Inspector Feiffer! I will take nothing you say *on trust!*"

And that was it, and it was all over, and he would never get close to the Dalagangan, or—

"Captain!" It was the voice of an old, old man speaking in Chinese, "Captain! *Captain!*" and as Feiffer turned as Miss Lim did and the security man came forward another step with his hand reaching under his coat, Mr. Lim, eighty-five years old, dressed in a scholar's long brocaded coat, appeared in the open doorway of one of the rooms at the far end of the hallway carrying something long and white in his hand and grinning a wide, happy grin.

He thought Feiffer was someone else.

Coming forward, waving the security man aside with a flick of his fingers, so happy his eyes filled with tears, Mr. Lim said with his hand outstretched to greet him, "Captain! It's been so long! I'm so happy to see you again! Come, come! Come into my little private room and see what I have to show you!"

In the Detectives' Room, with Auden and Spencer showered, reclothed, and re-armed standing beside him, O'Yee finally said to Bontoc, "What the hell's a Dalagangan? And what the hell does he *do?*"

There was a silence, then, speaking softly and slowly, one awful, lethal piece of information at a time, Bontoc told him.

For a moment, as Lim, ignoring his daughter completely, led him excitedly into the room at the far end of the hallway, Feiffer thought perhaps Lim thought he was his own father.

He was like a lot of successful old men: he had become interested no longer in what he had or what he could have, but who he was and where he had come from. The room off the hallway was his scholar's room, a quiet, wood-lined place furnished with a simple calligrapher's desk and two carved-teak benches set at right angles to each other in it, and nothing else—a place of quietness and contemplation.

Lim, pulling him in and sitting him down next to him at the junction of the two benches, still grinning, said, as happy as a child, "Look, Captain! Look what I have!"

It was a white, almost rectangular piece of what looked like thin stone or quartz two foot long by a foot wide with the curved top worked smooth and divided by deep incised natural lines into four equal segments.

The eyes were gone. He was no longer living in the same place or the same time, but somewhere else in some other, some better time. Mr. Lim demanded happily in Chinese, senile beyond redemption, "Do you know what it is, Captain? Do you? Do you?"

Feiffer said softly, "Yes. Yes, I do."

"I knew you would!"

He had never seen one before, only heard about them.

Lim said, reaching over and holding his hand and then patting it over and over again, "Isn't it wonderful? Isn't it . . . *won-derful?*"

Still smiling, still holding Feiffer's hand and patting it, Mr. Lim, holding the wonderful object against his chest, said in a whisper, "It's at least—at least . . . four and a half thousand years old! It's from the village of Hsiao T'un near Anyang in Honan Province in the far, far, mountainous part of northern China!"

Cracked and bleached and jagged, covered in pictograms and characters so ancient Feiffer could not even read them, it was a dragon's bone.

There were people who thought he was immortal, that he had lived and killed forever.

It was a notion, a terror, he did nothing to discourage.

On the back fire stairs of the fortieth floor of the fifty-story Enterprise Mass Media Associates Building on Beach Road, the Dalagangan, having climbed all the stairs without losing strength, but instead gaining it, paused for a moment and nodded to himself.

He was there: the top ten floors were the offices of Lim's Enterprise Mass Media Associates company, the very top, the fiftieth, Lim's own office and private museum where he displayed the great treasures of Chinese history and antiquity he had collected or had had purchased for him by agents all over the world.

10:38 P.M.

Standing in the half light of the stairwell with his hand resting lightly on the steel fire-door knob on the fortieth floor, the Dalagangan knew, because he had studied the man for over a year and read everything that had ever been written about him, that he had a little routine he never varied from.

He knew that every second night, at exactly midnight, Mr. Lim came to his office and museum and stood there for a long while looking out at the city contemplating his life and holding in his hand his latest acquisition before putting it carefully up in its place of honor in his collection.

He knew, because it was a private thing in his life and a thing of great peace and comfort to him, that he always came alone.

At the very least, while he was there in the house with him, Lim was safe.

In the dream he dreamed sometimes, while he sat with his father in his office in the house in New Territories, his father still lived and he was safe too.

In his dream, in his memory, he could not remember whether, when his father told him the wonderful things he told him about China and the Chinese and all the places one day they would visit together in China, his father had spoken in English or Chinese.

Mr. Lim's hand still rested on his. It was the hand of an old man the same age as his father would have been had he lived. It was a hand of softness and gentleness with the long grown fingernails of a man who did no manual work, the hand of a scholar.

Mr. Lim, with his gaze lost in the texture of the object in his other hand, said in an intimate whisper, "Of course, we know now that these objects are nothing more than the polished and worked shells of tortoises and the bones of cattle, but at the time—so long ago—we Chinese believed that just as the snake sheds its skin, so the dragon sheds its bones, and that these objects dug up in the fields by the poor farmers of the village of Hsiao T'un were the shed bones of the dragon, the creature so central to Chinese thought that at least one branch of the Buddhist faith, the ch'an, or, as it is called in the West, the *Zen*, elevates it to the philosophical symbol for the single great flash of truth that is Enlightenment in all things."

He patted Feiffer on the hand and smiled at him. "Before these bones were unearthed and discovered by scholars in 1899, the dragon and all the history that once was China's had become a myth, merely things of bedtime stories for children, and of pathetic import compared with all the power and the progress and the might of the West. And the opium the West brought with it was to addict and enslave a people with no past to fall back on for strength and therefore no future of their own to hope for. Do you agree with me, Captain?"

"Yes." He was quoting from the Changs' standard book on the history of the Chinese language. His own grandfather, his father's father, had been one of the men he spoke of, one of the opium runners. Feiffer said gently in Chinese, "Yes, I agree with you."

Lim, still quoting, said dreamily, caressing the bone, "A bulwark of cultural tradition three thousand years old was crumbling beneath the impact of Western scientific thought. Chinese writers were even beginning to publish serious articles claiming that their own people were inherently incapable of operating foreign machines, let alone inventing new ones. A mood of self-doubt, of dissatisfaction with old wisdom, extended into every branch of study. Goaded by occidental standards for scientific proof, Chinese historians scrutinized their ancient records with increased skepticism. Were the stirring histories of the earliest Yin and Chou dynasties only legends? Were there enough hard facts to prove Confucius really lived? Was even the foundation stone of China itself, its written language, even Chinese at all, or were Chinese characters not native to the Middle Kingdom at all, but imported from the Middle East in ages past?"

He heard his father's voice again. With his eyes half closed, Feiffer felt the touch of his hand on his and the sound of his voice as, together, they talked of great things and great discoveries and great places and snow-capped mountains so high they hung like icicles in the sky.

Mr. Lim said, "Then, when the farmers of Hsiao T'un began unearthing these 'bones' covered in characters of a script so ancient no one living could read them, scholars began to wonder again, 'But if all that has gone before is myth and story and fantasy, what is this?' What can this mean?" Mr. Lim said, "Finally, in 1905, the first of the bones was deciphered and found to be the record of a people who called themselves the *Shang* and ruled all the lands surrounding Anyang some four thousand years ago. The bones were found not to be the bones of the mythical dragon at all, but the scraped and polished tablets on which were incised royal questions from the Shang emperors to the spirits of their dead ancestors about the next year's harvest and the affairs of the realm and the health and prosperity of all the royal personages and members of the imperial court! They were fortune tablets, linked directly to the words of the gods, the four incised lines segmenting the 'bones' carefully drilled and formed after the questions were written down so that when heat was applied, cracks would appear, their length and shapes determined by all the ancestral spirits to indicate answers to the emperors' questions."

Mr. Lim said, "And in that moment, in that moment of decipherment, China reappeared from the mists and everything the Chinese had ever believed about their own ancient history was true!"

The bone was a treasure beyond value. Mr. Lim said, "The Shang was China's Bronze Age—by 1937 wonderful Shang houses and buildings and monuments had been unearthed, and objects and artifacts of breathtaking beauty and grace and civilization: decorated bronze vessels of artistry greater than even that of Cellini, entire burial suits of jade, and, like the once-thought-lost and mythical city of Troy, deep beneath the ground, entire Shang cities of wonderful and astonishing beauty and architecture."

Mr. Lim said, "Oh, Captain, I am so glad you are here again to share this object and this moment with me."

Feiffer said softly, "I am very glad to see you are still well, Mr. Lim." He thought Lim might say something to put a time and place to the time and place he thought he was in, but he did not.

Mr. Lim said happily, "I am well," but something about the eyes was wrong, and, resting the object carefully on his knees for a moment, Mr. Lim brushed his hand across his face and rubbed at his closed eyelids. Mr. Lim said, blinking, and then looking Feiffer square in the face as if for a moment he had forgotten who he was, "I am very well indeed, thank you."

"I'm glad." He still had Mr. Lim's hand in his.

Mr. Lim said happily, "Oh, Captain, the times you and I had together!"

"Yes." It was a soft, warm hand the way his father's hand had been soft and warm and without noticing it, he had been gently stroking and caressing it as he listened. Mr. Lim said, "They were wonderful times, just after the war, the best I ever lived."

"Yes." And it could have been his father he was talking about.

Mr. Lim said, "Your visits to me in my old house in Kowloon on Nathan Road, and my long, long trips out in the train to yours in the New Territories . . ." Mr. Lim said, "They were the happiest days of my life."

And he held the hand and would never let it go. "Yes."

Mr. Lim said in the sad, lost fog of his mind, "Oh, Captain, I thought—I heard— It's been so long . . . I thought you had died."

He had studied all of them: Wong, Yuan, Tam, Lee, and then he had killed them.

And the girl following Teddy Chang on Hanford Road: he had studied her, listened to her heartbeat as she hurried after him, and then, in exactly the same way, killed her too.

10:46 P.M. There were people who said that he was immortal, that he had lived and killed forever.

Waiting on the other side of the steel door on the fire-stairs landing to the forty-eighth floor, the Dalagangan, turning a box of matches over and over in his left hand, listened for the click of the television security camera in the passageway as it went off and the Enterprise Mass Media Associates security man in his little room on the fortieth floor found it clear and turned the camera on the forty-ninth to sweep it before moving on to the next.

10:47. He heard, although no one else alive would have heard it, the tiny switch inside the camera hidden behind the neon-light fitting in the ceiling click off as the security man moved on on his methodical, unchanging, never-varying, all-night-long routine to scan the fiftieth floor.

She had been standing there for some time. From the doorway, with the security man a little behind her to help her put him to bed, Miss Lim said gently to coax him back, "Father—"

He recognized her. Mr. Lim, looking up, said happily, proudly, "Ah!" He turned to Feiffer and taking his hand out from under Feiffer's, patted him on the arm in his joy. "Ah, Captain, I don't think you ever met my little girl, did you?"

She was a fifty-one-year-old unmarried woman with an austere, unsmiling face who had loved and worshipped her father all her life.

Feiffer said gently, "No, I never did." He stood up.

Mr. Lim said proudly, "My daughter—the great and crowning joy of my life."

Only he knew what and who he saw when he looked at her.

Mr. Lim said as if it was a thing of great moment, "Daughter, this is my oldest, my truest and greatest friend who I thought I would never see again, the Captain."

She had loved him all her life and in the last few months tried to hang on to him, to keep for herself some semblance in him of what he had once been. As she had always done, she loved him now, and, now, for that reason, at last, let him go.

Miss Lim, coming forward with her hand outstretched and a smile on her face full of light and gentleness and love for the old, lost man sitting on the bench holding in his hand what he thought was the greatest treasure he owned, said in the same formal tone, but with a look of sadness in her eyes that only Feiffer saw, "Good evening, Captain." Her eyes looked straight into Feiffer's. "I am very pleased to meet you. Is there any-thing—anything at all—either I or my family may do for you to assist you in any way?"

In the Detectives' Room, the phone on O'Yee's desk rang only once before O'Yee snatched it up and put it to his ear.

O'Yee said urgently, "Yes? Harry?"

He listened for a moment. O'Yee said, "Yes."

10:55 P.M. He glanced up at the Station clock.

O'Yee said, "Yes." He looked at Auden and Spencer and Bontoc and nodded.

O'Yee, still nodding, already on his feet and touching at his Colt Airweight in its Berns-Martin upside-down holster under his arm to make sure it was there, said urgently, *"Yes."*

15.

Reaching up into the blackness of night, Lim's Enterprise Mass Media Associates Building on Beach Road was an enormous, fifty-story monolithic aquarium of glass and steel and lights.

11:54 P.M. At the first-floor security desk, Feiffer, glancing at the bank of closed-circuit television screens that monitored all the floors of all the businesses up to the fortieth floor, said on the phone to the security man in his office on the fortieth who monitored the top ten floors that were Enterprise Mass Media Associates' alone, "Can you control all the elevators up to the fiftieth from your office?" Beside him, the uniformed first-floor security man, an ex–Hong Kong police sergeant Feiffer had worked with once, to Feiffer's unspoken question, said shaking his head, "I don't know him. He's Enterprise's man—"

The voice on the phone, after a moment, said, "Yes, I can."

Where O'Yee and Auden and Spencer and Bontoc waited, there was a bank of at least twenty elevators. Feiffer asked, "How many are there? How many go on to the executives' rooms and suites on the fiftieth floor?"

Either he had to think about it or he was getting nervous and becoming confused. The fortieth-floor security man said, "Um . . . the only ones that go all the way up to the fiftieth are elevators number one, two, three, and four, and Mr. Lim's private elevator—which you need a special key for."

"I've got the key." By the fire-stairway door, Bontoc waited with his axe out. Feiffer asked, "And the fire stairs? Do they go all the way up?"

"Yes." He sounded young. Feiffer had a picture of him in his mind as fat, smooth-faced, and mother-dependent, and, like most underpaid and unqualified security men, a gun nut. The security man said, "I'm getting a little frightened in here—"

At the bank of at least twenty elevators, Auden had his huge Python out, pulling out each of the rounds one by one and checking them before putting them carefully back into the cylinder, both Spencer and O'Yee had their revolvers out and held down by their sides, and Bontoc had his axe. If the security man had seen any of that, he wouldn't have been frightened, he would have been terrified.

Feiffer said, "Lock yourself in." He glanced again at the bank of TV screens. "Have you got full coverage of all the top ten floors where you are, or—"

The security man said, "No! I've got full coverage. I'm the only one here! The security office up here—" The security man, suddenly wanting either his mother or food, said with panic rising in his voice, "I'm not real security personnel according to my job description! I'm just fire watch and—" The security man said, "The cameras are on rotation: they don't cover everything at once. I've only got one screen and I have to switch to each one of the cameras by hand!"

"Okay. Have you got a hand-held radio?"

"Yes."

"Do you know the police tactical frequency?"

He probably did. He probably listened to it all the time.

The security man said, "Um . . . no."

"Switch your hand-held over to it and tell us if you pick anything up on any of your screens."

"What am I looking for?"

There was a pause.

Feiffer said, "A man. You're looking for a man." Feiffer said quickly, taking up his own radio from the desk by the ex-sergeant, "Elevators one, two, and three, and Mr. Lim's private elevator: when you register each of us pressing the button for the fiftieth floor I want you to take over control and make sure all the cars arrive there at exactly the same time." He said, terrifying the man even further, "Do you understand? I want them all to *ping!* together at exactly the same time as if it were just one car arriving. Do you understand what I'm asking you to do?"

"Yes!"

"Good." He had no more time for the man. "Set it up now."

Putting down the phone and switching on his radio, and moving quickly towards the bank of elevators, Feiffer said as an order to O'Yee, Auden, and Spencer by the elevators and Bontoc at the door to the fire stairway, "Forget the stairway. Cars number one, two, three, and four—Go!"

As all the lights on the panel above the door in Mr. Lim's private elevator flickered on and then off and then on again at top speed, as the elevator went straight up towards the fiftieth floor without stopping, the security man's voice said on Feiffer's hand-held radio, "I'm covering all the floors up here with the cameras one by one, but I can't see anything! All I can see is—"

On the panel, the light flicked on and then off for the thirty-ninth floor and, reaching the first of the top ten floors that were Lim's, flickered the light for the fortieth. Feiffer said, "Forget the other floors, just concentrate on the fiftieth." He knew what the man was doing: he was concentrating on his own floor. Feiffer said as an order, "Do not scan any of the other floors! We've got all those covered. Concentrate on the fiftieth!"

The light flickered on for the forty-first floor, then went off and the light for the forty-second flashed. Feiffer said, "Do you understand me? When we come out, I want to know exactly what's out there in the corridor waiting for us!"

The security man said, "I've locked myself in."

Forty-third. Feiffer said, "Good." He was sure the man still hadn't rotated the camera from the corridor outside his own room up to the fiftieth. Trying to think of a way to feed the man, Feiffer said dramatically, "Our lives are in your hands."

Forty-fourth and then forty-fifth.

The security man said midway between reality and fantasy, "Um . . ."

Forty-sixth, forty-seventh, forty-eight, forty-ninth.

Then the fiftieth.

There was a *ping!* as all five car doors opened at once.

And he must have done it.

The security man shouted in horror, "Oh, my God! Oh, my God! Someone just came out of elevator number four carrying an axe!"

The elevators were at the southern end of the floor framed by a huge tinted window looking out onto the sea and all the lights of the harbor and the floating restaurants along Hop Pei Cove and the old typhoon shelter. Ahead of them, the floor was a long wide corridor painted a soft teal-green color with closed office doors lining it on both sides and, here and there under the series of rippled thick glass covers in the ceiling that held the banks of neon lights that lit up the place, furnished with little tables and chairs for people waiting to see someone in one of the offices.

There was absolutely no one in the corridor at all, no movement and, as Feiffer listened, no sound. Like the lights, everything was recessed, out of sight, and there was not even the hum of the air conditioning that kept the place at an even measured temperature day and night.

It was the silence that got to them: Feiffer could see it on their faces. O'Yee, looking up and down the corridor, said as a question, "Harry? . . ."

He looked at Bontoc's eyes. They were flickering back and forth. Feiffer said softly, "He's a man. He isn't something immortal or supernatural, he's a man." He wasn't going to be in any of the office suites along the corridor because that wasn't where Lim came at night—he was going to either be somewhere in the main corridor itself or in Lim's private suite and museum. Feiffer said, "And what he does and how he does it isn't something miraculous, it's a trick—it's something—"

"I got a flash!" It was the security man yelling on the radio. "On my screen covering the far end of the corridor! I got a flash of light and then the screen went out for a second and then came on again! And then—" The security man said, "Oh, God . . ."

"Stay on this floor! Don't switch to your own! Stay on this floor!" He looked up, but the cameras, like everything else, were recessed and hidden and he could not see where they were. Feiffer roared as an order, "Sweep Lim's office! Is it in there? The flash—did it come from there?"

All Auden needed was something to shoot at. There was

nothing. With his Python held in both hands, the hammer back ready, Auden said seeing nothing, hearing nothing, "Harry? . . ."

On his radio, O'Yee said to the security man, "This is Detective Senior Inspector O'Yee—where was the flash? What part of the floor?" He looked up to the ceiling so the security man could see him on the monitor, but with no idea where the camera was, did not know if he saw him or not. "Which camera were you using? Give us a location!"

"I don't know! I—" The security man said in a gasp, "Your camera! The camera up there in the lights just behind you!"

"What sort of flash?" It was Spencer. He turned and looked back, but all there was behind was the tinted window overlooking the water and the five still-open elevator cars.

"It's gone again!" The security man, answering Spencer's question, said on the edge of panic, "I don't know! A sort of whiteout! A brilliant white flash as if something—" The security man said, not even aware of what he said until he heard himself saying it, "Like a ghost! Like a phantom suddenly appearing out of nowhere and then disappearing again!"

Maybe he was in one of the offices. Maybe he wasn't—they were all locked, and as the security man swept them one by one, they were all empty. At the far end of the floor, the corridor turned off to the left under the series of overhead lights to more locked rooms and, almost at the far end, the door to Mr. Lim's private suite and museum, and, if he was anywhere, he was there.

But he wasn't. He was somewhere else, and moving. On the radio, the security man, calling them off one by one, said, "Another flash! Halfway down the main corridor where you've just come—and another! Back a bit from the first! And . . . and another! Ahead of you! And another in the same place! And . . . and another and another—midway down the corridor—and another at the turn into the corridor you're in now!" The security man, starting to lose it, said in a whisper, "Oh . . ." The security man said suddenly, "I don't care who you are! I'm going to sweep my own floor! I'm not a cop! I don't get paid for this sort of thing! I have to look after myself! I've got a mother and a grandmother to support!"

If the flashes were him moving, he was everywhere and nowhere. As Feiffer looked back in the corridor and then ahead and then back again, Elizalde's voice came back to him: *There are only six basic categories of magic: Production, when something appears or multiplies; Transformation, when something changes in color, shape, or size; Transposition, when something moves from one place to another; Penetration, when one solid object passes through another; and—* Bontoc, all the stories and terrors of his youth coming back to him in a single culminating moment, said in horror, "Harry, he's in here with us, but we can't see him because he's *invisible!*"

"He's not invisible! He's—"

"You didn't see him in the hotel!"

"You saw an old man! You didn't see someone invisible! You saw—"

The axe was no good. Auden's and Spencer's and O'Yee's and Feiffer's guns were no good. A fleet of tanks with ground-to-ground missiles would have been no good. Bontoc, shaking his head, standing his ground, said, "No! No! It's *bangungot!* He's the Dalagangan! He can kill with a single look!"

He came back. On the radio, the security man said, "I'm clear. I'm—I'm back on your floor again and I—" The security man said, "A . . . a shadow. The whole screen just went dark and then—" The security man said, "A flash! And another! Right where you are—behind you! The entire corridor behind you! A brilliant white *flash!*"

He had his Python. It had always seemed all he would ever

need for anything. Holding it in his hand, glancing down at it for a moment as if it were nothing more than a water pistol, Auden said to Feiffer like a suddenly lost child, "Boss? . . ."

There was nothing in the corridor but a few chairs and tables and, above them, the lines of panes of rippled glass housing the lights.

He was not in Lim's office or in any of the offices anywhere on the floor.

He was not—

All there were were flashes of light.

All there was was Bontoc's terrified face.

Thinking fast, looking up, trying to see them, Feiffer roared into the radio to the security man, "The cameras! Where are they? Where are they hidden?" Turning to Bontoc, Feiffer said in the same breath, "You saw him! How tall is he?"

Bontoc said, "What?"

The security man, on the edge of fleeing, said, "In the ceiling!"

Bontoc said, "He's—" He was going to say eight feet tall and a hundred and fifty years old, but he saw Feiffer's face and changed his mind. Bontoc said, "Your height! About your height! Maybe an inch or two shorter because he's old and he—" Bontoc, fighting to think on the plane of the real physical world, said, "Your height!"

He still had the radio *transmit* button pressed down. Feiffer demanded from the security man, "*Where* in the ceiling?" Feiffer said before the man could answer, "They're up there in the goddamned light recesses, *aren't they?*"

"Yes!"

He was up there. Up there, there must have been a passageway that linked all the lights for maintenance. He was up there. Reaching up where he stood, Feiffer could just touch the catch that held the glass cover in place in the light recess above his head. He was up there. And he was moving.

On the radio, the security man said, "A flash! And now the screen's gone dark—and on again—and a *flash!* And another—!" The security man said on the radio, "Moving away! Moving away towards the elevators! Moving away to—" He thought he was coming to get him. "And another, and another, moving towards the elevators!" The security man said, "I'm taking all the elevators down to the first floor!" From far down the corridor there was a *ping!* as all five car doors closed at once. The security man said, "It worked! Another flash! And another! Now he's moving back from the elevators very quickly towards you!"

No, it was all wrong. In the corridor, the seventh light recess in a row swung down hard on its hinges with a crash and lit up Auden and Spencer and O'Yee and Bontoc waiting in front of it with their guns out, but there was nothing up there, and no passageway one from another, and it was wrong, and Feiffer knew the Dalagangan was not up there behind any of the lights but in Lim's private office waiting for him the way he had been out in the garden waiting for his father.

The security man screeched on the radio as another light came down and severed the camera cable up there, "Camera number two gone! And, on camera three, nothing . . . and on four—" Reaching up, Auden whacked at the catch on the next light plate in the row with the barrel of his gun and snapped it open. "—four gone! And a flash! A flash and then a shadow on camera five and a—"

Nothing. There was nothing up there except all the hanging wires for all the neon lights and the camera cable and what looked like a little motor to keep the camera turning.

The security man yelled as Auden hit the next one in the line, not one with a camera in it, "A flash and—" and then the next, one with a camera in it— "Camera five gone!"

And he had waited out there for him in the darkness by all the trees and the beds of flowers smelling all the smells and scents of the private place that was not his but his father's and he had waited and waited, and then . . . And he had never touched his father's hand again, and he had never been allowed to see his father's face again because of what had been done to him, and all his life he had thought that his father had been disappointed in him and shot himself because . . .

The security man screamed on the radio, "Another flash! And another! And—" The security man, suddenly alone and with no gun, screamed in terror, "They've all gone! All the cameras have gone! I'm blind down here! I can't see anything on the floor where you are at all anymore!"

And as he touched the knob on the door to Lim's private suite, he touched again the little brass levers on the French windows that led out to the garden in his parents' house in the New Territories all those years ago and smelled, not the smell of wood and carefully, scientifically monitored and washed air from the hidden air-conditioning system, but the smell of the trees and the flowers and the smell in his father's office of his cigarettes, and suddenly all the sounds of the lights coming down one by one were gone and all there was was silence.

"Harry—!" He did not hear O'Yee call to him in alarm.

Harry, Born August 13, 1948!

His father's soul was all wonder and gentleness and fine, beautiful, Waterman pens and drawings of snowcapped mountains in the north of China so high they seemed to hang like icicles in the sky.

His soul was all . . .

He had Mr. Lim's key.

He had, in his pocket, his father's gun.

He looked down and, unlike his father, he had cut all his fingernails down to the quick.

Thy rod and Thy staff . . .

Tossing his Colt Detective Special and hand-held radio together onto the floor of the corridor as O'Yee shouted at him in horror, *"Harry! What the hell are you doing?"* Feiffer unlocked the door to the garden and, back in that night, back in that time and place again to make it right, to make it not happen, to make it never to have happened, went into Lim's private suite and locked the door behind him.

He heard it. He heard the heartbeat he had been waiting to hear. From the outer office on the other side of the door to Mr. Lim's private museum, from where he hid, silent and unmoving, the Dalagangan heard the sound of the heart.

It was a man's heart, beating fast, full of trepidation and fear.

And then it changed, and he heard, just for a moment, the sound of a child's heart, beating faster.

And then, in an instant, it was the sound of a man again, and then a child, and then a man, and he had to strain to make sure what he heard was a single heart.

He was in the area of the ceiling of Lim's private museum where all the central circuit boxes for all the cameras were, and as he moved slightly to concentrate his hearing on the heart, he brushed yet again against a loose wire up there and made the connection between all the boxes that controlled all the cameras on the entire floor flash.

16.

Captain! Come, come! Come into my little private room and see what I have to show you! and, passing across Lim's Western-style office full of leather and mahogany on a carpet so deep and rich his footsteps made no sound on it at all, Feiffer unlocked the door at the far end of the room to Lim's private museum and was there again, back there in his father's office, in his father's world, on the night his father had died.

It was a long, dark room barely lit in the center by a single bank of underpowered soft-light neon tubes set under another one of the rippled rectangles. Closing the door behind him and hearing it click locked, Feiffer touched at the bank of switches to one side of the door jamb, and as lines and lines of hidden wall lights came on in a series and all the steel shutters on all the windows came up all at once he was in a treasure house, a repository of all the greatest and most beautiful creations of China over four thousand years, and, on the fiftieth floor with all the shutters up, surrounded by the sea of lights that was Hong Kong.

He was in his father's garden, his head full of all the stories of all the wonders of China.

Everywhere, there were things he had never seen but only heard about, jade carvings, statuettes, entire carved rocks lining shelves from one end of the long room to the other, Ming vases and plates with the glory of their glazes reflected on the black-lacquered floor as if in great ponds of still, dark water, entire sets of Imperial chinaware lining the walls between each of the clear, light-filled windows, scrolls and watercolors and drawings and hangings of such delicate material they hung like gossamer.

At the far end of the room, as its greatest masterpiece, there was a worked bronze urn from the Shan dynasty, all its facets worked in minute detail with scenes of life and poetry from four thousand years ago, its surface shining a dull, rich dark with the patina of age.

He saw, as he looked, a bronze flying horse of Kansu—the very symbol of the Shan—three and a half feet tall, of solid ivory, and, by it, an entire burial suit of royal armor of jade, and, next to that, another and another, and he was there, in his father's study as his father looked for words to describe the things he had seen and one day they would go and see together.

There were things in there of gold and silver so ancient and of such surpassing beauty he could not even tell what they were for the blinding light of their colors.

Harry, Born August 13, 1948! And snowcapped mountains far in the north of China so high they hung like icicles in a stark empty sky.

The Shan, the Ming, the Tang, the Chou, the Ch'in, all the centuries and millennia of China were there, gathered together in one room, and as he stood in his father's garden smelling the smell of the flowers and the trees and the coolness of the night air, he touched at another switch and all the back wall behind him on either side of the door slid back and lit up and everywhere on shelves and mounted on the wall itself were all the great scientific discoveries of the ancient Chinese: telescopes and lenses and clocks and instruments of unknown or lost function, and everywhere, on either side of them, arranged in categories all the manuscripts and scrolls and writings of all the men who had invented or discovered the instruments and their functions, all impressed and beribboned with huge, red and purple and yellow wax emperors' seals.

He touched another switch and looked up and all the ceiling except for the light and a dark-glass skylight behind it slid back and everything in the room, reflected back from the black lacquer of the floor, was full of all the stars of the night sky.

He looked up from where he sat at the bottom of the stairway with his arm around his brother's shoulder and he could not understand what had happened.

Lights and the night sky, and stars and all the wonder and awe of childhood: standing there just inside the door gazing, filling his soul with all the things of breathtaking beauty, Feiffer had to fight to get a breath and stop his heart from racing in his chest.

It was all there: everything his father had ever spoken of, all the things like fairy tales, like dreams they had talked about together in the study full of the smell of cigarette smoke.

He was a grown man, almost as old now as his father had been when he had died.

He was in the garden where, in a moment, it had all been taken away from him.

There was no sound anywhere in the room, nothing but an utter, timeless, sepulchral silence.

Up there in the ceiling, six feet down from the darkened black-glass skylight, there was the single recessed bank of lights, now gone out. Everywhere around him, through the windows, he could see all the lights of Hong Kong, and, on the floor, reflected and twinkling, all the stars of the night.

With an effort, he got his lungs to breath and stopped his heart from racing in his chest.

Thy rod and Thy staff, they comfort me . . .

With his hand in his coat pocket on the butt of his father's still-fully-loaded, freshly cleaned and oiled .32 automatic, walking across a universe of light and stars, Feiffer went slowly and carefully and deliberately towards the center of the room to where the light recess in the ceiling was.

At the door to Lim's office, the fortieth-story security man's voice yelled through Feiffer's radio still lying on the floor where he had thrown it, "I'm leaving! I'm not paid for this! I'm not a cop! I haven't got a gun! I haven't anything!" and O'Yee, bending down and snatching it up with the gun and pushing the weapon into Bontoc's hand, roared back, "Shut up! Shut up! Stay there! Don't you even think of leaving!" The door to Mr. Lim's office was locked and, pushing at it, shoving at it, moving it not a fraction, O'Yee yelled through it into the next room, "Harry, what the hell are you doing?" It looked like a standard, hollow-construction light-pine office door, but it was not; and as he pushed on it, it was solid, locked with a lock that nothing would dislodge except the key that had been specially made for it.

Auden, glancing between the door and O'Yee and Feiffer's revolver in Bontoc's hand, unable to understand why anyone would throw away a perfectly good gun, said both to O'Yee and Spencer at the same time in his confusion, "Um . . . what do we do now?"

On the radio, the security man's voice shrieked in Chinese, "I don't take orders from you! I—" It sounded, suddenly, as if he broke down and wept. The security man, his head full of fantasy and firearms and great deeds, screamed like a child, *"I want to go home to where people treat me with respect!"*

"Go!" On the radio, O'Yee screamed back, "Go! Go then!" and in the confusion, in the screaming, in the desperation of the moment, Auden, thinking O'Yee meant him, shoulder-charged the door with the weight of his entire body and, with a crash, splintered it from end to end and blasted one of the hinges off and sent it spinning up into the air.

Lost, drifting in and out among the lights and the stars and the silence, Feiffer, lost between memory and reality, forgetting why he was there, went a single step at a time towards the darkened light recess in the ceiling in the very center of the room.

He had killed his father, out there in the garden, in an instant, but it was not real, it was a trick, it was something mortal and human, and he had done it in some way his father had not been prepared for and . . .

Bangungot. It was not supernatural, it was a trick. It was something so sudden and awful and unexpected, so appalling in its appearance or in its aspect that . . . Moving across the floor, looking up, Feiffer said in a whisper to fill himself with the strength to resist it, "It's not real. Whatever he does isn't real. Whatever he does is . . ."

Out there, in the garden, he had killed his father. All martial metal and violence and power and strength: it had killed even *him,* and maybe he was not the man his father was or even the son his father had wanted him to be, and . . . And he was there in the garden again, lost, wandering aimlessly in it the morning after it had all happened, looking, gazing around, searching, hunting for some small hint of what had happened, but there was nothing, and suddenly time reversed and he was back on the stairs with all the people in the house and there was no answer and he would never know what happened and his brother, so small and vulnerable and uncomprehending, had his head down on his shoulder and he was sobbing, and he was . . .

In the room full of stars and memory, Feiffer said to bring himself back, "It's not real! He's not immortal! He's not the *mangkulam* of all the *mangkulams*, the Dalagangan, he's a man like any other man!"

He looked up and knew the creature that was Death was up there hiding in the darkened light recess where all the television cameras were.

He had nowhere else to be except where he was now, nowhere else to go, inevitably, nowhere else his entire life had been leading him a step at a time since he was eight years old.

Looking up, not knowing whether Death could see him or not, in a whisper only he heard, Feiffer said Death's name.

"Jesus Sixtus Caina."

He said his father's name.

Feiffer said softly, "Feiffer. Harry Feiffer. The same name as mine."

In the garden, looking up at the darkened light recess, he took the gun that had been his father's and was now his out of his pocket and with his thumb flicked the safety catch off with a single, clearly audible . . . click!

There was nothing! The door came down with a crash, but as they all went in together, there was nothing in there but an empty office lit stark-white and sterile by all the neon lights in the ceiling.

In the center of the room, trying to look in all directions at once as if the man was hiding from him and it was all going to be revealed any moment as nothing more than a child's silly game, O'Yee roared, "HARRY! *WHERE THE HELL ARE YOU?*" but there was nothing, and as Auden and Spencer wrenched at the huge mahogany desk in the center of the room and upended it as if Feiffer might be under it, there was nothing and no one, and he had gone and all there was were walls of leather-bound books and hanging brocades of good but not outstanding quality, and, in the far corner where Bontoc was with his axe and Feiffer's gun, some sort of modern carved wooden screen depicting the Eight Immortals in a scene from Chinese mythology standing together on a bare hill gazing out across a valley at a mountain covered in snow.

The screen was heavy—it must have weighed fifty pounds.

With a single swipe of the back of his axe, Bontoc had it down on the floor in a moment.

Bontoc roared, "A door! Another door!"

There was thin brass keyhole escutcheon in the lower left-hand side of the door and, taking a step back and kicking at it with all his force, Bontoc hit the wood around the lock hard enough to turn it to shavings, but nothing happened, and, as he looked, the escutcheon was not even marked, and it was not brass at all, but tungsten.

And the door itself was solid, three-inch-thick teak, and as he charged it a second time with his shoulder, it did not budge or give a single inch.

He heard it. Up where he hid in the ceiling—listening, waiting, preparing himself—the Dalagangan heard the heartbeat.

He heard it almost directly beneath him in the one spot, unmoving and stationary, beating hard and fast.

Up there, behind the glass recess, he was crouched by all the central circuit boxes that controlled all the television cameras in all the corridors and rooms on the fiftieth floor, and, moving his arm a fraction to take something out of the pocket of his coat, he brushed against the loose wire connecting the boxes and made them all spark in the darkness.

The first thing he took from his pocket was a little pack of four boxes of matches, held together by a single cotton thread tied across them like the wrapping of a parcel, and, holding the pack lightly in his left hand, without looking at it, the Dalagangan undid the knot on the thread with his thumb and forefinger and let the thread fall.

In all his nearly sixty years of killing, he had never lost the feeling of excitement, the joy at the horror of his victims his killing had given him.

It was his life, his pleasure.

In the darkness of the recess, with the spark from the circuit box jumping and fizzing as he moved, the Dalagangan touched at his face and his eyes were the green, black-slitted eyes of a lizard, and as the spark flashed again in front of him, they glowed bright yellow in the dark.

In Lim's office, O'Yee yelled, "Use the axe! Use the fucking axe! Get the door down *now!*"

And suddenly, standing there looking up at the light recess and seeing all the stars in the sky and smelling all the smells of the garden and the loss and the taste of tears and loss and desperation at the corners of his mouth, there was something wrong and he could not hold himself together any longer, and, alone, as he had been alone that next morning and all the mornings that followed it one after another, Feiffer looked down at the floor and felt all the strength and purpose go from his body.

And suddenly in that silent, wonderful room the voice of a small child said from nowhere to his dead father, not from him, but from who he had once been, "I'm sorry . . . I'm so sorry . . ." and again, this time too, he had been unable to do anything and over and over in the garden his father died and was taken to the church for the service and was buried out on a hill overlooking the harbor and was no longer in the house and was silent forever and was gone.

He had thought . . . Somewhere, in some sort of place where the past could all be rewrought, he had thought he might have been able to . . . but there was something wrong and he did not know what it was, but knew it was wrong and something in his mind merged and then melded and then became lost and he was no longer even sure where he was or what he was doing there or what he had intended to do.

Looking up for a moment at the darkened light recess and then down to the reflection of all the lights and stars and objects on the black-lacquered floor, Feiffer said in a whisper to the ghost of the man he had not been able to save then and could not save now, "I'm sorry . . . I'm so sorry . . . I'm so . . ." and in that moment, not from the neon light recess in front of him, but from the dark skylight behind him, the Dalagangan came down to kill, and with the bony, awful grip of Death, took Feiffer hard by the shoulder and spun him around to face him.

With the first blow, all the wood around the lock splintered, but the lock did not give, and O'Yee shrieked, "Hit it again!" and wrenching Auden by the arm yelled, "Phil! Put your goddamned shoulder to it!" and as Bontoc swung the axe again and made the metal around the lock ring, Auden threw himself against the very center of the door and moved it, he thought, an inch.

Bontoc was already swinging the axe. O'Yee screamed, "Again!"

There was another splintering, but the door did not give.

"Again!" and a sliver of metal flew from the lock in a shower of sparks.

"Again!"

God only knew what was happening on the other side of that door.

Out of time, out of alternatives, out of hope, O'Yee roared at Bontoc and Auden and Spencer as the three of them alternatively axed and charged the solid, three-inch-thick teak door and moved it not at all, "Again! Again! *Again!*"

"Oh, my God!" and he saw then, in that instant, what his father had seen. He saw what Wong and Yuan and Tam and Lee and Helen Lau had seen that had killed them.

It was not his, but his father's voice. Over the years, dying over and over and over and over and over, his father cried out in terrible final horror, "Oh—! Oh—! *Oh, my God!*"

There was a shower of sparks as the axe hit the lock escutcheon full-on, and, for a moment, O'Yee thought the entire lock had gone, but it had not and was still there, and it was solid, impenetrable tungsten.

"Hit it again!"

It was a litany. It was all he could think of to do.

"And again!"

Over and over, useless command after useless command, O'Yee, out of control, shrieked, "And again! And again! *And again!*"

It was not Lim.

It was someone the Dalagangan thought he had killed forty years ago—

—and now, in a sudden, blinding explosion of orange and red and yellow flame like a hundred phosphorous matches all bursting into flame at once, began to kill again.

The fire was in his hands. His hands came up above his head and met in the center and his whole face was lit up and wreathed in a roaring circle of burning light and the eyes through the light were yellow and glowing and they were not the eyes of a man, but of a reptile. Going down, falling backward, crashing into something behind him—some statue or carving or he did not know what—Feiffer saw the face, twisted and in aura, in epiphany, below those awful eyes, draw back its lips and bare its teeth, and then, reaching in at him through the afterimage of the halo of flame, saw the long, razor-sharp fingernails as they went for his eyes.

"It's not real! It's not real! It's a trick!" But it was happening in microseconds and he could do nothing but keep falling and falling and falling away backward as the thing came for him with a hissing sound so loud it was everywhere and filled the room. The eyes were green and yellow and lizard's eyes. Feiffer's mind shrieked, *"They're not real! They're contact lenses! They're—"* but it did not stop his body falling, and then there was a feeling like something coming apart in his chest and a terrible pain that paralyzed his left arm, and, somewhere deep inside him, his heart spasmed, could not start again, started again, and then went into spasm again and swelled all the great arteries in his chest and neck, contracted them and cut off their blood supply, then swelled them and then contracted them and then swelled them again and sent them into rupture.

He hit the floor so hard it blasted all of the last, precious air out of his lungs and he could not breathe.

"It's not real! It's—"

But it was real. It was happening. Above him, on top of him, hissing, his face twisted, the awful green-and-yellow eyes rolled back in his head like a creature at the peak of sexual ecstasy, the Dalagangan, reaching down for him, came at him out of all his nightmares and, with a force so hard it felt like a death blow, reached down, and with a single twisting, tearing movement, plucked both of his eyes out of their sockets at once, and with a hiss of triumph, held them out an inch in front of Feiffer's face so he could see them.

And he saw them. And he could not have seen them! But he saw them. Reaching up to claw at the sockets, what was left of Feiffer's brain shrieked at him, *"It's not real! It's—"* and there was something wrong, not right, but he could not get his brain to work fast enough as it all happened in an instant to understand and tell him what it was.

He thought he screamed, *"No—!"* but he might not have, and with his hands reaching up to his own face to claw at the sockets he felt his heart suddenly grow molten, burn in his chest, and fill all his chest with pain.

In that moment, as his fingers with their carefully cut-down fingernails clawed at the place where his eyes had been, and his brain, unable to take in the horror that his eyes saw the eyes that were no longer there looking back at him from the creature's hands, something seemed to explode in his head, and with all the muscles in his face locked in a look of utter, uncomprehending terror, his heart went into a massive, unstoppable series of spasms and began to fail.

☆   ☆   ☆

"Again!" and with a tearing, splintering crash of Bontoc's axe, all the top layer of wood around the lock came off and the entire lock mechanism in the door was exposed.

Screaming, roaring, shrieking the same thing over and over again, O'Yee ordered the man even as the axe came back for another blow, "Again! Again! *Again!*"

It wasn't real. It was a trick. It wasn't supernatural or immortal, it was a trick. It was some sort of faith healer's trick and there was something wrong, and as Feiffer saw his own eyes in the Dalagangan's hands, they were not his eyes at all, but the eyes of the man the Dalagangan had been waiting for.

They were not blue as his were, they were brown. They were Lim's eyes, and, somehow getting his body to work as it jerked and convulsed and died by the second, Feiffer yelled to his mind to keep it alive, *"No! It's not real!"* and, twisting, turning on the floor, reached into his coat pocket for his father's gun.

And then, above him, the reptile eyes rolled back and, glowing yellow and green, the lips drawn back over his teeth, hissing, sounding in his climax, the Dalagangan reached down hard with both hands into Feiffer's chest for his heart.

There was a thud against his chest that sent his heart into contraction and as he rolled away with the creature's hands still inside him, he got his hand around the butt of the gun and pulled it out.

The eyes the Dalagangan had held in his hands were gone. Whatever the eyes were he had held in his hands, whatever they were really made of, they were gone, disappeared like a magician's sleight of hand, and, using all his strength, Feiffer tried to bring the gun up, but his arm was paralyzed by all the dying muscles in there and he could not lift it, and he thought he felt the Dalagangan's hands touch his heart, reach around it on either side, and with an explosive hiss of power, grasp it in its cavity and, with a single movement of such violence it made his entire body convulse, wrench it free.

And then, in that same instant, as the hands came out, there was a single sound, like a blossoming, and the Dalagangan had Feiffer's torn and bloody heart in his hands and he was dead.

. . . He was dead in that room surrounded by all the stars of the night as his father had been dead in the garden, and the heart held an inch from his face was his own heart and everything in his body was dying and his brain could take in no more and was also dying, exploding in sparks and filling with an unbearable pain that had no cure and as he felt himself leaving reality, he thought as his father had thought—

He thought, *"It's not real!"* They were not his eyes, they were Lim's eyes. A blossoming, like tissue paper on a gift being . . . And as the Dalagangan, holding the heart, shook in power, there was no blood dripping from all the ripped and jagged arteries and veins still attached to the heart, and it was all just painted paper and papier-mâché as the eyes had been papier-mâché, and it was a faith healer's trick and the blossoming was the sound of the flattened and folded papier-mâché heart the magician took from somewhere in his clothing and held hidden in his hands as he appeared to reach into the chest cavity and then—and then—and then filled with air and expanded and filled like a suddenly inflating balloon with a single downward snap of his hands.

It was not real! It was an illusion!

It was all happening in microseconds, too fast to calculate, but he was not his father and he was not dead, and, somehow getting his hand and arm to move—or thinking he did—Feiffer got his father's gun out and with every last remaining ounce of his strength, pushed it out hard and got the muzzle up against the Dalagangan's forehead to blast his brains out the back of his head and kill him before, there, in the garden, he killed his father and left him all alone on the stairs with his brother's head down against his chest and sobbing in utter incomprehension and loss.

And in that moment, he saw the Dalagangan's eyes roll back and see what was happening, and he pulled the trigger and nothing happened, and pulled the trigger and nothing happened, and there was something wrong, and with his eyes filling with hot tears of frustration, there, in the garden, trying to save his father, the four-pound pull on the trigger was more than a child could manage and nothing happened, and nothing happened, and nothing happened, and his mind and body, convulsing, spasming, could not comprehend being in two places at once and, trying to decide between life and death, because the heart was there in front of them, decided on death.

He pulled the trigger and nothing happened.

He pulled the trigger and nothing happened.

All violence and martial metal. But it was not him. It was not what his father had been. What his father had been was a man who would have chosen to die rather than let his son kill to save him and, his father's son, he could not get the trigger to work, and in the last, the final moment of his life, drifting, starting to fade, all there was left in his head was the picture of an eight-year-old boy gazing out from the stairs with a look of awful loss and sadness on his face, and he was alone, dying there as his father had died, in the silence and sad, sad wistfulness of all the lonely and lost days that had followed, and he had no one, and—

And the gun in his hand, too heavy to hold, came down in a

slow-motion arc and he felt as his body surrendered and died that he would never see a mountain with snow on it and that all his life, he had never again ever had someone he loved and who had loved him and who had—

Harry. Born August 13, 1948! He had never had anyone, ever again, who had loved him like that, and he had never again ever had—

It had all happened, from start to finish, as it had happened in the garden, in a second.

Above him, his work all done, the Dalagangan straightened up and, with a flick, snapped the papier-mâché heart closed and reached up to his eyes with the palm of his hand and slipped the contact lenses free.

And then, looking down at the dying man on the floor, as he had looked at a hundred dying men before, maybe more, drew back his lips and smiled . . .

And he had no one to help him. And like his father, because he had had no one, he was alone in the final moment of his life, and he thought it was such a pity, that there were so many things he had left undone, so many things he could have said to his father, so many things he . . .

He had no one there with him who loved him.

He had at least four people who loved him. He had at least three who had been with him for almost twenty years and loved him, and he had one more, a man with an axe and his own gun who was the friend in Manila of his friend who had known and loved him for even longer, and with an explosion of teak and sparks and metal shavings, the entire lock came off the door and they were there, all of them, O'Yee, and Auden, and Spencer, and Baptiste Bontoc, all there in the garden in the last savable instant before his father died.

"HARRY—!"

He thought, in that instant, that it was his father's voice and he was there, in the garden, armed with his father's gun, to save him.

Harry. Born August 13, 1948!

Feiffer said in a whisper, "I'm here! I'm here! *I'm here!"*

At the open doorway, as the Dalagangan turned to face them with a look of terror on his face, O'Yee, Auden, Spencer, and Bontoc, aiming for the head, all fired at once.

17.

2:00 A.M.

In his car parked in Hop Pei Cove looking out at the darkness of the South China Sea, and far, far out, the lights of the junks fishing, Feiffer said gently on the car phone to Rebecca Pickering still on duty at the hospital, "I just wanted to—"

She was in the doctors' lounge of the OR, tired and with her voice low. "Yes?"

"—to tell you about—"

She knew something was wrong. Doctor Pickering said softly and gently, "Yes, Harry?"

"About that thing you thought you saw in your sleep that night in Africa—the panther."

Doctor Pickering said softly, "Yes?"

Feiffer said in a whisper, "You were right. It was real. But it's gone now." Feiffer said, "I thought I'd tell you so you wouldn't worry about it anymore and you could—"

Rebecca Pickering said softly, "So I could sleep at night?"

"Yes." He did not know what to say or how to say it. Feiffer said, "I just thought I'd tell you."

"Thank you, Harry."

"Yes."

And then there was a long silence, and then Rebecca Pickering, full of her own ghosts, said so quietly he had to strain to hear her, *"The Snows of Kilimanjaro."*

"Kilimanjaro is a snow-covered mountain 19,710 feet high, and is said to be the highest mountain in Africa. Its western summit is called by the Masai 'Negaje Ngai,' the House of God. Close to the western summit there is the dried and frozen carcass of a leopard. No one has explained what the leopard was seeking at that altitude . . ."

He could not think why she had said it. Feiffer said with a faint grin, "That's Hemingway, isn't it?"

There was another pause and then Rebecca Pickering said in a whisper so soft it was like nothing more than the sound of a faint wind rustling in the leaves of trees, "No, Harry. That's you. Every day of your life. And I thank you for it and love you for it more than I can say."

And then, in the same moment, like everything material and corporeal—like life itself—if not held on to hard and unyieldingly, and with determination—was gone . . .